"Blood might be thicker th[...] Cindy K. Sproles's touching [...] expected bond forms betwe[...] woman in the twilight of life and a young reporter who enters her remote world. Together, they explore the nature and meaning of family as they unravel their entwined past—all against the backdrop of a glorious mountain landscape, beautifully rendered by the author."

Valerie Fraser Luesse, author of *Under the Bayou Moon*

"Cindy K. Sproles is a master of the Appalachian story, immersing her reader into that distinctive mountain life once again in *This Is Where It Ends*. She invites her reader bit by bit into spitfire Minerva's life, then builds upon that relationship to weave a powerful and emotional story that will stay with you even after you've read the last word. After all, how long *does* a body keep a promise?"

Sue A. Fairchild, freelance editor

"This is the fourth book I've read by Cindy Sproles. Each time I think, *This is the way Christian fiction should be written*. The message of God's love is embedded in the storyline and characters; it's not a crude attempt to impose the gospel message. At times the story is sad, but it's also highly inspirational."

Cecil Murphey, author or coauthor of 140 books, including *90 Minutes in Heaven* with Don Piper and *Gifted Hands: The Ben Carson Story*

"In *This Is Where It Ends*, author Cindy K. Sproles again gives readers unforgettable characters that feel like family. Few can find the richness in a scene of seeming deprivation and poverty like Sproles, who draws beautiful images in a slanting screen door and a slanting sun, a worn porch board and worn-through patience, even the aching bones of a woman aching for heaven. Sweet and sharp, drawn out like hard-to-come-by forgiveness, *This Is Where It Ends* provides readers with insights they didn't know they needed."

Cynthia Ruchti, author of *Afraid of the Light* and *Facing the Dawn*

"How long do you honor the promise to keep a secret? To the grave? *This Is Where It Ends* is a remarkable and beautiful character study. You'll question your own morality when it comes to such, but you'll never question Minerva's."

Eva Marie Everson, CEO, Word Weavers International, Inc.

"Cindy Sproles breathes life into paper and ink to create Minerva, a memorable flesh-and-blood mountain woman who realistically confronts deception, betrayal, rejection, and her own mortality. While written about another time and place, it is thoroughly relatable to modern readers."

James Watkins, award-winning author and speaker

"Cindy Sproles writes about the hardscrabble life of the mountain folks of Appalachia. Her characters are real and gritty and winsome in their own ways, and her stories explore themes that reach far beyond the mountains to touch her readers wherever they call home. It was well worth the wait for this novel."

Nancy Lohr, retired editor, JourneyForth Books

"I laughed. I cried. I enjoyed. Cindy Sproles perfectly captures the voice of Minerva, a fiery, elderly Appalachian Mountains mamaw who embodies the internal strength of twenty men. This story sneaks up on you. At first, you're amused, even intrigued. The next thing you know, you're laughing out loud and crying—sometimes at the same time. By the end of the story, your life is richer for knowing Minerva."

Zena Dell Lowe, author, director, actress, and creator of
The Storytellers Mission podcast and online platform

To Ruth Ann

This Is
Where
It Ends

Blessings

Cindy K. Sproles

Books by Cindy K. Sproles

What Momma Left Behind
This Is Where It Ends

THIS IS WHERE IT ENDS

A NOVEL

CINDY K. SPROLES

Revell

a division of Baker Publishing Group
Grand Rapids, Michigan

© 2023 by Cindy K. Sproles

Published by Revell
a division of Baker Publishing Group
Grand Rapids, Michigan
www.revellbooks.com

Printed in the United States of America

Library of Congress Cataloging-in-Publication Data
Names: Sproles, Cindy, author.
Title: This is where it ends / Cindy K. Sproles.
Description: Grand Rapids, MI : Revell, a division of Baker Publishing Group, [2023]
Identifiers: LCCN 2022035623 | ISBN 9780800740795 (paperback) | ISBN 9780800744687 (casebound) | ISBN 9781493441433 (ebook)
Classification: LCC PS3619.P775 T55 2023 | DDC 813/.6—dc23
LC record available at https://lccn.loc.gov/2022035623

Scripture used in this book, whether quoted or paraphrased by the characters, is from the King James Version of the Bible.

Baker Publishing Group publications use paper produced from sustainable forestry practices and post-consumer waste whenever possible.

23 24 25 26 27 28 29   7 6 5 4 3 2 1

Dedicated to Linda Bambino, Wendy Smith,
and M. D. and Elvera McCue.
Your love for the elderly has changed
and continues to change lives for the better.

ONE

SHOAL MOUNTAIN, KENTUCKY, 1872

My eyes focused as best they could. "Stately!" I shouted. "Stately!" In our fifty-some years together, I hardly ever caught the man sittin still. Something was wrong.

I'd swear the man was growin deaf. That, or he just chose to ignore me. Momma used to call that selective hearin when she was talkin to Daddy. I just never dreamed it would happen to me. But that's been Stately's habit through the years. Dragging me to this blessed mountain and stickin me here without a body outside of himself to talk to.

"Stately Jenkins, you getting hard of hearin? Answer me!"

I inched my way down the bank to the fence line. A blurry shape hunkered over by the water trough never budged. My eyes were weak, and it was hard to tell if it was a person or just something leaned against the barn.

"Stately!" I hollered again.

My heart raced as fear seeped into every pore of my body. Surely to goodness, that couldn't be my husband, but the closer I got to the barn, the clearer things become. Stately was on his knees, one arm rested on the trough, and his chin hung to his chest.

"Lawsey mercy." I grabbed hold of his shoulders, and he fell into my arms, graspin hold of his chest. His eyes were glassy, but I could feel his hard gasps for breath. "What happened?" I tried to pull his arms from his chest, but his hands were stiff. It was like he'd been struck by lightning and the surge still raged through his body.

He finally grasped my hand. "Too late," he whispered. "Keep the secret. It's up to you." His words were weak yet stern.

Panic shot through me. "What happened? Did your legs give? Is it your heart?"

He nodded. Stately's legs were weak from bein hurt in the war. He'd fall at the drop of a hat.

"Oh, lawsey, lawsey." I pressed one hand against his. "Stately, open your eyes and answer me."

He stretched his hand to my face. "You promise me. Keep the secret?" His voice grew soft. "Promise to keep the box a secret?"

"Secret? I ain't worried about no secret, and why would you? I'm frettin over you."

His skin grew a pasty grey. All I could think to do was talk. Momma always told me I could talk a blind man off a ridge. I'd use this gift, or curse, to talk Stately outta dyin!

"Don't you die on me! Don't you dare die on me," I squalled. "Stately Jenkins, you hear me? Now ain't the time to ignore me."

His body grew heavy, and his arm dropped to the ground.

"Oh lordy, what'll I do? Stately. Open your eyes. I married you fifty years ago, trustin you'd always be with me. I followed you up on this mountain where there ain't a soul within miles. You ain't about to leave me here alone. There's work to be done. The garden fence needs mendin. How do you suppose I can see to do that?"

His lips took on a blue tint. His mouth gapped open.

Tears commenced to slip off my nose. "Stately, you know I ain't a woman that cries over spilt milk, but I need you. You got responsibilities here. You blessed ole stubborn hound dog. Don't you die! Stately, please don't you die on me." I pulled his head close to my chest and gently brushed his long, white beard. "I'll not tease you no more about the skin that shows on top of your head. Hear me? Stately, you hear?"

My talkin wasn't doin no good. I couldn't guilt him outta dyin.

"Promise me?" His voice hissed like steam from the coffee kettle.

I felt his chest heave, and a groan seeped from his mouth. His fingers wadded the tail of my apron into his palm. His hand balled into a fist, and his lips opened.

"Promissssse." The word pushed out of his mouth.

Even with my poor sight, I could see his pupils shrinking. I was losin the one thing I depended on.

"I promise."

Stately's head rolled loosely into the bend of my arm—his life gone from him.

I wrapped him tight in my arms and bellered loud as I rocked him. The only person in my life was gone. Gone.

The mornin breeze brushed over me, blowing strands of hay from the barn floor. They took to spinnin like a windstorm, then as quickly as it come, the wind died. It was like they swirled around his body and lifted his soul right out. Just like that, Stately died. A slow sigh melted into a breeze. It wrapped around me, then vanished.

In the distance, the peaks of the mountains lifted toward the heavens. There was a peace about the quiet here, a lovely peace, but it seemed to come with a price. Hardship. Loneliness. A streak of lavender pulled across the deep blue of the sky, and I wondered if that was Stately's soul makin its way to heaven. Could a greedy man even make it to heaven?

There ain't a soul alive that's found their happiness in the almighty dollar. Money, gold, possessions—all act like a coiled snake. They build up their fire, strike, and then they're spent. A body's happiness, the real prize, is found in the folks they befriend. Stately had been caught on a barb—some sort of secret—and the irony was, it only served to cause me grief.

"Stately, open your eyes," I sobbed. But he didn't crack an eyelid.

I rocked him and screamed curses at the birds that soared so effortlessly overhead. It felt like ever part of me ripped into pieces.

"Don't you die. Stately, don't leave me alone on this mountain. Please don't die." He wouldn't hear, for he was done gone. Still, I tried to convince him to come back. "I got soup beans stewin. You love soup beans and corn bread."

I grasped his hand, and his fingers relaxed, openin so I could see his wedding band. The one thing we owned was wedding bands. They weren't much, but it was never taken off his finger over the years. Liftin his hand, I kissed his fingers, then pulled the band over his wrinkled knuckle. I knew better. No amount of talkin could keep his stubborn soul here.

It took me a right good bit, but I pulled Stately into the barn and closed the door, then I commenced to walk the five miles down the mountain to Barbourville. It like to have killed me. I squalled and cried every step of the way. There were times I cursed even though cursing wasn't something I usually did. I felt like I earned the right as I mourned. The one man I'd loved since I was a youngin . . . was gone.

"Minerva? That you?" A voice come to me from across the path. "That you? It's Robert. Robert Blessing."

It wasn't no secret on the mountain that my eyes were poor. Most folks, what few I saw, was good to tell me their name if I couldn't make them out. Despite my eyesight, a body manages. They do what they must to get along. But when Robert took hold of my arm, my legs give and I went to my knees. He wrapped his arms around me and eased me to the ground. The two of us set there huddled like a storm was comin.

"What in the Sam Hill has happened?" Robert asked. "Nerva, talk to me." He pulled me tight against his chest. His hug was like a sweet, warm blanket. I buried my face into that blanket and wailed. There was a comfort in his hug, in his presence—one that twisted at my heart.

"Stately's dead." The words dripped outta my mouth like molasses. "His heart, I reckon. It took him," I muttered into his shoulder. And that was all I needed to say. In his kindness, Robert sat there holdin me whilst I cried.

Before long, Robert's wife, Mary, come runnin. Somewhere betwixt the tears, she helped me stand and walked me to her cabin. Robert gathered some of the men in town, and soon they brought a wagon round to take me home. Mary rode by my side, never once lettin go of me. She cuddled me like a momma cat snugglin her kittens.

This mountain can be a godforsaken place. Folks is spread far apart. Visitin ain't something that happens a lot, but folks, they know one another, and they never fail to come together when they need to. They buried Stately. Even made him a headstone, which was right kind. The women brought me food, and after a couple of weeks, they were all gone back to their lives.

Except for me. I was left on this mountain alone. Broken and sad—angry. Partly because I'd lost the only man I'd ever loved and partly because I was left here to tend a pea-sized farm dug out of the side of the hill. All for a box that held a secret.

What Stately called gold, even if it was gold, was nothin more than a burden. I never laid eyes on it and had no intentions of ever doin so. Only asked once what was in it. Never again. It was nothing but a curse to Stately Jenkins, and now he made it my burden, my curse, my chains, by forcing me to promise to keep his secret. What kind of man does that to the woman he loves? Just to guard a secret. A secret that was never mine for holding to start with. A secret I wasn't right sure was real.

Two

I set up straight in the bed. The dream. The one of Stately's dyin. It hung in the back of my mind. Early on, it haunted me every night, but as the years passed, only occasionally. I reckon that's our way of healin the hurts—livin them over and over in our dreams until time puts a patch over the emptiness, keepin the hurt at bay. Every once in a while, the ache seeps through when the heart lets its guard down. You'd think after thirty years, it would vanish like his soul did. Still, his presence haunted me every now and again.

I pushed my face into my palms. The memory of his hand graspin hold of his chest like he could pull out the pain and toss it over the ridge hung in my memory. I reckon his heart give out and he fell. That quick, his soul left the shell of a man he was and seeped over the ridge into the clouds.

It galled me that in his last breath, all he could think of was that secret. A secret I was plagued with now. What was I to do with it? Keep it from who? Why? It wasn't ever my secret, and I never wanted a part in it. A secret ain't nothin but a dishonest seed layin in wait. Somethin just waitin for the right soil, the right water, the right amount of sun to make it sprout its roots. When it does . . . Lord, help us. There ain't no sucha thing as a good secret. Nary a one.

There's times a body ought to think before they speak. I reckon that day was one of them. I should have thought before I made Stately that promise. But I didn't. The agreement just fell outta my mouth, and I promised him. A promise is something to be valued, so I reckon I've made my bed and now I have to sleep in it. I'd keep his secret, be it right or wrong in my eyes.

I washed my face, scrubbin hard enough to take the memory, then dressed for the day and made my way to the garden. My eyes were no better now than they was the day Stately took flight. Things were blurry, but I could see good enough to take in the blue of the heavens dotted with an arrow of ducks. I sucked in a breath of cool mountain air—cool as the river water when you scooped it into your palm to drink.

It wasn't the mountain or the beauty nestled in her crevices that I despised. She was always kind to oblige my frustrations or to hold me close in the bend of her river like a momma caressing her baby. What I despised was the loneliness. The seclusion. The emptiness of no sound.

I pushed open the gate and took hold of a broke hoe. Droppin my basket at my feet, I went to pluggin at the dirt, searchin for taters.

Ain't been no stranger worth their salt make their way onto my land in years without an invite. Short of that sweet couple that brings me smoked meat ever now and then, even neighbors are sparse. So when old Satchel crawled beneath the fence and cocked his head toward the path at the end of the garden, I knew someone was close. His nose went up in the air, and that mouth twisted into a rounded shape just as he let out a howl.

I glanced toward the split-rail fence, then patted my sweater, feelin the revolver tucked beneath. I got the perfect "friend" to send a stranger packin. Come on. Just a little closer. I'd give him a few more steps whilst I dug up some fresh taters. I might blast his backside and I might not. That was to be determined.

"Minerva! Minerva Jane Jenkins?"

A tall, dark-haired man clad in a fancy suit and bowtie dodged his way through clots of red clay and into the garden. His jaw was lined by a thin, neatly trimmed beard, and his shoulders were broad. As he grew closer, I could see he was lean and skinny. Dressed right fancy. A city fella, without a doubt.

"You Minerva Jane Jenkins?"

I ignored him, pickin up a tater with my hoe and droppin it in my basket. Diggin taters was getting harder with every birth year that passed. I'd done made my way to ninety-four, and the hunch on my back wouldn't straighten up these days. Still, Stately made good and sure his woman could manage for herself. He taught me farmin and, better yet, how to wield a weapon. I smiled and patted the revolver again. Don't reckon my age mattered, just so I made my own way. I could do what I needed to do to get by.

The man inched closer. "Ma'am?" He pushed a dinky round hat away from his face. "I suppose you don't hear me, considering your age and all." He cleared his throat and raised his voice a notch. "Minerva Jenkins, I'm Delano Rankin. I've come here all the way from Lexington. You are Mrs. Jenkins? You have heard of Lexington? Right?"

I stabbed my hoe deep into the soil and yanked up another tater. Once I dumped it in my basket, I straightened as best these old bones could and pressed my finger into his chest. "Listen here. I'm old. I ain't stupid. Not deaf either. No need to shout!" I shouldered him as I snagged my basket from the ground. He took a step back. "What the Sam Hill does a fancy-clad man like you want with me? I'm an old woman livin on the side of a mountain."

"Well, are you Minerva Jenkins?"

I stopped at the edge of the garden and faced the man, shakin my head in disbelief. Was he slow? "You look like a right smart man, bein from the city an all. I've lost count of the times you've called my name. What do you want me to do? Tie a ribbon around your pinkie so you can remember? Reckon you got me unless you feel the need to call my name . . . again." I pulled my sweater back and showed Mr. Rankin the outline of my best friend through my apron. I winked so he knew I might be serious and I might not.

The color of his face went from pink to white. I went to chucklin. *City folk sucker ever time.*

I balanced my basket on my hip and motioned the man toward the house. It was hard to talk for my laughin. "Don't get many folks up this direction. Makes for a little fun to mess with a body when they show up." I set my basket on the porch and dusted off one of the three pine rockers Stately had built years ago. "Take a load off." I winked again and grinned. I figured I might as well be polite despite his makin light of my age.

He hesitated, so I egged him on by pattin my best friend. Just when I didn't think a man's face could get any whiter, his did.

I slapped my leg and let out a loud laugh. "Oh, hogwash. Pull up a rocker and set down," I said, and he did.

"Delano Rankin." His hand shook as he gingerly extended it.

"Is that hand a peace offering?" I cocked my head.

"No, ma'am. Just trying to be friendly."

I eyed his hand, then spit on mine and swiped the dirt onto my apron. Grabbin his hand, I shook right hard. Stately always told me a strong handshake shows a body you are right confident. And confident I was.

Mr. Rankin stared at his hand. I wasn't sure if he stared because I had a little dirt on my palm or because I spit on my hand. Either way, he went from a right pale color to green around the gills.

"Mr. Rankin, what brings you to my mountain? What do you want with me? I'm done well past the marryin age by seventy years or so." I batted my eyes and straightened the strings of hair that dripped down my face. Then I let out another laugh. "Lordy mercy. One thing is for sure. You done made me laugh more than I've laughed in the better part of thirty years." I leaned closer to him. "What's a man like you want with me?"

I stared straight into his eyes. The sight in my right eye was just plain poor, but what good sight I had in my left eye went by the wayside years ago when my old rooster spurred my face. I hated the old bird, but I did try to give him the benefit of the doubt. The old cuss doubted his way right into my stew pot. Wasn't a thing I could do about it except take it as an apology for messin up my eye and appreciate his sacrifice to make dumplins. To this day, that eye bears a white cloud over the pupil. I reckon it looked a bit queer, but I didn't have no husband to look at me day in and day out anymore, good Lord rest his soul. Beauty was the least of my worries.

Mr. Rankin cleared his throat. "I've been doing some research, and you and your husband surfaced."

I cocked my head and twisted my mouth to the side. "Research? What is there to research on me? If you'd done very much search-ing, you'd know Stately passed on several years back."

"Uh, yes. I knew that. I'm sorry for your loss." Mr. Rankin wiggled in his seat.

"Whatta you need to know about a peaceable woman like me?" I let my sweater pull back just enough that my revolver peeked out. The stranger could see I might tease with him, but overall, I meant business.

"Well, it's about, uh . . ." He pointed at my revolver. "Can we put that away? I mean no harm."

I scooted closer to him. Looked him up one side then the other and covered my friend. "Just so you know, I got this little friend that takes right good care of me." I patted my apron and grinned.

"Yes, ma'am. I can see that."

"So I'm askin you once more, and it'll be the last time before I send you hightailing it back down the mountain. What sort of research are you doin on little ole me?" My eyes fluttered like a butterfly in spring just to make him antsy.

"Actually, it's more your husband I am interested in." Mr. Rankin swallowed hard, then coughed whilst he choked on his spit.

"Reeeally? Well, Stately's been gone the better part of thirty years. I never was right good with arithmetic. And just so you know, on the mountain, we don't talk raw about the dead."

Mr. Rankin pulled out a small pad of paper and pencil from his coat pocket. He touched the lead to his tongue and commenced to write. I could see he was a nervous sort, for he pressed so hard on that pencil, he snapped the lead. "Oh, I'm sorry. I have a knife. Let me sharpen this real quick."

He fumbled around in his pocket for a bit before I grew weary of his huntin and yanked the pencil from his hand. I pulled a knife from my boot and scraped the wood down to a new point. Shoving it toward him, I grumbled, "Can you go any slower? Get to the point. Are you a youngin or a man?" I nudged his knee, teasing him.

He eyed me, lookin a little confused. "I'm thirty. I think that qualifies me as a man. Is it different on the mountain?"

I shook my head. Poor city boy, didn't know how to take this old mountain granny. I snickered. Momma always taught me it was best a stranger couldn't cipher the difference betwixt teasing and serious. I could see I had the gentleman puzzled.

"The point," I said. "Don't you catch it, or did it fly over your head like a hawk after a squirrel?" I rolled my fingers into a gentle fist and tapped his head.

He touched the pencil tip to his tongue again and scribbled the number one on the page. "I'm tryin to get some facts on a story about a box of gold."

"Gold?" I raised my brow. "Well now, ain't that just something. You come all this way to ask *me* about a box of gold?" I pointed at my rickety house. "You can see I've spent it well. The holes were a gift from the woodpeckers." I grinned, right proud of my comeback.

"I can see you're quite the character. Real sense of humor." He grunted out a fake laugh. "About the box. I know this gold came from a vein of gold on the Ohio River, down by Lexington. It was claimed by the Bishop family, who said a box went missing after your husband and a friend worked their land."

My nose flared. "Well, Mr. Rankin, I'm born and raised a Kentucky girl, and the truth be known, if I was ever caught lyin, my daddy woulda horsewhipped me. I got no idea what you're talkin about. That's the truth as I know it. And you still ain't answered my question about why you come here."

"Yes, I . . . I'm getting to that. I have information that your husband and his friend might have taken that box of gold and stashed it away for safekeeping. Keeping it for themselves would have been tempting, especially since the Bishops were not known for being good to their farmhands. There are all sorts of tales about what happened to the gold, but only this one seemed to have any worth."

A snarl twisted my lip. "Worth? Ha! Like I told you, Mr. Rankin. Just look at my cabin. Does it look like I have a box of gold? Stately's been gone long enough that if they were even a hint of gold, don't you think I'd have spruced up my place? At least fixed the holes, bought me some frilly pantaloons. Looks like common sense has left you."

"No, ma'am. But my research shows me that one Stately Jenkins"—he flipped through his pad to a page of notes—"turned up missing along with one Allan Gumble, and that they were last seen in Lexington bragging about their worth at a tavern."

I furrowed my brow and come close to Mr. Rankin's face. My mouth twisted, and before I could stop myself, a puff of air and spit flew out. "Bull!"

THREE

I SLAPPED MY KNEE and busted into laughter. "You think Stately hid a box of gold?" I groaned as I lifted my bones outta the rocker. "Mr. Rankin, I think your business is done here. You're barkin up the wrong tree. If you can't look around and see for yourself what that gold bought us, then it's time for you to leave."

He stood and his rocker banged into the back of his leg. He jabbed his hand into his pocket. "No. No. I'm not climbing a tree."

I shook my head. The boy seemed a bit dense.

He pulled out a paper and unfolded it. "Do you read?"

"Do I read? Lordy mercy, you go from one hornet's nest to the next. Truth be known, you're startin to irritate me. First you holler at me like I'm deaf, then accuse me of lyin. If that ain't enough, you insult me by askin if I can read. What's wrong with you, boy? Got no manners?" I stood and took my basket of taters, then pulled open the screen door. It squalled like a wildcat. "We'd be done here. I'm sure you can find your way back to where you came from. Goodbye, Mr. Rankin."

Rankin slapped his hand against the door and pushed it closed. "Please, Mrs. Jenkins. Hear me out."

I felt the hair on the back of my neck stand straight. My jaw tightened and I gritted my teeth. I could fun with the best of them, but this feller had just crossed the line. I yanked his hand away from my door and come toe-to-toe with this city boy.

"You listen here." My tone changed to right hateful. "There ain't a man alive that can put his hand on my door and keep me outta my own house. Now, here's what we're gonna do." I dropped my basket of potatoes on the porch and wrapped my feeble fingers around my revolver. I pulled it from my apron and shoved it against Rankin's chest. "You, my friend, are gonna step away from my door and get your caboose off my porch and then off my property." I pulled the hammer back, and it clicked in place. "And if you think for one iota that an old woman can't make haste while the sun shines, you keep standin here and testin my patience." I pressed the revolver harder into his chest.

His hands went up. "Hay. Isn't it hay? You make hay while the sun shines?" As soon as the words left his mouth, he realized he'd done made a mistake in correcting me.

My nose flared again. I eyed him as his hands shook above his head. "Raisin them hands might be the smartest thing you've done since you got here. Lord knows it ain't your mouth. Now go on. Git from here." I tilted the gun and fired toward the garden. "Next round will put you in the ground. That what you want?"

"I'm leaving. Just read this. Maybe I'll check back tomorrow and see what you think." He stuck a crumpled piece of paper toward me.

"Don't bother, I won't be here," I snapped.

"You're going somewhere? Maybe I can take you."

"Lordy mercy, boy, you left your smarts in Lexington." I nudged him toward the edge of the porch. His hand shook as he tried to hand me the paper. I held tight to my gun.

Rankin folded the paper in the middle and hung it over my revolver barrel. "Just read it. I'll be back tomorrow when you're in better humor. Just don't shoot that gun anymore."

I tipped the barrel, and the paper dropped to his feet. He backed off the porch and down the steps.

"That's right, you mosey right on back to Lexington." I pulled the hammer back a second time. It clicked into place, ready to fire again. Rankin took to runnin.

I waited until I couldn't see him anymore, then eased the hammer down and blew on the end of the barrel to cool it down. I groaned and bent to grab the paper. Givin it one last glance, I slipped the gun and the paper in my apron pocket. I'd look over it later. There were more pressing things at hand.

I moved my creaky bones down the steps and around the back of the cabin to the stand of vines Stately had planted. Takin my hatchet in hand, I run it three or four times over the whetstone, then chopped away the vines that crawled toward the house. Derned ole kudzu vines.

"Stately Jenkins, I told you this would come back to haunt you! I reckon it's time you and me have a chat."

Them stems coming off the trees reminded me of the long, slender-like legs of a granddaddy longlegs. I cupped my hands around my mouth and hollered into the darkness of the twisted labyrinth, "Dadburn it. I didn't die soon enough. Somebody's come huntin that blessed box. Move over, Stately, I'm comin." I stepped up to the shadowed path and went to wielding that hatchet, cutting away enough vines so I could step through. My chest ached after a few swings, and I dropped the hatchet back in its spot. I'd have to make the trek back to Stately tomorrow. Liftin my hands in the air, I hollered, "Lord, just take me. Take me now!"

The mornin mist laid heavy on my arms. I rested a hot cup of coffee on the bench next to my rocker. The rumble of a bear messin in my garden echoed up the bank. Most days, I'd grab that gun and fire it in the air. Scare the beast off. But today, my body ached too bad to fuss over a tomato or two. "Just leave my vines standin. Don't rip them outta the ground," I shouted. The bear let out a soft grumble and made his way down the hill.

There was always something sweet about the mornin mist on the mountain. The way the white fog danced over the river, givin me a peek ever now and again at the water that rushed past. If a body was good and kept quiet, they could hear the trout slappin in the water, snapping at the morning bugs lightin for a drink.

I slid my finger through the handle of my cup and tilted it for a sip. Ain't nothin like a good cup of coffee. Ruby sleeked up the steps and swiped around my legs, leaving a good portion of yellow fur hooked to my skirt.

"Hello, kitty." I sipped the coffee, and one eye drew tight. "Lawsey me. That's so stout it could stand and walk. Stately used to say, 'The stronger, the better. Puts hair on a man's chest.'" I smiled. I missed the old cuss. Can't help but miss the man you spent the bigger part of your life with.

I run my hand into my apron pocket and pulled out the slip of paper Mr. Rankin left. "Huh! Can I read? Man's got gumption." I squinted hard to see the words on the page. *Ohio River Gold—Truth or Lie?*

My eyes skimmed the page best they could. Readin was never my issue. Seein the words was.

Recent information suggests a vein of gold was discovered in a tributary just south of the Ohio River. Freelaw Bishop and his nephew Travis laid claim to the vein, according to papers filed to the Kentucky Division of Land Assessments. It was noted that the vein was small, yielding approximately 20 ounces of gold, and that the gold went missing after two hired hands, Mr. Stately Jenkins and Mr. Allan Gumble, vanished from the Bishop farm. A warrant was issued for their arrest.

There wasn't nothin to do but chuckle. I never wanted Stately to keep that box. Didn't want a thing to do with it. Blood money was what I called it, even though there was never nobody killed—leastways that I knew of. Stately called it a freein opportunity—a secret. Either way, I had nothin to aid Mr. Rankin's search and no intention of eggin him on. Stately had buried the thing, and I never laid eyes on it after that. Never asked. Didn't care. It was none of my business. Momma taught me there was a time to run my mouth and a time to keep it shut. When Stately told me about the box, I figured it was my time to keep my mouth shut. What I didn't know wouldn't hurt me. Or so I thought.

I'd read what I could. Rankin got a good bit of the words right. That bothered me. Bothered me right bad. If he could put enough pieces together to find his way to this mountain, then they'd be somebody else who could do the same, and I was too old for this malarkey.

Easin outta my rocker, I took one last sup of coffee and tossed the rest over the rail. I made my way right slow around the house. There on the ground laid a coiled-up rope. Reminded me of a rattler twisted and ready to strike. I grasped hold of the rope and tied it around my waist, then give it an extra yank to double-check it was knotted good and tight. The way back to Stately's resting place was flat, but it could be right dark under them kudzu hangin down. That rope, because of my poor eyes, was the way out if I was to get lost in the overhang. I give the rope one more tug, reassuring myself it was snug.

"Stately, you better pray there ain't no varmints gnawed through the knot tied to the stake. I hate those vines. They're like the devil himself, slinking around things and choking the life outta them." I stepped into the dark thickness.

I reckon the best part of livin alone on this mountain is I can talk out loud and there ain't a soul that cares. "The only three people that count is me, myself, and I. And I reckon we know I ain't crazy." I let out a hearty laugh that pitched me into a coughing fit.

The mornin sun shimmered through the vines, makin streaks of rainbow lights. Just enough for me to see my way to Stately. There was one thing for sure, the leaves that glistened with sunlight and dew was lush and green.

"Lord, I'm askin You to keep the teeth of these leaves to themselves. You know I hate these things. They grow like nobody's brother. I'd swear they had minds of their own. Evil minds. Be ready to pull me outta here, Lord."

Everybody knows that leaves ain't got no teeth, but these vines were odd. Purt near as odd as old Henry Tennison down toward Barbourville. His one crossed eye made him look like he was crazier than a fruitcake. I used to laugh at him until my own eye went south. It was hard to throw stones at a body once you come up with the same affliction.

I took my hatchet and whacked my way through the tangled mess of roots and creepin leaves till I found the edge of Stately's tombstone. The fine leaves and vines wrapped tight around it forced me to beat away at them until I could see a name chiseled in the rock.

Herman Stately Jenkins
1805–1872

I run my wrinkled fingers over the fading letters, and a sadness crawled over me like a shadow in the night.

I laid the axe against the tombstone and used the blade to scrape away the tiny veinlike legs of the kudzu. "I reckon folks would call me crazier than a fritter, coming into these vines and all to visit. Talking to you like you was still livin." I nodded and pulled more tentacles away from the date on the rock. "I suppose I do miss you. Didn't always agree with you." I chuckled and pointed my finger at his grave. "Rarely agreed with you, but I miss you. Still gets my hackles up that you never give me no child to love. Now, look at me. An old woman and alone. Since you had the gall to up and die, I'm left alone to die without a soul. And just so you know"—I snugged the rope tighter around my waist—"ain't a soul gonna know where to bury me. I reckon I'll just give out and go to dust where my bones hit the ground."

I took the blunt end of the hatchet and give that stone a good whack. "As you well know, I can use this hatchet too, now, can't I?" My fingers gripped the leather on the handle tight as I shook it at the stone. I slipped the tool, sharp end first, into my apron pocket.

Bendin my arm, I commenced to roll the remainder of the rope from palm to elbow, palm to elbow. "Stately Jenkins, I just wanted you to know that box, *your* secret, has come back around to bite me in the rear, you old . . ." I yanked the hatchet from my apron and slammed it against the stone again. The jolt shook ever tooth in my head.

"Lordy, lordy, forgive an old woman her anger. I'd ask you to forget what I almost said. Though them words never left my mouth, you saw them in my heart. Forgive an old woman her bitterness."

I squatted to the flat ground, dustin away the dead leaves and dirt. I measured two hands to the left of Stately's stone, then I went to diggin till my fingers touched the wood. A sigh of relief seeped from my lungs. Still there. I covered the hole and smeared a pile of leaves over it, then turned to make my way back through the tightly woven overhang. Despite this Mr. Rankin coming around, I had no desire to know what was so precious to Stately. I guess even after thirty years, I was still a little miffed over Stately making me promise him to keep it a secret.

"Just so you know, Stately Jenkins, once more, I hate these vines. I hate every leaf, every root, every twist they make as they crawl over the mountain. You shoulda never planted them. I ain't to blame. If you wanted to graft a plant, you shoulda stuck to roses. You should see my rosebush. Grafting to this mangy plant only sped up its growin. This sin is on you!"

I wagged my head from side to side and mumbled. I knew when that government man come along and offered Stately a little money to plant these varmints, something was wrong. When a plant nearly doubles in a day or so, it couldn't be no good.

"Comes from the Orient," the man told Stately. "It'll help stop the dirt from washin down the mountain."

All I could say was, "Good for the mountain, my foot! It's like a swarm of locusts overtakin anything in sight." And I was right.

"Mm-mm. Good Lord have mercy on your soul." I give Stately one last glance, then took a few steps and stopped. Moving back to the stone, I gently brushed my fingers over his name. *Herman Stately Jenkins*.

"I try to be mad at you. Try to blame you. Truth is, betwixt me, you, and the fence post, there ain't been no man I've loved more." I felt a twinge at my heart.

"I reckon my snideness is comin from you dying. How could you die and not take this old woman with you? You always promised you'd come back. And you always did . . . until death." Tears leaked from the corners of my eyes. "You ole dog."

Stately had made sure I was blind to what he was doing. I knew about that box, but I was never sure exactly what was in it. Never opened it, and Stately never showed me. He told me it was gold, but he never said what or how much. Tried to justify his doins. But there wasn't a lot of talkin about it. In his own way, I think he was tryin to protect me. From what, though? I never figured that one out. So he didn't mention it much, and I asked even less. That's what a good wife does. By the time I figured out he was secluding me on this godforsaken mountain, there wasn't a thing I could do about it. Nothing but live and die here.

I picked up that rope and commenced to rollin it around my arm, using it as a guide to find my way back to the cabin. When I finally stepped out of the mess of tangled vines and limbs, the sun lit the mornin with a brightness that looked like heaven. In front of me, Mother Nature in all her glory. Behind me, the gates of hell.

FOUR

A WOODPECKER rubbed his head against the well pump. His bright red, black, and white colors busted up the incessant green of the vines. I nabbed the bucket and hung it under the mouth of the pump. My arms and back ached like they were thorns sticking in me.

"Don't make me pump twice. Fill this bucket the first time, you rusty old pipe," I muttered. The water gurgled and spit from the pipe, stopping just below the edge of the bucket. Lifting one hand to the sky, I thanked the good Lord for the water that sloshed from the pipe. "And thank ya, Lord, that I didn't have to prime this rascal." I wrapped the edge of my dress around my palm to pad the rusted bucket handle, then slowly made my way around the cabin.

"Let me take that for you?" Mr. Rankin come from behind me.

"Woo!" I shouted. "You scared the bejeebers outta me. What are you doin here? You were done warned."

"I'm sorry. I didn't mean to scare you," Mr. Rankin said.

"Well, you did scare me. Especially since most of my view is lookin down at the ground thanks to the hunch on my back." I craned my neck to see Mr. Rankin reachin for my bucket.

"I can get that for you, Mrs. Jenkins."

I eyed him right good. He'd showed up a little less fancy. He was fitted in old trousers and a plaid shirt, and his shiny shoes were traded for a pair of muddy boots. He took the bucket from me.

I rested my hand on my hip. "I thought I told you to get off my land yesterday. Whatta you want?"

He bowed just a bit, then offered me his free arm to help me walk.

Without takin my eyes off him, I warily took hold. "You see I got myself another friend now?" I patted the handle of the hatchet.

"I didn't expect any less. Everyone needs a friend like that. They're always good to have." He twisted his head away to hide his smile, but I'd done seen that sneaky grin, teeth shinin behind them lips.

That remark took me back. There was somethin about this Mr. Rankin. Somethin that put me on edge, but at the same time, somethin that was right kind about him. Right son-like. The mischievous sort.

I learned years ago, trust ain't somethin you put easy in a man. The good Lord was the only one I ever put much trust into, and I'd guess if you were to ask Him, He'd tell you my trust coulda been better.

"Mr. Rankin, you outright ignored my warnin. You're either dumber than a box of rocks or the bravest man in the world. Which is it?"

A grin tipped his lips upward, and when he turned, crevices as deep as the valley dented his cheeks. "Maybe a little of both. You do scare me, though."

"I can see that's a lie, but you see that you continue to make me think you're terrified. Are we clear? I ain't a woman to be reckoned with."

That smile raised, and the dimples at the corners of his mouth deepened. "Yes, ma'am. I believe you." He set my bucket down on the porch and helped me step up. "I noticed there were some things around your farm I might be able to help you with. I'm positive you could manage on your own, but I have come all this way. Might as well prove my worth. What do you say? Let me stay around and help?"

I pulled my shoulders back as far as they could go and tilted my head toward him. I squinted to pull my eyes tight enough to see the man clearly.

"Oh. Wait. I brought you something. May I?" He waited for my nod, then he reached to retrieve a large leather bag he'd left on the stair. After fumbling around for a minute, he pulled out a small leather box and opened it. "Look what I brought you. Glasses." He took them from the box and held them to his mouth. He huffed a dab of warm air on them, then wrapped his shirttail around two fingers and shined them. "I'm not sure they'll be perfect. But I had an extra pair in my bag. I noticed you were squinting yesterday. See if these help."

Mr. Rankin eased next to me, and my hand went to my friend in my apron pocket. I pulled the hatchet up just enough so he could see it.

"Hold on. Don't go slinging that hatchet. Let me slip these on."

I held tight to the handle but leaned slowly toward him. Mr. Rankin slipped the contraption on my face. The wire pieces curved just enough to fit around my ears. I went to lookin all around me. Up, down. Toward the barn, the garden. Things was still fuzzy but not like they had been.

"Well, I'll be." Laughter popped outta my mouth. "Slap my knee and call me cornpone. I can see. Leastways better than before."

"They're called glasses—spectacles." Mr. Rankin stepped back and looked at me. "Pretty nice. Like I said, they aren't perfect, but they should help a bit."

"I know what they're called. I ain't stupid. I just couldn't see them. They work right nice."

"Mrs. Jenkins, can we start over? I'd like to be your friend."

Bein my friend was not somethin I'd heard since Lillian Goins passed. She was my friend. Good woman. Me and her got into a lot of mischief together. We were both lonesome young girls that found comfort and fun in the antics of one another.

I wrapped my fingers around the handle and tugged at the bucket of water. Mr. Rankin quickly took it from me.

"Can we begin again? I apologize for anything that might have offended you yesterday. I was nervous about meeting you. It seems all the wrong things came out of my mouth."

"I might consider acceptin your apology. You are polite, after all. That means you was raised good."

"Yes, ma'am. My mother was a stickler about manners."

"Mother?"

He looked taken back. "Yes, my mother. Edna Kathleen Rankin. She was a fine woman. A seamstress by trade. My father worked for the railroad in Lexington."

He'd called his momma *Mother*. I'd not heard that since the last time I saw my own momma. When I climbed on that wagon with Stately Jenkins, my momma wiped a tear and said, "Minerva Whaley, don't you forget your mother."

That was the last time I ever saw my momma. Stately, bein the man he was, said the good book tells us to leave our parents and cling to one another. I reckon I didn't think that would mean forever. Time gets away from us, and I reckon it run like a scared rabbit from me. I made one trip back to Lexington, and all I could find was a headstone. *Viney Clair Whaley*. There wasn't even no date.

Warm memories of hot tea steamin on the potbellied stove and the scent of fresh-made bread filled my mind. Things that were pushed clear to the back of my soul wiggled their way to the front.

"A good mother teaches her son the ways of a gentleman." I reached for Mr. Rankin's arm. Who was I not to accept?

"Mother was a wonderful woman. She made sure I learned the things I needed to know."

"'Train up a child in the way he should go: and when he is old, he will not depart from it.' That's what the good book says."

Mr. Rankin smiled as I looked across the mountainside. The

colors of spring painted the peaks—lilies, daisies, sunflowers, sparrows, groundhogs. I could see them all. I'd not seen their real beauty in years. I closed my eyes and took in a deep breath. The air that filled my lungs was like the sugary taste of honey. Fresh, cool. Tender memories commenced to fill my mind.

I felt a tender spot in my soul open. A stranger. A complete stranger had started a crack in the hard shell of my heart. A shell that had formed over thirty years. I didn't usually let a body in early on. Maybe it was the realization that I was old. Maybe there was something familiar about this young man. Maybe I didn't realize my loneliness until I found myself rockin on my porch alone, talkin to the night air. Still, this Mr. Rankin had a spell to go before I trusted him.

I slipped my hand into my skirt pocket and felt the wadded slip of paper he'd given me. The one that contained the partial path of Stately Jenkins and that blessed old box. Mr. Rankin's job was to figure out if that box of gold was a fable or truth, and I wasn't about to tell him one way or the other. Instead, I wanted to see how a real man behaves.

I pulled the slip of paper out and slipped it into his chest pocket. "Just so you know"—I made my way up the porch steps—"I read right good."

FIVE

THE SUN PEEKED THROUGH the slats of my window shutter, formin what looked like stairs up the wall. Ole Satchel begin his bellerin out in the barn, and that fool rooster went to squawking. Easin to my side, I rolled and dropped my feet over the edge of the bed. Every day is a blessin at my age, but them blessins come with curses too. Things like feet and legs that hurt like porcupine quills was stuck all over them. Still, just to see the sun squirm through the cracks of the cabin was a joy.

It took me a minute to get my balance, but once I got my bones movin, I raised the window and pushed open the shutter. There it was in all its beauty, the outline of the mountains. Dots of smoke rose over the pass. That was the reason the Cherokee rightly named these mountains Smoky. A gust of mornin air put a chill to my skin, raising the hair on my arms. I closed my eyes and took in a breath of the mornin. The scent reminded me of fresh-cut maters and boiled corn—enough to bring a sting to set my mouth watering. Then come that twinge of hunger gnawin at me.

I ladled out some water into my wash pan and washed my face and hands. My skin was thin from age, and the more I rolled that lye soap around in my palm, the more it stung. A good lye cleans deep, but it ruins the flowery smell of a mountain mornin. I slipped on clean drawers and a fresh dress, then washed the dirty ones in the basin and hung them by the fire. I stirred the cinders in the fireplace, dropped on a new log, and set my pot of coffee on the grate.

Every day was the same anymore. Despite my love for the mountain, the loneliness took the sweetness away.

The cat stretched and swiped past my leg.

"Mornin, kitty."

I commenced to fry me an egg even though the thoughts of it turned my stomach. I was hungry but I wasn't, all at the same time. I dropped a slice of ham at my feet for the cat and split my runny yellow egg—part for me and part for Satchel. The old dog would set by my feet, knowing that I'd be lucky to eat half of my half. His tail would slowly swipe on the floor whilst he waited for me to scrape my portion onto his plate.

"Eatin ain't what it used to be. My stomach growls, but my appetite says no. I just ain't got the stomach these days."

Still, eatin keeps this old woman alive, so I forced down a few bites. Stately always said I was a cook worth havin, but somehow these days, the things that used to cross as tasty just ain't anymore. My body was payin the price for just nibbling too. My clothes just kept gettin baggier.

I poured my tin cup to the half with coffee, then wrapped the tail of my skirt around the cup so I could hold it. I leaned against the table and pushed the plate closer to the dog with my toe. "Go on now, Satchel. Eat up. Don't leave no evidence of me not finishin my portion. Only leads to guilt." Taking a few steps toward the door, I rested an elbow against the mantel. The quilt folded on my cane-backed rocker called to me. Sitting in that rocker, watchin the sun come up, I had fond memories of Stately—tender moments of rockin with him.

These days lots of memories come to me. There were things that hadn't come to mind since I was young, and to beat all, they was vivid pictures in my head. Many were things that brought a smile to my lips, and then there was those few. The ones that haunt you. Like holding Stately Jenkins in my arms as he took his last breath.

Hearin him say, "Promise me you'll keep the secret," instead of "I love you." Bittersweet, yes, they were. Even more hurtful.

I lifted my face toward the rays of the sun. The need to speak to the good Lord come over me.

"Are these memories Your way of remindin me of a hard but sweet life? Or are You passin my life before me? I've heard folks say before a body dies, their life, all the good and the bad, passes before their eyes. I am right old, and I'm smart enough to know my body is wearing down. Dyin don't scare me, but dyin alone does. Good Father, I don't mind leavin this world. I just don't want to do it alone. Is that too much to ask—don't let me die alone? I can hardly eat these days. Walkin is harder. My chest carries twinges of hurting. I know what's comin. Just don't let me die alone."

I rocked a few more times and took in the warmth of the sunshine. Who'd have ever thought there was such joy in rockin? I forced down a sip of coffee.

Mr. Rankin come to mind. There was something about that Delano Rankin that made me curious. I wasn't sure if it was his incessant desire to know about that box or if it was the fact he was company. Much as I hated to admit it, I needed company. Any company.

Mable and Harley Russell come up the mountain every other week and bring me smoked meat. They're good like that. I suppose that's when the reality of bein old sinks in. When folks wander by to make sure you're still alive. They see to it that an old woman has food, but they rarely stay long enough to get in much talkin. It ain't that I'm not grateful. I am, but a body grows lonesome for chatter. I seemed to have took a shine to this stranger—this Mr. Rankin—and his chatter. He certainly never hushed.

I chuckled. Even when I scolded him, he kept right on yapping. I can't say that in two days I'd grow to trust him, cause I won't. But he was an interesting sort, educated and all. I'd need to string him along enough to see just what he really knew about Stately. I did promise to keep that gold a secret.

Still, findin that box was the least of my worries. Ain't a soul in their right mind would fight their way through them kudzu vines searchin. Stately's secret was buried right by him. Wouldn't a body anywhere find either one under that evil kudzu. That stuff would creep and crawl like a snake across the ground, clinging to anything it could and snuffing the life outta it. I've said it more than once—when I die, I'll rot where I hit the ground. But I might change that thought. Them kudzu would wrap around me, devourin me in days. I cringed.

The best way to see a man's intentions was to see him work. Since Mr. Rankin wanted to pull his weight around here, I figured I might as well let him. Momma didn't raise an idiot. He thought he had me hornswoggled—that I didn't know why he was offering to help out. Oh, I knew. Like I said, I was smart enough to know when to pet the cow to get extra milk. If I could keep my patience with him. Lord knows they was plenty to be done on this square of land.

I smiled. "This square of land." I stood and eased to the porch rail. Around the side of the cabin came Delano.

"Morning, Mrs. Jenkins. Nothing like the sunrise on the mountain, is there?"

I furrowed my brow. "How long you been there?"

Ole Satchel growled from his pallet by my bed, but I figured he was grumbling it was that grizzly in my garden again.

"A bit. I made my way up from Barbourville before the sun did. I figured I'd help you some more." He pushed his hair back and pressed his hat tight on his head.

I grunted and reached for my hoe resting against the doorframe. "Mr. Rankin, I ain't never met a reporter. I reckon now is about as good a time as any for you to start explaining why you think my Stately had anything to do with this goose chase you're on." I hobbled toward the garden and took to diggin at the weeds. He followed like a pup nipping at my heels.

"Here, let me help you with that."

It only took a minute for him to take my hoe and commence to dig. His desire to help set me on edge. He went to swingin that tool hard into the dirt.

His face turned the color of a cherry. "I was raised in Lexington. We don't do a lot of hoeing in town. But I'm very willing to learn." He went back to diggin ankle-deep holes.

"Stop it," I snapped. I eased to his side and pressed my fingers around his hands, then went to guiding him. His arms were stiff. "Ease up. Don't be so tight." I wiggled his arms, tryin to loosen them up. "Just tap the ground enough to pull up the weeds. We ain't diggin a grave here."

He nodded. "I see."

I could tell that he did. It was like lighting a lantern in the pitch dark. The man went to digging like nobody's brother.

"Pace yourself. Sun gets hot when you're workin. Won't be long till your tongue will be hangin out like a thirsty dog. Now, why are you really here?"

"Mostly curiosity. I am a reporter. I love the story."

"Mr. Rankin, you were askin about gold. That's more than curiosity. That's more than a story." I furrowed my brow to be sure he saw I wasn't bitin the bait.

A bead of sweat formed on his brow. He grimaced when he snagged a rock. "To start with, please call me Del or Delano. I'm not accustomed to the formality of using my last name. Please? Call me Del."

I shrugged like I didn't care if I called him anything. I know how a spider catches her prey, and I could play right coy when necessary. Seeming to not care might draw out some answers.

He waited, I think, for me to give him permission to call me Minerva. Not yet. We wasn't that good of friends. He'd be stifled to wait.

"For me, it isn't about the gold," he said. "It's about the story. Besides, I doubt there is any gold. But the story . . . now, that is fascinating." He rested his arm on the hoe. "It's the challenge of seeking out the truth. But it's the mystery that makes a good story. It's the people along the way. Their thoughts, wants, desires. That's what makes a good story with meaning."

"Well, ain't you all smart and whatnot?" I teased and pointed at the row of weeds to be dug. "Like I said, sun sneaks up on you."

A soft breeze brushed past us. Something Mother Nature was good at doin in the spring. She gives you just enough wind to cool you while you work.

"Feel that breeze?" I pointed at his shirt. "Best loosen that collar, let that air in. You'll need it if you keep hoeing at that speed."

Del stopped and undid the top two buttons on his shirt.

"Thattaboy. A man that works the land don't care if he's wearin an ironed shirt."

He smiled and undid a third button. He was already sweatin like a pig at Sunday lunch.

I leaned against the fence post, keepin my nose high in the air. Clouds danced across the blue horizon like the whitewash drippins along the edge of a barn. I squinted and let my eyes focus. The shape of a rabbit formed in a cloud. A bird soarin across the sky busted a hole right through the middle, making my rabbit look like buckshot hit him.

"Go on now . . . Del." I hesitated to call him by his given name. Since Stately Jenkins died, I'd never let nobody any closer to me than their last name, but I figured at ninety-four, what the hay?

A sneaky grin spread across my face. I got nothing to lose. I had something to hide, but not a thing in the world to lose.

SIX

DEL WEEDED TATERS for a spell while I sifted through the fresh dirt and pulled out the stragglers. I felt a bit bad that the man was workin up such a sweat, so I made my way to the spring that seeped up through the ground. I'd planted my garden by that small bubbling of water for a reason. That spot of ground was hard to till in the beginning, but once it was done, I had that little sip of fresh cool water when I needed it, and it was there for my garden when the summer days grew dry.

I took the ladle from the fence post and caught Del a taste of the cool liquid. "Best take you a sip of livin water before you drop." I nudged his arm with the ladle.

He swiped his forehead with his handkerchief and smiled. "Thank you, Mrs. Jenkins."

Now was as good a time as any to hit him up for his real intention. "Tell me about this gold and how you found your way here."

He tilted the ladle to his lips and went to guzzlin.

"I wouldn't swaller that all at once unless you want your head to split open."

My warnin was too late. Del grabbed his head, and his eye squinted shut.

"Told you." I grinned.

He plopped down in the dirt and hung his arms over his knees. "Oh my. Can't say I've ever had that happen."

"Icy water does it ever time. A body's got to sip, not gulp." I rested my hand on his shoulder and worked my way into a squat. I finally went to a firm splat to the ground. "Unh!" I groaned. "Lordy mercy, I'll never get up." I straightened my dress over my knees and dug the heel of my boots into the dirt. "Come on, tell me. How'd you end up on my mountain?"

Del leaned back on his elbows and stretched out his legs. "The story came to me from a typesetter."

"A what?" I cocked my head to one side. "I can't say I've heard of a typesetter." I pushed the spectacles he'd given me tight on my nose.

"Oh, I'm sorry. Remember, I told you I was a reporter. Once we have the news stories ready for the paper, we have to set the words in metal so we can print them on paper. A man sets at this machine called a Linotype." Delano waved his hands back and forth, drawing a picture in the air. "He spells the words line by line, then they are molded in lead. He's called a typesetter."

"I'll be," I said, scratchin my head. "Beats the life outta me. That's how the words get on the page. Huh."

Del grinned. "Anyway, this typesetter—his name is Colton Morris—got wind of some treasure hunters and the possibility of gold. He got drawn into the hope there might be a vein of gold. One thing led to another, and he'd found some information on Melba Bishop, the wife of Freelaw. Colton was so struck by the thought of gold that he was determined to find it. I liked the story—two men taking off with a wealthy man's gold but never spending it. There had to be more to it. The idea of a series of articles intrigued me, so I thought I'd follow up on this end of the story."

It was a hot spring mornin, but when I heard the name Melba Bishop, my skin went cold. I knew that woman. Stately Jenkins knew her too.

My skin crawled. Thirty years dead, and there was still a jealous streak in my heart over that man. That Melba Bishop was mean. Selfish. A temptress—and one that managed to lure a handsome young man like Stately Jenkins into her arms. She didn't care who she stepped on to get what she wanted either. Including Stately Jenkins's wife. I felt my lip curl.

There was the reason we ended up on this mountain. Melba Bishop was the reason Stately was sworn to secrecy. She was the one who took my dreams. She was the one—*is* the one, I'm ashamed to admit—that I hate. Harsh words, I know. I'd pushed that thought to the back of my mind a lot. Hate was not something I wanted to dwell on, but the truth is, I felt there was good reason to dislike the woman.

There were a thousand reasons why Stately shoulda never had that box—reasons he kept such a secret and never let me know what was what. It was news to me it was stole, though his wantin to keep it a secret led me to think that. I just never imagined my hunch was true. Or was it? I didn't know what to believe. I needed and wanted to know more.

Thoughts run through my mind like a bobcat on the trail of a rabbit. Somethin wasn't right. Why would Stately hide the box instead of usin the gold to build us a comfortable life? Unless it was given to him to protect or there wasn't no gold to begin with. He shoulda never took answers like these to the grave. More so, he shoulda never made me a part of his deception. I could feel the anger twist my stomach. Still, it is what it is, and like I always say, hindsight is always clear as a bubblin creek.

"Mrs. Jenkins, you all right? Mrs. Jenkins?" Del waved his hand in front of my face.

"Of course, I'm fine. Why wouldn't I be?" I snapped.

"Well, it was like you drifted off into deep thought."

I cocked my head to one side. "Del, do you plan to make a mountain outta a molehill every time I take to ponderin a thought? Cause if you plan to, you're gonna be wastin an awful lot of good energy that you could be using to hoe up weeds. Now, you was sayin . . . about Melba Bishop?"

"Oh, uh, yes, ma'am. Her husband was a coal tycoon from upper Kentucky. That was something else that bothered me. Why would a man already filthy rich from coal mining care about a small box of gold?"

"You mean besides greed?" I nudged Del. "What was Melba's husband's name again?" Though his name slipped my memory for a second, I couldn't let on like I knew too much.

Del reached into his pocket and pulled out a small notebook. He thumbed through the pages, and when he got to the right spot, he run his finger down a list. "His name was Freelaw Bishop."

That name rung a bell. The old hag had got her claws into a man she deserved. As soon as that thought entered my mind, I knew it was sinful. But still . . .

"And here I thought you was a smart man." I belted out a laugh and bobbed back and forth until I was able to roll to my knees and stand. "You think you can believe a bunch of greedy treasure seekers just because they say my Stately was a part of this? Hogwash. Ha!" I went to slingin my head from side to side. "If there was anything to this gold story, do you really think those who were charged with takin it would tell a soul? Do you really think if Stately had a part in any gold, he woulda told me?"

I glanced toward my shambles of a cabin. What Stately had told me years earlier was one word. Gold. He'd never mentioned it again. Just because he said that one word didn't mean he was tellin the truth. Like I'd said before, a body could just look at my house and see how much wealth Stately Jenkins had. It didn't make one iota of sense that he really had any gold. There was more to that box than gold, and I aimed to figure it out. I wanted to know what Stately was hidin.

Pain shot down my back clean to my feet. I grunted. Delano grabbed my elbow to steady me. I couldn't tell if it was pain from bein old and decrepit or if it was the foot of the good Lord in my backside for misleadin—no, let's call it what it is. Lyin. If there is a good reason to lie, it would be to protect, I suppose. Or would it?

"They might have told their families," Del said. "And you're right. Stately didn't say for sure, and your house is a shambles." He grinned as he pointed to my cabin. "I would have thought a man with any kind of money would have at least spruced up his house."

I couldn't hold my laughter. I put my finger in his chest. "I was married half a lifetime to a poor mountain farmer." I pointed at my house. "Let me remind you that the house you see on the bank is not a house at all. It's a shack. Does that answer your question about my Stately or me hoardin some wealth? Besides, a thief won't never tell his secrets. He'll take them to the grave." I swallowed hard, knowing if my Stately was a thief, then ever word I'd just uttered was true.

Delano stared at the unpainted, worn boards that formed the sides of my cabin.

"Ain't a man alive wouldn't give up that? Riches tend to make the wealthy stingy. Greedier. I don't live in no fancy house," I said, bumpin against Del's arm. "Ain't nothin to be had here. Stately was a hardworkin farmer who did the best he could to get the necessities of life. He was lucky to be alive, no thanks to the war. When he was done, he was crippled up and bitter. We come here to this mountain to get as far from folks as we could." I shook my head. "Look right good at my cabin and tell me to my face that that's the home of a man hoardin gold. And for how long . . . thirty-some years the man's been gone. I ain't got no wealth, Mr. Rankin. Just maybe you need to put these spectacles you give me back on your own eyes." I pointed at the cabin. "That ain't wealth." My dander was gettin up.

Del pulled his hat off and wiped away the sweat. He never blinked. The man just stood and stared. I wondered if my ruse was enough to convince him Stately had nothin to do with that gold. I might not have exactly lied, but I didn't tell the whole truth either. And that still makes me accountable in the good Lord's eyes.

Still, this man was raisin questions about Stately and Melba that I couldn't put together. I knew Freelaw and Melba were married and they had a son, though his name was not somethin I knew. I knew Stately worked for the Bishops and then quit right as we got married. I didn't think they was anything more to it. My husband said we was movin and I moved. I reckon I'm not sure now.

I swiped the sweat from my neck. "Lordy me. It's gonna be hot today. I don't know where you come from in Lexington, but us mountain people live on what we got. And that ain't much more than a little common sense and ingenuity." I smiled right big. "You didn't know I knew such a big word, now, did you, Mr. Rankin?"

It took a few minutes before Del said a word, but when he did, I could tell by the tone of his voice he felt right sorry for me.

"Mrs. Jenkins, I'm sorry. I certainly don't mean to offend you when I ask questions."

"Aaah, it's all right. I might get the least bit testy." I picked up the hoe and went to diggin around the tomato plants. Del offered to take it, but I held tight, diggin at the weeds that tried their best to swallow my maters. "You got a reason for starin me down?" I asked.

"Uh . . . no. I mean, I'm sorry. I guess I just feel bad that things are so hard for you."

I leaned against the hoe. "Listen here, Del. You got no business feelin bad for me. You're right, I didn't choose this life. Stately did. Still, I agreed to it. It's my life, like it or not. But despite the hard times, these mountains are home."

"Why here?" Del asked. "Why did Mr. Jenkins choose here? This mountain. What I read in my research said he was working on the Bishops' farm in Lexington."

"Well, that's true. That's where I met him." My mind traveled back to a time long ago. It felt like an eternity. "Stately was a fine-lookin man. Fresh from the war." I pulled my hands to my chest and remembered. "He swept me clean off my feet. It only took one wink from them deep-green eyes to set my heart throbbin."

"Why, Mrs. Jenkins, your face is turning red. Are you blushing?"

I fanned my cheeks with my apron. "You need to wear your own spectacles. You're seein things. It's hotter than a fritter out here. I'm burnin up."

Del grinned, and I could tell when he covered his mouth with his palm that he was hidin his laughing. But what we don't admit to can't be held over us.

"So, you met Mr. Jenkins in Lexington. When did you marry?"

I could see the wheels turnin in his head. I needed to be careful to not slip up on my story.

"Let me see." I twisted the tiny gold band on my finger. "We met in the spring of 1822. He was seventeen. Seems it was about two or three months later we were married and Stately decided to move. And we did. I didn't put up no fuss."

"Two or three months?" Del's voice turned louder. "That wasn't very long."

I thought a minute before I answered. "When the right glove is slid up on your hand and it's a perfect fit, you wear it. Now, pull us one or two of them tomatoes and a cucumber, and I'll fix us a bite to eat." I pushed open the garden gate. "Or are you done snoopin in my business for today?"

"Ma'am?" Del cleared his throat. "Did you know the Bishops?"

I eyed him right straight. "Workin makes the time fly. It's done lunch."

As the sun neared straight overhead, I realized just how fast time had passed. I shaded my eyes, grateful this stranger had given me spectacles that cleared my sight some. I scanned the mountainside and remembered the first time I stood on this bank looking across the way. Stately had slipped his arm over my shoulder and twisted me in a circle. "Every bit of this beauty is ours. As far as you can see." Thing that struck me that day was that Stately never cracked a smile. I remember that. He didn't smile. It was like he wanted me to be pleased, but he wasn't satisfied. He was right proud, best I remember.

A tear dripped from the edge of my eye. As I scanned the valley and the meadow below the cabin, I could truly say little had changed since the day Stately Jenkins brung me here. Across the field below the garden stood grass up to my hips, and dotted inside the swaying green was patches of white daisies and yellow black-eyed Susans. Close to the creek stood cattails bendin in the breeze, their tan fuzz turning loose and ridin on the wind. Vines of honeysuckle crawled alongside a small stand of pine saplings, givin off such a sweet smell that your mouth would water. Toward the barn, the old oak tree lifted its arms upward to the heavens. It never seemed to mind the rope swing Stately had hung from its lower branch. I smiled as my imagination let me see the plank seat that had long since rotted from the ends of the ropes.

Things I'd not thought of in years kept pourin back, and I wondered again if the good Lord was remindin me of a life well lived.

I shook my head and turned toward the porch. "Get them vegetables if you're hungry." I pressed the handle of the hoe into the ground and used it as a cane to climb the hill to the house. When I'd almost reached the porch, I turned and pointed my finger at Del. "No. I didn't know the Bishops."

And I hadn't known the Bishops. Leastways not personally. Never met them face-to-face. That wasn't no lie. But I knew *of* them, and that was more than I cared to carry.

SEVEN

DEL STOOD at the far side of the garden. If anything, he was good at doin what he was told.

"Mrs. Jenkins, where's the cucumbers? What end of the garden?" he shouted.

I sighed. Did the man ever have any life outside the city? He was a nuisance, but at the same time, he was a blessin. Just proof, I reckon, the good Lord heard my cries to not let me die alone on this mountain. I wasn't blind enough to ignore the fact my days was numbered.

I lifted my finger and pointed toward the south end of the garden. "Down on that end. Up against the fence. They like to climb." I pressed my hand against my knee to give me some support and took a step when something come to me. "Lordy mercy, I forgot to tell him about the hole."

About the time I got turned to holler and warn Del about the low place in the ground by the lower fence, I heard a loud grunt. He'd fell knee deep into the dirt where the bank give way. Though I felt bad I'd just thought of it, it was a sight that made me laugh out loud as he bounced and rolled down the bank into a stand of blackberries.

"I'm sorry, Del. I forgot about that—"

"Hole!" he shouted. "The big one by the cucumber plants. That the one?" He stood and dusted himself off, then picked up the vegetables that had strewed everwhere whilst he rolled down the hill. I could see his mouth movin, and it didn't take keen hearin to know the words comin out was less than clean.

I giggled. "Watch your mouth."

I made my way to the steps and sat hard on the first one. It was just minutes till Del plopped next to me. He laid three tomatoes and two cucumbers in my apron. "That enough?"

I eyed him, then leaned back on my elbows and went to hollerin and laughin. "I really did forget about that bank givin way. Like to have killed me in the early plantin when the dirt broke loose and give with me. I'd have moved the seed, but they were done in the ground and covered with what dirt that give way with me."

"It was a surprise. After I got past the shock, I remembered the fun I had rolling down a hill when I was a boy." Del grinned.

"You takin back all them foul things that come from your mouth as you climbed back up that bank?"

He nodded. "Now that I think about it, it might have been fun."

"Well, whilst I fix us something to eat, why don't you run down there and take yourself a second tumble." I pointed down the bank.

Del chuckled and pulled up his trouser legs. There wasn't much hide left on them knees, and blood trickled down his shin.

"Mm-mm. That looks like it hurts." I stood and headed into the cabin. "You hobble on around the cabin to the pump. Wash them knees up and your hands. Dinner'll be ready in a few."

I pulled open the screen door and inched through. My knees and feet looked like melons. I leaned against the rough wall and lifted one foot at a time to pull off my boots and rub ever toe as best I could. My feet were swelled like nobody's brother, but I managed. I walked on inside, poured some water in the basin, and washed my hands. I pulled a sharp knife from the salt block and scrubbed it a few times against the rough side to get a nice sharp edge. It took me a minute, but I carried the basin to the back door and tossed it. "A body needs clean water to wash the food in," I said.

49

Del grabbed the basin and carried it to the pump. He rinsed and refilled it.

I dipped the vegetables in a pan of water and washed off the dirt, then went to slicing. Juice from the fat red tomatoes oozed over my fingers, and the smell made my mouth water. I'd lost a lot of things in my old age, but my sense of smell could still make my mouth water or my stomach turn. I touched my fingers to my mouth, tastin that sweet juice, then dipped them in the water and wiped my fingers on my apron. Cleanliness was next to godliness—that's what Momma taught me.

I commenced to cut the cucumbers into strips. Stately Jenkins never liked a cucumber cut in rounds. It was the silliest thing I'd ever seen. Man wouldn't touch a round-cut cucumber, but slice them longways and he'd eat till he made himself sick. I popped a slice in my mouth. Nothin better.

It felt good to cut a whole cucumber. I might gnaw on a quarter of one, but to have another person share a full cucumber . . . well, that felt warm and special. It had been a long time. Course, it took from Satchel's portion, but I figured he'd make do.

The screen door whined, and Del come through. "I made sure I got cleaned up while you were cutting up vegetables. Wooo, that water, cold as it was, set me on fire when I washed my knees."

I giggled under my breath as I lined tomato and cucumber slices along a plate.

"Mrs. Jenkins, I didn't know mountain water was so versatile."

I looked over the spectacles and cocked my head to one side. "What?"

"Well, earlier, you gave me a swig of cold water, and my head felt like it was going to split in two. Then that same spring water set me on fire when I washed my skinned-up knees."

"You think that set you afire. Wait till I dab you some camphor on it. Pull up a chair and sit."

I laid out two plates, two knives, and two forks just like Stately Jenkins liked them. Handing over a plate of leftover fried taters and the tomatoes, I nodded for Del to take some. I watched as he gently scraped potatoes onto his plate, and it hit me just how long it had been since I'd fried up taters for my husband.

"This looks good, Mrs. Jenkins. Thank you for taking time to make it up." Del cut his tomato and started to shove it into his mouth.

I took hold of his hand. "Wait a cotton-pickin minute. In this house, we pray over our blessins."

Del's mouth shut like a bear trap snappin down on a limb, and he laid his fork and knife to the side. "I'm sorry. I didn't know."

"Wasn't you raised to pray over your meal?"

He shook his head. The blank look on his face told the story.

"Just as I was beginning to think your momma did a good job. Bow your head." He did, and I went on. "Good Father, You have brung me into another year and, well, another day. I welcome You here in my house to share what You have give me at no cost. Thank You, sir. Amen."

Del harbored an awkward look when I finished my words to the Almighty. It let me know that a piece of paper from a fancy college didn't teach what a man really needed to know about right livin.

"I might have a couple more questions," Del said. "May I ask while we eat?"

"Lordy mercy. More questions?"

"I'm finding out you're quite a unique soul."

I stopped chewing and pondered a minute, then bit into a tomato. "I've been called a lot of things over the years. Unique was never one. Ask your questions. I might or might not oblige you."

"Did you leave Lexington right after you married?"

I could answer that question without worry. "Best I remember, it was another month or so. My daddy worked with the railroad, and Momma worked three days a week at the general store. I was fourteen, give or take a year or two. Needed to finish school."

"Mrs. Jenkins, you came from society? Your daddy was a railroad man?" Del asked.

I stood, walked to the basin by the window, and went to cuttin a second cucumber. I looked out of the window across them vines and toward the ridge. Then I leaned toward one side of the window and peered toward the mountain range. The sun bounced off the ridge like flashes of lightning. As far as I could see, the mountains raised and fell like someone had squished bread dough betwixt their fingers.

"You know"—I pointed across the way—"I'm sure when the good Lord created these mountains that everywhere a ridge rises is like Him steppin in mud with it seeping up between His toes. And them twists and turns the river makes . . . I think the good Lord set Himself down and took one finger, drawing a squiggly line that become the water's path. But then, that didn't answer your question, now did it?"

"No, ma'am, but it painted a beautiful picture. I might need to borrow that from you when I write my next newspaper article." He stuck his fork in another slice of cucumber.

"We wasn't rich by any means, but Momma and Daddy made a living that kept us comfortable. Daddy worked for the railroad, but he was just labor. I made it to tenth grade before Stately Jenkins come around."

"I thought you had to finish school." Del shoved more taters in his cheek. He looked like a chipmunk cramming food in his pouch for winter.

"I did. Tenth grade was as far as our town school went. I met Stately, and he took me as his wife with Daddy's blessin. I finished up the last few weeks of school, and as soon as I was done, we married at the courthouse." I scratched my head. "Maybe it was the other way around. I'm old, things mush together these days. Anyway, me and him took a wagon and made our way from Lexington." My voice quivered, and I choked up. "Momma took her white linen and lace tablecloth and made me a veil. She told me it would make my plain blue dress look like a wedding dress."

"Mrs. Jenkins, did you want to stay in Lexington?"

I straightened my shoulders and bucked up. "I wanted to be a good wife, and that meant goin wherever my husband thought was best. But truth is, I was a youngin. Fourteen. Stately Jenkins was seventeen, almost eighteen. We were children. Stayin close to my family would have been . . . well . . . nice." I scraped the last of the potatoes onto Del's plate. "You can finish that spoonful, can't you?"

He eyed the potatoes and nodded. "You never told me. Why here? Why did Mr. Jenkins choose Shoal Mountain? What was so special about here to take you away from your family?"

I felt myself growin uncomfortable with the questions. Del was troddin too close to news I didn't want to share. Too close to truths I didn't even know. How was I to answer this question without causing concern?

I waited till Del got that last bite of tomato in his mouth, then I snatched his plate. My wash pan held a dab of warm water left from washin up breakfast dishes at daybreak, so I rinsed off the plates and swiped them with a towel. Years earlier, I'd stitched tiny leaves on the corners of my rags. The years of use had frayed the stitches.

My mind run over a fair way to answer Del's question without breakin my promise. Without givin away Stately's secret. Lawsey, how I wished I'd have thought before I made that promise. *Lord, forgive me for what I say if it turns to a fib.*

Then it come to me. The truth without lying.

"The land was given to him. I don't know by who, but it was given to him. It was his to do with as he pleased, so he brung me here to start a life, or at least what life could be had. I never figured we'd stay long. Like I told you, his legs were bummed up from the war. I didn't think he could manage here. But a body does what a body needs to do. And I become the wife I needed to be whilst Stately Jenkins become a farmer."

Del twisted in his seat, then leaned up on his elbows. He clasped his hands together and rubbed them. "Sounds like you were torn about leaving Lexington." The legs on his chair squealed as he scooted away from the table. He come to stand next to me by the window. "Do you still miss Lexington?"

I felt all sorts of emotion rise from deep inside me. Things I'd shoved over my shoulder, turned away from, left to forget. I nudged him, and we walked out to the porch. "Del, things is what they is. The two shall become one. That's what the judge said when we were married. I took to that. I loved Stately. I hated to leave my momma and daddy. After all, I was a youngin in her prime. It would have been a disgrace to marry after sixteen and have my folks be the parents of a spinster. I was given to a man who loved me and wanted to do for me, so I followed where he wanted to go."

"One more question, and then I'll go back to work on whatever you need me to do."

"Law, help. You're worse than a youngin askin so much. What else?"

"I'm out of time to stay in the inn in Barbourville. Can I make a bed in your barn? You still have a lot of work that needs to be done to fix up this place, and I want to help."

"Fix up my place? I didn't ask for no fixin to be done."

"I know. But I see things that you need. I'm not the handiest man alive, but I have a heart and determination. Besides, I like you, and you've taught me a lot about farming in the last couple of days. I want to learn. There could be a good story in all this."

We walked on the porch, looking over the farm. There were things that could use a little sprucing up, and I guessed some hands, even if they ain't the handiest, is better than none. I could feel a nudge in my heart as if the good Lord was remindin me He was my provider. I learned years ago to listen when the Almighty nudged. Maybe Delano was here for a reason. Maybe, just maybe, he'd hold my hand and usher me into the arms of God Almighty.

This Mr. Rankin was a different bird. I'd only known him a short time, but he seemed to be an old soul. He reminded me of a young Stately Jenkins—stubborn, but the right kind of stubborn.

He even set his jaw just like Stately would do when he was ponderin something. I reckon men must just naturally have a stubbornness about them—certain actions that only men do. I can't say much. I reckon I set my jaw pretty stiff when I know I'm right. My head reminded me of what Stately always said. *Don't trust no stranger.* My heart, though, said something different.

Stately was gone—had been gone for years—and I realized at that moment I was still holdin on to the ways of a man who was dead. Maybe you can teach an old dog new tricks after all. I only wished I could turn loose of that secret that haunted me.

I pointed toward the barn. "Stately built a room in the loft for travelers. You go check it out. Let me know if the mice have eat the quilt all to pieces or not. There's a straw broom in the barn. Clean up the loft." Wary as I tried to be, the truth was, I wanted someone around. Despite Stately's warnings about strangers, I knew a body had to come to trust.

It eat at me that this man I hardly knew felt so familiar. I'd prayed that the good Lord wouldn't let me die alone, for a person to bury me so the critters don't eat my dead body. Despite it all, I called this man a provision. Del didn't seem to have an ill bone in his body. He was truthful, honest so far. He was good as any, and my body was tellin me my time was comin. Alone ain't how I wanted to die.

Del placed a hand on my shoulder and squeezed. "Mrs. Jenkins, if I was to have ever known my own grandmomma, I would hope she would be like you. Thank you for letting me stay. Letting me help. This is my pleasure."

The grin on his face let me know he was tellin the truth, and I had a good feelin in my gut that lettin him stay was right.

Del winked and then smiled a toothy grin. A chill swept over me. For a minute, a fleetin minute, I felt like Stately might just approve of this young man helpin me out.

Del took a few steps and turned. "You know I'm a reporter, right? Stories are what I write. And you, my sweet friend, are a story worth reading."

I waved him away and headed into the house. There was nothin I could do, so I went to blubbering like a sick cow. There was someone who wanted to spend time with me, and it felt right nice. This old woman, lonely as she was, felt a little warmth in a budding friendship.

I turned, cupped my hands around my mouth, and hollered as Del headed across the field to the barn. "And just so you know, I ain't your maid."

EIGHT

THE SUMMER SUN begun to take its toll. The days were hot, and the nights grew muggy. Rain had held off, and my garden was waning. There were even a few leaves on the trees turnin brown right early. Summer heat does that. Curdles the leaves. My momma called these hot July days "dog days." It was hot inside the cabin and hotter outside. The air was so thick it felt like you were breathin in the dew. Despite the weather, Del was up before Wallace could crow.

A couple of months had passed, and Del hadn't come at me with more questions about that gold. That told me my gut was right in lettin him stay. I needed the company. Maybe he really did want to be my friend. Maybe I was important to somebody.

I didn't mind his stayin, but I commenced to wonder if the man had a family, and if he did, wouldn't his wife wonder why he was gone so long?

I set a cup of coffee on the porch steps and then eased down one by one. It took more and more time for me to get up and down them blasted steps, but I managed, and once I was at the bottom, I took hold of a cup and headed across the field.

Del was settin out late potatoes to get me through the winter. He stopped digging. "Morning, Mrs. Jenkins."

I nodded and reached the cup toward him. "A body's gotta wonder if settin out late taters is worth the effort."

"Why would you say that?" Del leaned against his hoe and took the cup.

"Look at me. I ain't a fine picture of health these days. I can't eat much. Can hardly walk. I ain't gonna be here to eat late taters."

Del shook his head. "Live each day to the fullest. None of us know when our time will come. Even you, Mrs. Jenkins."

The man was right, but then he didn't have ninety-four years kickin at his rear either.

"I've been ponderin," I said. "Ain't you got no family? And best I remember, a man can't just walk away from his job for weeks at a time."

"Oh. Well, so much for thinking up new jobs for me." Del blew the steam from his cup and took a sup. "I suppose I owe you a little history."

"You reckon?" I asked as I nodded toward the cabin. "Breakfast is ready. Come on and eat." We walked to the house whilst Del begin to talk.

"I'm not married. Wanted to be." His smile dropped. "But she didn't have eyes for me that I had for her."

"Did you ask her to marry you?" I blurted out.

"Actually, yes. She walked down the aisle and right on out the back door for an opportunity to live in Atlanta. Her timing could have been better." Del hung his head.

I patted his arm. "I'm sorry to hear that. You seem like a right nice young man."

"I'd like to think I am. But she wanted more than me or Lexington could give her. And as for my job, well, I'm a reporter. Reporters travel and do research on their stories. I promised my boss I'd send him weekly stories on life in the mountains of Kentucky, and he agreed to keep me on the payroll. I told you, it's all about the story, and my boss is all about selling papers. These articles would move papers. Win, win."

"So you ended up here on my doorstep?" I bumped his arm.

"Figured if I was going to work, might as well work for a cranky old woman." He grinned real big, proud of his snide little joke.

"You think you're right smart, don't you? It ain't becomin to be smart to an old lady. And I might be old, but my memory serves that you were the kitten that begged to stay."

His free hand come up and took hold of mine. He squeezed my fingers gently and kissed them. "An old lady that makes a good cup of coffee."

I pulled my hand away and tried to ignore his humor. "You keep callin me an old lady, and I'll turn you from a rooster to a hen faster than lightnin."

Del went to laughin.

"Like I said before you interrupted me, I've been ponderin and prayin, and I believe I've decided it's all right if you call me by my name. Minerva. But let's get something straight. You ain't to misuse it or run it in the ground. I'm tryin to be accommodatin here."

You'd have thought I hit him square between the eyes with a stick, for he stood there with his mouth open. "Really?"

I furrowed my brow and squinted. "Did I stutter when I said it?"

After breakfast, we walked onto the porch and set a spell. The smell of fresh coffee swirled in the breeze, and the hens wobbled their way to the porch, waitin for their bits of biscuits.

"I see you fixed them rotted fence posts." I gazed out over the garden as I crumbled a leftover biscuit in the grass. The hens clucked like a bunch of church women scurryin over and makin their spot on the front pew—nobody takes your pew in the church. I snickered.

"Yes, ma'am. Took me a bit to figure out how, but even you said I was smart." He pulled his shoulders back right proud.

"I said your mouth was smart. But that's a battle for another day. I'm obliged at the work you've done. Thank you. I see you

59

sickled down the knee-high grass from the house to the garden and barn. Place looks right nice."

"Glad you're happy. Since I've already put in a half day's work, I thought it might be nice if I hitched up the wagon to Belle and took you down to the river. It's cool by the water. Might be nice to enjoy it. Wait here." He rushed into the barn and come out carryin two poles. "I'm so smart I made us a couple of fishing poles. Are you up for a ride?"

I couldn't find words. I'd not been down to the river in years. I closed my eyes and remembered when I was young and Stately Jenkins took me there for a picnic. We'd spread a blanket under the willow tree, stretched out on our backs, and watched the clouds pass. The smell of purple wisteria blooms hanging from their vines that inched up a maple tree filled my lungs. It was a good day until Stately started to go on about needin to graft a vine to cover where he'd buried that box. He went on and on till he was pacin along the riverbank almost preachin about that box. I listened till I couldn't hear nothing but a muddle of words, then I packed up my basket and walked home.

Hours later, I gazed at the river from the porch, and Stately was still pacin back and forth, preachin about the box. He'd rant and gripe about all them Bishops took from him. I wondered why. Still, bein a good wife, I never asked. Stately give me one hint on the day we left Lexington. That was the last I was to ask.

The best I could do was stand on the porch and look from a distance. I loved him right deep. When he was with me, it made my heart shine, but it was like walkin into a cave with no light when he got like this. The deeper you walked, the darker it got, till there was no light to be had. I learned to turn around and walk back, elsewise I'd be hung in the darkness forever. Lost. Them days was when I noticed Stately's hand took to shakin a lot. From time to time, his head would bob. I figured he was just in a worrisome way, but deep down I knew they was something wrong for him to have these fits like this.

There were times Stately would take off. He'd be gone for days, and I had no iota of where he'd took to. Robert Blessing would pass by and see Stately was gone. Our cabin set up on the side of the hill, above the path that led to town. Robert could glance up and see if the wagon was settin by the porch. If it wasn't, the man was right kind to climb the bank and check on me. He'd see to it I had meat and flour. Sometimes he'd just sit and talk a spell. Guess he noticed Stately's manners too—him goin off and leavin me for days or weeks to fend on my own didn't hit Robert as right kosher. Sometimes I was left with no meat. I reckon Stately thought I'd kill myself a rabbit. Just because he taught me to shoot didn't mean I was gonna head out huntin.

Still, Robert and Stately was good friends. I reckon Robert's need to check on me was his just bein kind to Stately and feelin a little sorry for me. He'd become a dear friend to me too.

I brought myself back from the memory. "What's my price?" I asked as I eyed Del right stern. "Must be a price for a fishin trip."

"Price?"

"Yep, what's in this for you?"

Del kicked a clot of dirt. "Conversation. Fishing. Cool breeze off the river. No work."

"Conversation?" I asked. "You mean questions?"

"Might be a few. But I thought you'd like to know about me. I've learned a lot on this farm the last couple of months. Wouldn't you like to know what you've taught me?"

"You know this little invitation sounds like you're tryin to butter me up, right? Besides, I'm an old woman. You ain't married. It might look like your intentions ain't pure."

Del took to laughing. He bowed and took my hand. "Would you like this to be an attempt to court you, or would you prefer to simply enjoy good company?"

"I'd rather know the questions you're gonna ask so I can practice lyin." I took one of the fishin poles. "You ain't fished until you've fished with me. Give me a spell to get ready. A ride down the mountain might be pleasant." I give that pole the once-over, runnin my hands up and down it, checkin the string. "Looks right nice." I winked with approval and then leaned against the porch rail to scratch an itch on my back. "There's one good thing about these things."

"Yeah, what would that be?" Del commenced to check his stash of worms.

I rubbed my back against the porch rail again, then took the end of that fishin pole and slipped it down the back of my dress. "Makes for a good back scratcher." I scraped the long stick up and down my spine. Chills run up my arms. "And tell me, Del. You're all educated and whatnot—why is it when you scratch an itch, it just gets worse?"

He raised his brow and chuckled. Since I had him chucklin, now might be as good a time as any to pick his brain about that typesetter feller.

"You never finished tellin me about that typesetter. I done forgot his name," I said, handing him back the fishin pole.

Del held up his finger, motioning me to wait. "Did you just ask *me* a question?"

I thought a second and come back at him. "No, I didn't ask no question. I told you that you never finished tellin me about that typesetter. I'm assumin there is more to that story." I pulled myself up the steps by the rickety rail.

"Let me help you up." Del dropped the poles on the ground and grabbed my arm. "What's my price for answering your question?" He swiped his forehead.

"Ain't no price, smart mouth, and besides, I done told you, it wasn't a question." I headed inside the house.

"Wait a minute. I see you can dish out the tomfoolery, but there isn't much room for taking it." He grabbed the screen door and held it open. "On the way to the river, I might just finish the story."

I elbowed his stomach. "Smart mouth." I needed to catch my breath, so I slid a chair out from the table and set to rest.

Del sat across from me and rested his arms on the table. "Colton Morris was the typesetter I worked with. Still do. He had some papers he'd found from a visit to Richmond, Virginia. Amongst them was a stack of warrants. I didn't tell you this part, did I?"

I shook my head, but already I could feel my stomach turn.

"Like I said, Colton was all about finding the gold. Anyway, one of the warrants had papers attached and was handwritten by the sheriff there in Lexington. Told about two young men that worked the Bishop farm. It said they were bent on payback. Something about one of their parents was hurt and Mr. Bishop left him to die."

"Was Stately's name mentioned?" I tried to act as if I didn't know.

"His name and Gumble's were both listed. But nothing was said about whose parent died or if that was true."

"And you are tellin me that Stately Jenkins's name was on that paper? Hogwash! You don't seem to understand that Stately was all crippled up from the war. He could barely walk, much less come up with some plan to get even or steal gold." I felt my anger rise. "And Stately's daddy died of the fever. There was no 'hurt' to his dyin other than a fever hotter than the fire of hell."

Momma used to tell me that the quickest way to know a body was lyin was to watch how fast they got mad. Quick to anger usually meant they was coverin something. I reckon that was true, for the more I tried to think of a way to ward off Del's words, the harder it got and the madder that made me. I waved my hand at him as if to send him away.

This promise was goin to be the death of me. Despite my telling the truth about Stately's daddy, I'd failed to finish the story. The Bishops left Stately's daddy to die when he dropped along the railroad with a fever high enough to fry an egg on his forehead. Best I recall, Stately pleaded for them to put his daddy on the pump cart, but they wouldn't—there was no time to help the weak. They were dead weight. Stately never forgive the Bishops for that. And just like he made me promise about that box, he promised his dyin daddy he'd make things right.

I felt my teeth grindin together. Ever muscle in my body tensed. It was all I could do to keep a level head.

"You best go hitch up that horse," I said. "She ain't had a yoke on her in years. She might protest."

"But you need help gathering things to take to the river," Del said.

"I'll be fine. I've been doin for myself for ages. Today ain't no different."

"But I thought you wanted to know about the typesetter." Del cocked his head to one side. "Miss Minerva, did I upset you?"

I swung my hand, swattin at a fly that pestered me. "No. No. You didn't say nothin wrong. Not this time. Now, go on. Hitch up that horse. You keep in mind, I don't talk raw of the dead." I stood, took a few steps, and turned. "And you forget I'm an old woman. I grow impatient and cranky when I have to ponder too much. Stop readin things into my actions. You hear?"

Del stammered around, tryin to find the words he thought would ease my distress. "Are you sure I can't help you gather what you need to take fishing? I can help."

I stomped my foot. "I. Am. Sure. Hitch that mare!" I hobbled to my pantry and pulled down a basket. *The man can be right slow at times.*

Del shrugged and made his way toward the barn, and when I was sure he was far enough outta sight behind the barn, I walked outside and around the house. I took my hatchet. Tying the rope to my waist, I mumbled a prayer for protection, then I hacked my way through that wretched kudzu to Stately's restin place. The axe needed sharpened, but it cut the vines enough that I could get a finger under them and pull them from Stately's stone. They'd grow over it in a day.

I brushed my thinning white hair from my face. Sweat dripped over my brow.

"What have you done to me?" I leaned against the stone. "Stately Jenkins, this young girl loved you. Trusted you. Why would you do this to her?" I slapped my fist against my chest. My anger boiled. "Ain't enough that you died, but to make me hold this burden makes me wonder if you ever loved me at all."

It was my custom to pull all the vines from Stately's stone and scrape the dirt from the letters of his name. Not today. Today, I come to realize Stately Jenkins wasn't quite right. The burden of that box had weighed so heavy on him that it took his mind.

For years, I'd shoved what I knew to be true to the rear and counted it as my being selfish. Del bringing up them memories only served to show me the lie I had believed for years. It didn't mean I didn't love Stately, for I did with all my heart. But the truth about him was covered deep in my soul. He was never right after the war. And I was a fool.

In the distance I heard the wagon makin its way up the hill. I pushed my way through the vines and out. I hung the axe by the pump, rolled up the rope, and set the bucket on top. I went to pumpin to prime that thing as Del worked his way around the house, hollering for me. I commenced to splash some water on my face like I was washin up.

"There you are," Del said. "Mare hitched up good. It was like she remembered everything necessary. You all right?"

"Yes. Yes. I just wanted to wash up in some cool water. There's a pitcher behind you on the well house. Why don't you fill it? We'll have us some good cold water to take."

Del reached for the pitcher whilst I pumped. The cool water bubbled and splashed into the pitcher. I turned toward the house.

"Miss Minerva, watch out. Don't catch your foot on that root." Del yanked the axe off the hook by the pump. With one whack, he sliced that vine in half. He pulled till he broke it loose from the dirt and tossed it into the thick stand of twisted vines. "Those vines are a mess. Maybe I ought to cut a few out tomorrow."

"Ain't worth the effort. They just grow right back. Don't

bother," I said, prayin that he'd let the idea go. "Besides, they keep it cool back here."

Del nodded and took the pitcher. "You ready to go fishing?"

"Lead the way. I'm slow, but you go on ahead. There's a rag and twine you can tie up that pitcher with to hold in the water."

"Yes, ma'am."

Del meandered around the side of the cabin, and I stopped and turned back. "What have you done to me, Stately Jenkins? What have you done?"

NINE

I SQUINTED THROUGH the spectacles Del had given me as we bounced down the rough wagon trail toward the river. Ruts as deep as your ankles snagged the wheels, causin them to lurch hard as they hit bottom. Tree roots pushed across the trail, refusin to give our backs and necks any peace.

It had been a spell since I'd been down this trail—since I walked the five miles to Barbourville when Stately Jenkins died. Since I'd fell against the chest of Robert Blessing and howled in hurt. I don't recall even noticin the rush of the river or the roar that its rapids shouted. But as we neared the flatland, the river's voice commenced to speak to me. *Remember when you were young? Remember when you'd sit by my banks and dream about a family? Remember?*

The thoughts brung tears to my eyes.

"You all right, Miss Minerva?" Del gently bumped my knee with his. "What's runnin through your mind?"

I pressed two fingers beneath the glasses and dried a damp cheek. "Ahhh, ain't too much to think about at my age." I tapped my forehead. "Empty."

"Empty is the last thing in your head. Why don't you tell me about when you used to come to this river?" He pulled the mare to a halt and leaned on his knees. His eyes scanned the deep blue water that pushed over the rocks. "The river's beautiful, isn't it?"

He leaned against the wagon bench and rested his arm on the back. "I'm sorry, Miss Minerva. I didn't mean to interrupt. You were about to tell me about coming to the river when you were young."

"Ain't much to tell. I always loved to fish."

"So you aren't new to fishing? Worms don't make you sick to your stomach?" Del pressed his hat tight on his head.

I huffed. "I could hook a worm three times before it got out its first wiggle."

"I bet!" Del chuckled and gently rubbed my shoulder. His touch was reassurin.

"There was a time when I snagged a carp longer than your leg. It fought me like the devil himself was stuck on my hook. But bein as I had feet and dry land, the varmint lost the war. He was supper for two nights."

"Carp, heh? Can't say I've ever eaten carp." Del tapped the reins and nudged the horse on down the trail. He reached across my lap to steady me over a bump in the path. "Hang on."

"Boy, you ain't experienced nothin, have you?" I shaded my eyes from the sun. "Best I can tell, you've lived a pretty boy's life. Didn't know nothin about hoeing. Nothin about buildin. Less about gardenin. And now you're tellin me you ain't eat carp? Land sakes." I shook my head in disbelief.

"In all fairness, I've eaten bass and trout."

"Whoop-de-doo!" I snickered. "Well, a man ain't a real man till he bites down into the tough meat of a carp. They're . . . well, they're right chewy. It's what Stately called a poor man's meal. When a body's hungry, even carp is tasty, that's what he'd say." I let out a belly laugh. Holdin my hands up, I eyed my bent fingers. Years of work and pain had twisted them out of shape. "Don't think these fingers got the strength in 'em to fight a carp these days." I showed Del my pointer finger. The first knuckle turned toward my thumb. "Truth is, Del, I'm gold."

He looked at me right funny. "You givin yourself a pat on the back?"

"What you mean, a pat on the back?"

"You said you were gold." Del stood from the wagon bench and pulled up on the reins to get the mare movin again. She needed remindin about the feel of the bit in her teeth. She shook her head, adjusting the bit, then stepped forward.

"I said that? I meant old. Not gold."

"My paper publisher always says the first thing from your mouth is what you really meant. You must be thinkin about that gold."

I felt a rush of blood to my cheeks. If things such as that would slip from my lips, I could just as quickly give up Stately's secret. Givin up that secret was not an option.

"Hogwash!" I snapped. "Gold wasn't on my mind at all. It was a slip of the tongue. Your friend is wrong."

"Maybe, since you brought it up—albeit through a slip of the tongue—I might just ask you a question about that gold."

"Afore you ask me a question, I need the mud cleared. See, I was thinkin on that story you told me about the Bishop family. Are you thinking that child of Melba's belonged to someone besides Freelaw?"

Del's eyes grew wide. "It was a pretty twisted story, but yes, it seems that child might have belonged to someone else."

My mind led me back to the day I saw Melba kiss Stately across the river. Maybe it was just a goodbye—they was friends. He worked for them. I never asked. He'd married me. But . . . was there more?

"Maybe this man that was with Stately really fathered a child, and old man Bishop was out for revenge. I mean, maybe there was more goin on with that slice of land than a little box of gold. Just something to chew on. You're the reporter." I crossed my arms, right proud of my conclusion.

"Do you think Stately could have been the father?" Del asked as he pulled the wagon to a halt.

"Absolutely not!" I drew back and smacked his arm. "And don't you never talk ill of my husband again."

"I . . . I . . ." Del looked a bit taken back. He flipped the reins again against Belle's back, urging her to keep a slow pace down the path. He said very little for quite a spell.

I commenced to feel a bit bad about smackin the man, so I eased my hand onto his cheek. "I reckon I crossed the line. I shoulda never smacked you. That was wrong of me. I guess I just let my feelins step in. I'm sorry, Del." I gently brushed my fingers across his cheek.

He smiled. "Naw, Miss Minerva, I was out of line myself. The thought just crossed my mind that maybe the secret was never gold to start with." He quickly hushed. The look on his face give me every indication why—he was about to crawl right back into the hole he'd just got out of.

Thing was, this news from Del really was news to me. Miss Melba was one to sow her oats everywhere. The woman was married to the richest man in Lexington, but she was always on the prowl for happiness. She was never faithful to her husband, and everyone in Lexington assumed that—except for her husband. Guess it's true, riches can't buy you happiness.

I just had to piece together how and when Stately became part of this. Nothin made sense. Could he have fathered a child? Her child? No, impossible. I tried to shake the thought from my head.

If Del was out to plant seed, then he did. I never once, in all our years, was unfaithful. Stately wasn't always the husband I wished he was, but fatherin a child with another woman was not something I'd considered. All those times he just took off . . . Del had planted a seed as tough as that kudzu, and it just sprouted and commenced to take over.

Since the only thing Stately ever really told me was to keep that box a secret, there suddenly come some questions I needed to answer. Could Stately Jenkins have been in love with two women? Did he steal that gold? Was there really any gold, or was this secret just a lie? Was it a child? My momma once told me some things was best left lying on the back porch. After all these years, maybe this was that thing. What I didn't know certainly couldn't hurt me. Or could it?

I'd been glad to leave Lexington, even though it meant leavin my family behind. Nothin would have been worse than losin the man you loved to a harlot. A wealthy harlot at that.

My hands commenced to shake the more I thought about Melba, and these days, holdin back my intent grew harder. I was to the age that it really didn't matter a hill of beans what I said. My days was short anyhow. I'd just try not to think about Melba. Try not to think of her kissin the only man I ever loved. Of course, once the seed was planted, I couldn't get the roots pulled.

I slipped my arm through Delano's and tugged. "There. Over there. See them purple flowers hangin? Them's wisteria. They're nice and shady."

"Then the wisteria is where we stop." Del tipped his hat. With that, he directed old Belle to a shady spot and unhitched her. He pulled out the pitcher of water and the small basket of ham and biscuits, then he spread a quilt on the ground. He went to his knees and rubbed out the wrinkles in the blanket. The man was one to get the details right. If he'd rub out wrinkles, he'd find a sneaky way to trick me into givin up Stately Jenkins's secret.

"If I wasn't so old, I'd swear you was tryin to court me! But I've said that before. Must be something to it, heh?" I rared back and let out a laugh.

Del raised a brow. "Maybe I am." He helped me outta the wagon. I stood and watched as he unloaded the gosh-awfulist bunch of stuff I'd ever seen—a bag filled with dirt and worms, one with extra hooks, and one with line he'd found in the loft. Line from Stately's fishin pole.

"Did you bring the feedin trough too?" I teased. "Some worms and a stick is enough."

"Nope. But I brought you a stool to sit on by the water."

"Well, la-di-da! Ain't you just the smart one." I rested my hand on my hip.

71

"I've been told I was smart."

"Again, what you heard was you was a *smart mouth*. Them's different things."

This Del was right fun to spar with. There were times I'd look at him and swear he had the green eyes of Stately Jenkins, but them was just thoughts messin with what little mind I had left. The boy was kind. He made me laugh. And I was startin to believe once again that the good Lord had answered that prayer for me. The one where I prayed not to die alone. Nothin scared me more than dyin alone. A body woulda thought that was the least of my worries since I'd lived alone, holed up on this mountain, for over thirty years. I was smart enough myself to know my days was short. I felt a chill run up my arms, so I wrapped my hands tight around me.

"You cold?" Del asked. "We can move into the sun."

I stared at him before I spoke. "No, son, I ain't cold, but I got a chill. A chill from a memory. Seems you've drudged a lot of them up lately."

He brushed off the stool and helped me down, then handed me a pole and the bag of worms. "Want to tell me about it? Or is it none of my beeswax, as you say?"

"I ain't sure tellin you is worth the effort." I nodded and threaded a worm onto my hook. After pullin the line away from the pole with one hand, I leaned back and tossed the worm and hook into the water.

"Nice toss," Del said. "I may have met my match."

"We'll see," I said. "We'll see who can outfish the other."

We sat quiet for a spell, pullin in and tossin out them lines, before I felt a nudge on my hook. I yanked hard and felt the line dip deep into the water. "Got me a carp."

"How do you know it's a carp?"

"Went straight to the bottom." I reached the pole toward him. "Pull it in. And don't you lose it. We're eatin carp tonight."

The chill that climbed my back wouldn't leave me. It stuck

hard to my bones, but I wasn't about to lay my heart out on the ground for a stranger.

Del rushed to the riverbank and fought at that fish for a few minutes before wrangling it up on the rocks. The fish flopped helplessly, tryin to flip its way back to the water.

"You get on them slick rocks, and I'll be haulin you outta that river," I said.

Del struggled to grab the line and snag the fish.

"Oh, for Pete's sake!" I hollered. "Pick it up. Then slam it on a rock."

"Do what?" Del dangled the fish like he was doin a dance along the river.

I strained to stand and walk the few steps toward him. I yanked the pole and fish up into the grass, then took the slippery beast by the tail. I rared back and slammed it against a rock, and its body went limp. I snorted and swiped my hands on my apron. "And that is how you kill a fish."

We'd fished pretty near most of the afternoon, catchin little ones and tossin them back. Nothin beat the carp I snagged, and I knew it wouldn't.

Words were few. It seemed Del sensed my mind was wandering over old times with Stately. Before I knew it, he'd built a fire and cleaned that carp. We sat takin in the smoky scent of fresh-baked fish. As the sun eased toward evenin, I finally decided to talk.

"We ain't stayin down here too late, are we? That path is hard in the dark."

"I know. I figured I could walk and lead Belle. I put a lantern in the wagon."

"Of course you did. I wouldn't be surprised if you had half the house in that wagon."

"Now whose got the smart mouth?" He chuckled.

I leaned back and rested my feet against a warm stone. "What is so important about that box of gold? The way you talked, it wasn't much more than a handful."

Del eyed me as he finished off the last biscuit. It was easy to see there was more on his mind. "Minerva, it's the story behind the gold. If, in fact, there is any gold. It's the intertwining of the lives of all these people that makes me curious. How the decisions they made affected one another. And exactly who are the others involved? We're all connected, you know. I like to connect the lines."

"Ain't you a deep thinker? I bet finding that box would make you a hero, wouldn't it?"

Del leaned back on his elbows and commenced to chew on a stick. "Naw, I doubt it. The way the stories go, it was more about paying off someone who wanted what they couldn't have. Getting even when there was nothing to get even over."

"You ain't makin no sense."

"Miss Minerva, did you know Melba Bishop? Because best I can figure, she is the key to this whole story."

I stared into the fire. I wasn't sure I could answer his question—leastways, not how he wanted me to.

My mind went to the day I caught Melba's arms wrapped around Stately's waist. I could see them across the way, her mouth flappin like she had something real important to say. She stuffed something in his coat pocket and patted it to be sure it was safe. Stately hardly said a word from what I could see. We'd only been married a few weeks. And when he glanced across the way and saw me standin there watchin, he pushed Melba away and acted like he never saw me. But he did. Our eyes met, and I knew then and there I was never to mention what I'd saw. Never. It wasn't long after that Stately up and moved us to this mountain.

I didn't answer but picked up my stool and tossed it in the wagon. Del followed suit, and it wasn't long before we were on that bumpy road to the cabin. He walked beside Belle just like he said he would, guidin her around the holes, and once we reached the cabin, he helped me down.

He bowed, hat in hand. "It has been my pleasure, Miss Minerva. Thank you for your company. It's going to be a long time before I forget what carp tastes like."

"I bet it will." I giggled. I sat down on the steps and rubbed my knees. "It was right nice. Thank you for doin this. I might not get back down to that river again before I die."

"Awww, you got five or ten more years in you." He plopped next to me on the step.

The moon lit the night, outlined the trees and the distant mountains. Crickets waged a shoutin war to see who was the loudest, and down toward the garden, the *whooo whooo* of a barn owl echoed up the hill.

"Beautiful, ain't it?" I said. "I never tire of peace on this mountain—the voices that give it life."

"Yes, ma'am, indeed it is."

"There's times I hate this mountain. Well, I hate bein forced to stay here, but I never tire of the beauty. When I go to feelin sorry for myself, I count my blessins by sittin right here on these steps. Sittin quiet. Takin in the scents of night. Countin the stars. Listenin to the voices that only speak when it's dark. The good Lord gives me rest in this. Yes, He does." I lifted my head and took in a long, deep breath.

Del stood. He leaned over and kissed my cheek. "Miss Minerva, you are an amazing piece to this puzzle." He took Belle by the harness and tapped her tenderly. "Hup, girl." He tipped his hat as he stepped her toward the barn.

I made my way up the stairs and leaned over the rail. "Del." I raised my voice just enough for him to hear. "I knew of Melba Bishop. That's all. Just knew of her."

TEN

I'D MANAGED NOT TO LIE. That meant I could lay my head on my pillow and sleep sound. I never met Melba Bishop face-to-face. I truly did only know *of* her . . . that and the fact she coaxed Stately Jenkins into her arms.

The fire had died to embers, so I stirred them right good. I pulled a couple of logs from the stack and dropped them into the glow. Yellow and red bits of flame floated up the chimney. I took the bellows and squeezed it a few good times to catch the bark ablaze.

It had taken me three days back last spring, but I managed to move my bed close to the fireplace. I was glad I did. These days my bones kept a chill. It was getting harder and harder to reach my feet, but I managed to pull my shoes off. I'd learned a few years back to keep a bedpan under the bed, bein the outhouse was just too hard to see in the dark. After I relieved myself, I crawled into bed and pulled the covers up. The flame grew warm, and since I'd stoked the fire with applewood, it would burn hot but slow through the night.

My Bible laid next to my pillow. It seemed to be the best bedfellow an old lady could have. It was Daddy's Bible. He'd slipped it in my bag when me and Stately Jenkins rode off from Lexington. Its pages were yellowed, and the lines and notes Daddy had made was so dim after all these years, I could hardly make them out.

My fingers grasped tight around the tattered leather cover and pulled it to my chest.

"Good Father, what say Ye tonight?" I whispered as I buried my bent finger into the pages and opened the book.

Seek ye the LORD *while he may be found, call ye upon him while he is near.*

"You never fail to answer me, do You?" I licked the tip of my finger and straightened the wrinkle out of the page. "Isaiah, huh, Lord. He's as old as me!" I chuckled, but as I stared at the fifty-fifth chapter, I could see how the good Lord reminded me to keep lookin. I'd find Him near.

"You know my body is tired, but now that this man has come around and started snoopin, draggin up things I'd shut away, there's too many questions for me to die yet. I need to know what is buried in that box besides a fistful of gold. That too much to ask, Lord?" I was realizin kept secrets would come back to bite you.

I rolled to my side and gazed into the flame. The crackle of the fire eating at the wood lulled me in and out of sleep. Just as my eyes closed again, I heard the creak of the screen door. The spring cried as the wooden frame opened. My heart stirred, and I run my hand along the edge of my pillow, lookin for my best friend. Delano had grown comfortable around my house, but he had yet to just waltz in without a holler or a knock.

Be calm and quiet. If this was Delano sneakin in my house to hunt for that box, I'd burn his rear good with buckshot, then send him and his deceitful ways off my property.

A figure edged around the door into the room. A tall, lanky man much bigger than Del eased around the foot of my bed. He run his hand along my hearth, feelin for somethin.

I took in a deep breath and held it, hopin he'd move away. My fingers grew tight around my revolver, and I prayed there was a bullet in the chamber. Ever so gently, I pulled the hammer back. It clicked into place, and the man jumped. I laid my covers back and pointed the gun in his direction, hammer set to fire. He tripped over the rocker. As he stood, I did somethin I ain't done in ages. I pulled the trigger. And I did it before I give him a chance to speak.

The gun fired, and the man squalled. He fell into my table, tippin it on its side. My door slammed, and I could hear the poundin of horse hooves. Runnin wasn't somethin I did, but I reckon the good Lord give me a spurt of energy, for I was on my porch before I knew it. I pulled the hammer back and fired again. And a third time. And a fourth. A fifth.

My hands shook and my knees grew weak. I heard Del shoutin from the barn, "Minerva! Minerva Jane!" But I didn't have no voice to answer.

I dropped to my hands and knees and commenced to crawl toward the door. All that energy give to me by the good Lord was used up, and I ended up belly down, sobbin on the porch.

Things were foggy, but in the background, I could hear Del hollerin. The next thing I knew, he was sittin next to me on the porch, cradling me like I cradled Stately Jenkins when he died in my arms.

My eyes focused, and in the darkness, I could see the fear wrote on Del's face.

"Miss Minerva. Wake up. Please open your eyes."

I sat straight up. "Del?"

He stood and helped me to my feet. When I didn't move fast enough, he scooped this old bag of bones into his arms and carried me to my bed.

"You all right? What happened? I heard your gun. What happened?"

My throat felt like I'd swallowed a wad of sheep wool. The words stuck hard. "There was a man come in my cabin."

"A man?" Del seemed confused. "What did he look like?"

"Tall, skinny. Stood a head above you," I muttered. "He run his hands across my hearth, and when he got close to my bed, I pulled the hammer back on my revolver. The click give him a start. He fell over the rocker. Turned it over."

Del pressed me back into my pillow. "Calm down. Lean back. Take a breath."

I lifted my hand and pointed. "He fell over the rocker."

"Miss Minerva, what rocker? The only rockers are on the porch."

"What? What the Sam Hill is wrong with you? I've had a rocker by my fireplace for years."

Lookin around the dimly lit room, I could see there was no rocker. My eyes grew wide and my mouth fell open.

"I've had a rocker by that fireplace for thirty years. Where'd it go? What on earth happened here?" I whimpered.

Panic filled my chest. I knew my body was commencing to fail, but my mind had always been sharper than a fresh-whetted blade.

"He fell over that rocker and my table. I fired my revolver at his rear. Then I got a spurt of energy. I reckon fear does that to a body. I come on the porch just as he hopped a horse and headed down the path."

"Let me get you some coffee." Del patted my arm. He pulled the pothook over the flame and set to warmin the mornin's coffee again. "Minerva, I know this has you upset. But do you think this could have been a dream? When I came in, the rocker on the porch hadn't been moved, and I never remember seeing a rocker by your bed."

I come off my pillow and wagged my finger at him. I still had the gun in my hand. "I shot ever round outta my revolver. All five. See for yourself." Anger blew through me like a winter wind as I tossed the revolver at him.

He caught it midair and spun the cylinder. "No doubt you shot it five times. But, Miss Minerva, there isn't a rocker in this room, and look, the table is fine. How could he fall over what isn't here?"

My teeth clinched and my nose flared. "I'm tellin you he fell. He was runnin his hands over my hearth. Them ten fingers looked like spiders crawlin over the stone."

79

"Calm down. Please calm down. Let me pour you some coffee."
Del took a tin cup from the cupboard and poured it a fourth full.
He gently wrapped my stiff fingers around the cup. "Blow it. It's
hot. We'll figure this out. Let me take a lantern out and walk
around. See if I see any signs of someone." He rubbed my arm
with all the tenderness of a loving son. "Take a sip. I'll be back in
a minute." And with that, he headed outside.

I knew what I saw. I saw a man messin around—lookin for
somethin. Probably that fool box. I saw him with my own eyes.
It took me a spell to simmer down, but every time I run them
thoughts through my mind, I got bent outta shape again.

After a few minutes, Del come back. He opened the door and
hollered in, "Miss Minerva, it's me. Del. Don't shoot me."

"Oh, bull," I said. "I ain't gonna shoot you."

He winked. "I walked down the path pretty far. I didn't see
anything. But I need to ask you a question."

"Go ahead. Ask. But I ain't up to talkin gold."

"No, ma'am, I don't want to know about the gold. I want to
know where Satchel is. Where was the dog? Did he bark?"

I leaned back, stunned. "I . . . I . . . he . . . he was curled up by
the door when I went to bed."

"Did Satchel bark? Did he come close to you? That dog is on
your heels most all the time. I'd think he'd light into a stranger."

I dropped my stare to the floor. "No. Satchel didn't bark." My
voice grew as weak as my stomach felt.

"Could the man have fallen over Satchel, and you thought it was
the rocker? I mean, when we get scared, things look and sound
different."

It didn't take much to see that Del was bein as polite as he could
be to an old woman who . . . who must be losin her mind.

"You don't believe me? You think I was dreamin?"

"I don't know. What you say isn't adding up. Satchel was all over
me when I came in the door. He knows me now. But a stranger . . .
he'd be eating a stranger alive." Del shrugged.

80

"Truth is, you think I'm losin my mind, don't you?" I shouted. "Just cause I'm old you think—"

"No, ma'am. I don't think that. All I'm saying is things don't add up. I believe something happened. I can see you're terrified. But I can't put the facts together to figure out what happened."

"That's the reporter in you? Figurin how to make an old lady seem crazy?" I growled.

Del paced a few steps, rubbin his head. I tossed my empty coffee cup on the floor, then opened the little table drawer by my bed and pulled out a leather pouch filled with bullets. I reloaded my friend and tucked it under the pillow.

"Miss Minerva? It is the reporter in me to find the facts and make a conclusion. It's not to set out to make you look crazy. You're the farthest thing from that ever." Del leaned close to me.

I turned my back and laid down.

"I'll drag that rocker inside and keep watch, maybe doze in the kitchen. Will that be okay with you? If he comes back, I'll be here."

I never said a word. Just pulled up the covers. I know what I saw despite what Del said. A dream. Huh!

Del dragged the heavy pine rocker from the porch into the kitchen. He called Satchel to him, and I could hear him whisperin like the hound was a person. I commenced to settle, and my heart slowed to regular.

Delano eased to the fire and poured himself the last of the coffee. "I'm right in the next room. Just call if you need me. And, Minerva, we'll figure this out. Rest."

I rolled over. "Drop another log on the fire. I'm cold."

ELEVEN

DELANO WAS UP and outta my kitchen before that blasted rooster crowed. I pulled the quilts up to my chin and rolled to my side. I don't suppose it was cold, bein it was headin into midsummer, but the chill that had climbed my back the day before was still there.

The mornin sun spilt betwixt the boards in the wall, shootin strands of color across the room. Shades of yellow formed shapes of things I knew in my mind I needed to do. Crazy as it seemed, they nudged at me, eggin me to rise and get dressed. As I gazed at how the colors filled the room, I wondered if this was what the golds of heaven was like.

Gold. There it was again. Hauntin me. Naggin at me. I hadn't lied yet, but keepin this secret was eatin at me like I had.

Maybe if I was to lay it all out for Del. Take him back to Stately's grave. Dig up that box. Maybe that would ease my worry about that blessed promise I made.

"I was old enough to know better," I whispered. "I shoulda known not to make a promise like what Stately was askin. Shoulda known it would haunt me." A body ought to think right hard before they force a burden like a secret onto another person. I've come to think it's about the most selfish thing someone could do.

A peck on the window by my bed forced me to turn over. I could see Del's hands circlin his face as he tried to peer through the smoky glass.

"Miss Minerva. You awake?"

I pulled my pillow over my head. The man grated at my last nerve, but at the same time, I liked the old cuss. I eased to my elbows and then pushed myself up. My joints ached like somebody took hot irons to them. They quivered with the weight of my body. I slid off the bed and into my shoes, then managed to loosely tie the strings.

"Oh, lordy, have mercy. What'll I do when winter comes? I'll never be able to tie my shoes." My legs were swelled the size of fence posts, and my feet barely fit in my shoes, they were so tight with fluid. There was a time when I was right plump, but not these days. Now my clothes hung loose, and I tied them tight against my body with my apron.

I held up my arm, and the skin dangled like a sheet blowin on the line. What was there to live for? That question hadn't much more than formed till I answered it.

"Delano."

It seemed odd that in the short time he'd come to stay with me, he'd weaseled his way into my heart. I could spar with him, tease him, smart off, and the man just rolled with the punches. He'd more than proved his worth on the farm, and though he worked hard, I still guarded the secret he was curious about. Still, he didn't push. Didn't keep at me. Apparently, there was more to him than gold. Integrity.

"You awake? Can I come in?" Del pecked on the window again.

"Well, if I was asleep, I sure as whiz ain't no more. Come on in."

I heard him click the heels of his boots on the steps before he come into the house. Once again, a sign his momma had raised him well. And he knocked. Didn't just barge in. That spoke to his upbringing as well.

His head peeked around the door. "I warmed you a bucket of water. Thought you might want to wash off a little." He lifted the bucket and poured my basin full. "And here's a fresh bar of lye soap. I'll leave you to clean up."

I leaned against the bed, and a smile tipped my lips. This was somethin I'd never had before. Never once in my adult life did Stately Jenkins even consider pourin warm water for me. I nodded my approval, and Del turned to head out.

"Satchel. Come on, boy," he said. The hound come to his feet and trailed out the door on Delano's heels.

That was a first. The beast never left my side until Del.

I dipped my hands in the water and filled my palms. The hairs on my arms stood up from the warmth. Leanin toward the basin, I washed my face in the tenderness of someone who seemed to care about me, and it felt right nice.

"Is this what this is about, Lord? You sendin me a child to care for my needs? Lettin me know what it's like to have a son? Givin me a taste of what I missed? Ain't sure if it's a blessin or a curse."

Still, it was like my prayers hadn't fell on deaf ears. The good Lord seemed to be answering them right here. Right before I died. Nothin like perfect timing.

I giggled. "The good Lord has a sense of humor." I wiped my face with the clean towel on the basin stand, then leaned against it. "You do have a sense of humor and a heart. I'm grateful for this sweet young man You've sent."

I finished cleanin up and made my way to the kitchen. There on a plate was a strip of ham and a slice of sourdough. Coffee steamed on the pothook. My tummy was still full from the few bites of carp I'd choked down the night before, but I forced down half a ham slice. It would have been ugly to turn my nose up at the man's kindness. I'd have taken the whole slice, but I couldn't slip the other half to Satchel since he'd gone with Delano.

I pushed the screen door open with my elbow, tryin to balance my cup of coffee, but despite my efforts, my fingers just didn't have the strength to hold the cup steady. Settin the cup on the rail, I used both hands to walk down the steps.

Del was mixin mud and ladling it into a bucket from out in the field. He waved.

"What in tarnation are you doin?" I squawked. "I thought you was too old to play in the mud. You're makin a mess by my spring."

He lifted the bucket and met me halfway. "I noticed the cabins down in Barbourville used mud to seal the cracks between the logs. I did a little research around town and found out how to make this thatch. A little mud, a dab of hay, some chopped-up corncob, and there you have it." He sunk his hand into the bucket elbow-deep and pulled out a handful of the mess for me to see. "You needed some holes filled before winter comes. Figured I'd fill them cracks and then coat the inside wall."

I was dumbfounded. "You're gonna do what? Is this how you buy information about gold that don't exist?"

Del let out a laugh. "Naw, truth is, I'm going to make another trip into Barbourville. Send a wire to my publisher. Ask him to send me my pay up here. I've written some articles on living on the mountain. I'll send those for the paper by courier."

"How long you plan on moochin off an old lady?" I grumbled.

"Long as I'm needed."

"That right?"

"Yes, ma'am. I like it here. I like learning the ways of the mountain. This makes great stories for the paper, and, well . . . it makes me happy. Besides, I might like you." He held up his thumb and forefinger as if to measure.

I slapped his arm. "You've done enough, Delano. I don't expect you to stay away from your home."

"Don't you like my company? Aren't you happy with the work I do?" The expression on his face drooped.

85

"Of course I like you, and yes, you've done a good job. I just don't want you to stay away from your normal life very long."

He set his bucket down and plopped to the ground. "Now we get to the story. You want to know about my family. Isn't that right?" Del wiggled a finger for me to come closer.

"Well, I don't suspect a boss would be happy with his reporter off on some mountain dotin over an old woman for months." I pointed to some dried grass. "Mix that in with your mud. It makes the thatch strong."

He sat down and laid back in the grass, stretchin his arms over his head. His teeth gleamed in the mornin sun. He blew a long sigh, and when I looked again, he had a piece of dried grass and was pickin at his teeth. The man was doin his best to be a country boy.

"I'm what the city folks call an 'open book.' Trouble is, Miss Minerva, my pages are blank. I'm not married. Thought I might be once. I told you that. Marybeth Townsend was her name. Come to find out, she liked the son of the postmaster better than me. Left me sitting at the altar. Guess being left behind was better than being trapped in a marriage you didn't want."

I could certainly understand that. Especially now.

"Well, that was right selfish of her. Guess the life of a reporter was too excitin, heh?" I pointed a crooked finger toward him.

"My parents died some time back. Mother insisted childbirth wasn't what it was cut out to be, so there was only one. Me. That covers it. Questions?"

I thought my life was borin. Listenin to the ho-hum of Del's day-to-day explained why the girl he wanted to marry took after someone else. Still, I wondered if there wasn't more to this man. He was kind, gentle. Grant you, a little on the unexciting side, but just what he'd done for an old woman he didn't know from Adam told me there was more to this man than he was letting on. I reckon he'd be like eatin an apple. One slice at a time till you reach the core.

"How long you gonna lay there before you start patchin holes?" I asked.

He crawled to his feet. He chuckled off and on as he carried the bucket to the house.

"By the way," I hollered, "I did tell you to add more hay into that mix of mud for it to harden right, didn't I?"

"I know, you told me, remember?" His hand went up to let me know he heard. It wasn't long before he was slappin mud into the very cracks that let the mornin sun climb my inside walls.

I pushed open the gate to the garden, and that was Satchel's cue to rush by me and wind his way through my mater patch.

"Find you a good one. They ain't gonna last much longer."

The animal nosed his way through the vines until he found himself a bright orange mater. He plucked it off the vine like he had hands, then laid down to gnaw away.

I pulled several tomatoes and picked my apron full of green beans. They would make a nice supper. I tied a knot in my apron to hold the vegetables, tucked the pouch in at the waist, and made my way back. Just as I passed the cornstalks I glanced to the ground, and there at my feet was the tiny glass dish my momma had given me for my sixteenth birthday.

I like to have fell, but instead, I went to squawlin. "Del! Del! Lord have mercy. Del, come here."

He dropped his bucket on the porch, leaped over the railing, and tore down to the garden.

"Look!" I cried. "Look." I pointed to the ground.

"What? Look at what?" He dropped to his knees and went to scootin dirt around.

"Careful. It's my dish Momma give me."

"Minerva, where? I don't see a dish. Show me with your foot. Maybe I covered it over by accident." He picked up a flat white stone and dusted it off. "Is this what you saw? It is white."

I had no words. The dish I saw had seemed to disappear into the dirt. It was a . . . rock?

"Minerva." He took my arm, but I yanked it away.

"Leave me be." I'd argue with the best of them that I saw my momma's broke dish in the garden, but when all we found was a rock, it told me my eyes and my head was at odds.

Delano stood silent as I slowly walked to the house. I stopped halfway to the cabin and sat on a stump of an old elm tree that Stately had cut down years ago. A few posies bloomed around the trunk. I'd planted them some years back. The heel of my shoe mashed a bloom. My apron loosened at the band, and the vegetables dropped to the ground. There was nothin I could say. Nothin I could think of to explain what I saw. Nothin except the realization that my mind was leavin me. It was no surprise. I'd expected old age to be hard, but I never expected my mind to turn on me.

Del picked up the maters and gently placed them in my apron. He held them taut in the cloth until I stood, then he sweetly tucked the knot in at the waist. "We better get these to the house and wash them up. They'll make a great supper. Add some of your fatback to these beans, and they'll be somethin to write home about." He rested his arm around my waist, and with the other hand, he clasped his fingers tight around my elbow. "I'll get you settled at the house, and then I'll go back and look for your dish. Sound all right?"

I nodded. "When was you goin into Barbourville?"

He stopped and scratched his head. "Thought about going later today, but it can wait until tomorrow."

"Today is fine. Mind if I ride along? I ain't at my best today."

"I'd be honored. I'll hitch up the wagon."

"Del?" I took his hand. "What was it you come here to ask me about?"

His eyes glistened, and I saw a dampness at the corners. "In the beginning, I came to ask you about Stately Jenkins and his part in taking a box of gold. But I know there isn't any gold." He patted my arm. "The gold is right here." He pulled my wrinkled hand to his lips and tenderly kissed it.

That one sentence drew a tear to my eye. I could see in them few words that there was somebody who cared about an old woman on her way to meet her Maker. And it meant the world.

I felt my hand take to shakin. Shakin like Stately's hand did, and I suddenly knew what was to come.

TWELVE

I DIDN'T SAY MUCH as we bumped and bounced down the path toward the river. Once we hit the level road that run alongside the water, things commenced to change. I ain't sure if it was the smell of the wisteria we'd set under the day before or the river's song, but things cleared up for me, and I felt the need to converse.

Satchel climbed over the wagon bed between me and Delano, plantin his rear against my side. He rested his head on Del's knee.

"I ain't sure what you did to my dog, but he's become like a silly schoolgirl gushin over you." I scrubbed my nails up the dog's back in an attempt to win him back. His tail and nose pointed to the sky, a sign he enjoyed the feel of an old lady's nails. "Don't you forget who feeds you." He switched his head to my knee.

"Me either. He just took to me. Maybe he felt sorry for me since you were mean by making me work like a . . . dog!" Del busted into laughter. "You catch that joke?"

"I tried not to," I said, but listenin to the man laugh at himself become contagious, and it wasn't long before I felt a smile come on. Then a chuckle. "You're a mess. Ain't you?"

He nodded.

I lost my smile as the thoughts of the mornin come back over me. "You didn't see my dish, did you?"

Del stared straight and took his time answerin. "I have to be honest. I don't think lying to you is the right thing to do."

"Much obliged." I stuck my hand in my apron pocket, pulled out a handkerchief, and dabbed my nose. "I expect honesty. But let me say it for you. That's two things I saw that you didn't. So either you're tryin to make me think my mind is slipping, or the hard truth is . . . it might just be. I am old, after all."

"Minerva, I don't think you're losin your mind. You might slip up on a detail or two, but I believe you saw something last night. I can't explain why the dog didn't bark, but that doesn't mean you didn't see something."

"What do you think?" I rested my elbows on my knees, stretchin out my back.

"I think two things are possible. First, you were asleep and dreamed this. Dreams can sometimes feel completely real. Or, who-ever came in your house didn't fall over the rocker. They tripped over this rascal. And let's face it. Satchel here isn't a spring chicken. Maybe he was sleeping hard and just didn't catch the noise. I've hollered at him before, and he didn't acknowledge me. His hearing may be growing weaker with age. Truth is, we may never really know."

"You're just tryin to make me feel better," I growled.

"No, Minerva. I'm not. I believe you, but I wasn't there, and the things you tell me don't add up. It don't mean it didn't hap-pen. It means I can't fit the pieces together. And as much as you don't want to hear me say this, you are older. It's common for thoughts and happenings to get twisted. It's just part of grow-ing old."

"Then what about my dish? Why couldn't you see my dish? It was plain as day." I felt myself workin into a tizzy.

He looked me in the eye and pulled the reins tight. Belle come to a stop. "I think you saw that white rock. It's not uncommon for folks to mistake items when their eyes are failing. And you know your sight isn't good, even with the glasses I gave you. So, I believe you. Like I said, we'll figure this out. Whoever came into your house will have left something behind. I just have to find it."

I took in a deep breath. My lungs hissed out the air. "You really do believe me, don't you?"

"Yes. I do. We just have to sort out what really happened. Now, can we talk about something else? I don't want you getting all worked up. I'll figure this out. It's my job, after all." He nudged me.

Oh, brother, I could feel it comin. I was ripe to answer more questions about that gold.

"So, you knew *of* Melba Bishop?"

"That's all. I knew who she was. Knew that she was married to a rich man across the river from our home. Knew she had a reputation of ill repute that followed her. Had always heard she was a real ringtail tooter."

And those things I told Del was the truth. Melba was known for being a floozy. I never could figure what Stately saw in her. I'd run that memory of her flappin her mouth and waggin her finger in Stately's face over and over. Then that kiss. I won't never forget the hurt that stung my heart when I saw that. I had no idea what she was sayin to him. Stately never spoke of it. I did recall we had one conversation about it. We were in the wagon and on the way to the mountain.

"Stately, just tell me one thing," I'd said.

He smacked the reins on the horse's back and grunted.

"Do you love that woman across the way? Do you wish you'd married her over me—that Melba Bishop?"

He never uttered a word. Instead, he rolled his eyes and spit over the edge of the wagon. Now that I think about it, that was right rude, but when you love someone, you don't always question. More so, you learn when to talk about things and when not to. That spit on the ground was Stately's way of sayin it wasn't open to discuss.

That was the first time I saw the box. It jutted from under Stately's coat, no bigger than a loaf of sourdough bread. I remember starin at it, wonderin for the longest time before getting the umph to ask.

"Stately, what's in that box?"

"Gold," he whispered. Then he pressed one finger against my lips. "Shhhh. It's a secret. And it's one you have to keep. Can't a soul know about this."

"Where did you get it?" I asked.

"Ain't important. What's important is that you keep the secret. And you keep it to the grave."

"To the grave?"

"To the grave." Stately nodded and spit again.

He'd never opened that box in my presence, but if the truth was known, I ain't right sure I believed it held gold, for we lived poor as dirt for half a lifetime. There'd be times I'd see Stately hunkered over that box, rubbin it. Ponderin openin it. I can't say I ever saw him do it. Instead, he just hogged it like it held some gosh-awful curse.

"Minerva. You with me?" Del nudged me. "You drifted off there."

"I was thinkin. Why do you want to know so much about this Melba Bishop?"

"Well, I'm not sure. In those papers Colton had, her name kept showing up. Oddly enough, there was never anything attached to her other than your Stately."

I shook my head. "Stately never mentioned that name. Never." That was the truth. Even when I had asked Stately Jenkins if he loved that woman, he never spoke her name. Never once.

"It seemed that Miss Melba's husband and nephew Travis had come upon a small vein of gold. It couldn't have been much. Gold was not something that was commonly found around Lexington.

At least not raw gold. So when Melba's husband turned up floatin down the Ohio River facedown—"

"What? Her husband was dead in the river?"

"Yes, and there was evidence that connected to Travis. He was a bit greedy and the most likely to do anything necessary to claim the gold as his own. Remember I told you the papers said Stately was wanted for stealing the gold? That was all he was ever accused of doing."

Del had said that earlier. It just didn't sink in. There was so much to take in that I wasn't sure I was catchin the half of it.

"Anyway, Travis pointed the finger at Stately and his buddy, Gumble. Said they took his box of gold."

I took a start as his words sunk in. My chest commenced to ache. Stately hadn't been a talkative man, but I might be seein why. Seems he was like an onion. We just keep peelin back layer after layer of mystery. Maybe that was why I despised bein on this mountain. I'd felt alone even when I was with my Stately.

I turned to Delano and eyed him. "Now, hold up here a minute. Even that piece of paper you give me to read never mentioned a man bein killed. You think my Stately killed a man?"

"I don't know, Minerva. That's why I was trying to locate him. I figured I could get to the bottom of the story myself."

"But that was years ago. What makes you think you'd find the answer? And Stately's been gone for over thirty years. Did you know you'd find me? And if you did find me, what made you think I'd tell you about Stately Jenkins or a box?"

"Don't get all worked up. I didn't know anything. Only what the papers said. I told you, I'm a reporter, and stories make me curious. I didn't know anything about Stately Jenkins except that the trail pointed to Barbourville. Once I got here and asked, the owner of the general store sent me to you. That is all I know."

"Well, my Stately wasn't a violent man," I grumbled. "He mighta been a bit selfish and cautious, but he was not a violent man. I never known him to run from anything or anyone, much less hurt a body."

We turned the bend in the road, and the tiny town of Barbourville come into sight. I looked to my left and saw the general store. To my right, the farrier. Then four houses and the one-room church that become a school durin the week. Just past that, a tiny cemetery. Such memories.

We come to a stop in front of the store. Things had changed some. No, things had changed a lot.

Del eased me down from the wagon. We walked onto the porch of the general store. Inside, two children giggled and chased one another around a shelf centered in the room. A woman snagged one as he dashed past. The other took hold of my waist and hid behind me. I teetered to gain my balance. Del took the child by the arm and sent him toward his momma.

I walked to the counter and tapped my nails on the slick wood. A man in his mid years raised his head from behind the shelves. "Can I help you folks?"

"I'd like to send a wire to Lexington." Del handed the man a slip of paper and a fifty-cent piece.

I grinned. "I never knew you had money on you. I mighta asked for pay for your stayin in my loft."

The man took the paper and nodded his head toward a room in the back. "Back this way."

Del followed, and since I was nosy, I trudged along. I watched as the man tapped out clicks and dashes.

```
Send pay to Barbourville. Stop.
Sending two articles by courier. Stop.
Several to come. Stop.
Delano Rankin. Stop.
```

"There you go. Done as a slice of bacon in a skillet." The man handed Del a signed slip of paper. "Hang on to that. That's your receipt. Anything else?"

"Yes. I'll need to set up a mail slot. And when my pay is delivered, will you send someone up to Miss Minerva's to let me know?"

The man scribbled himself a note and then slid a card across the counter. "Fill this out." He nodded at me, then stuck out his hand. "Am I to assume you're Miss Minerva?"

I eyed him a spell, then took his fingers and shook them. "Minerva Jenkins. I'd like to speak to Robert Blessing."

The man's smile dropped. "Uh . . . well, that might be hard to do."

"Ain't nothin hard about talkin. Where can I find him?" I growled.

"I'm Robert Junior, but if you're referring to my daddy, that would be Senior, and he's over there. Under the poplar tree." The man pointed across the street.

I glanced toward the tree where he pointed. Centered in the cemetery, it shaded a tall stone cross and several small ones.

"You mean Robert is dead?" It had never occurred to me Robert could be dead. I'd not been off the mountain in years. I guess my memory was just as bad as my eyes.

"Yes, ma'am. Been dead about twenty years now. I know for a fact."

The air left me, and for a moment, I felt . . . lost. Heartbroken. I stepped onto the porch and looked over the tiny town. It come to me. Everybody I ever knew here was most likely in their own plot of ground. But Robert—he kept vigil with me. Checked on me. Rubbed my back when I cried. His was a special place in my heart.

Had that many years passed me by? And when did Robert stop visitin? It was comin clear to me—my stayin hid away on the mountain had caused me to lose track. I felt a rush of sadness come over me. Not for Robert, though I was sad he was dead, but for me, that I'd not bothered to look past my own front porch to see how life had changed.

I straightened up and hardened my brow. I cleared my throat.

Del helped me down the step and onto the dirt road. I caught his nod toward Robert Jr. Like he felt sorry for me.

"Well, ain't that just peachy?" My heart ached. Two men I cared about had had the gumption to up and die. I kicked the dirt with the toe of my boot. "Ain't that just peachy?"

THIRTEEN

THE BREEZE WHIPPED MY SKIRT tight around my legs. I stood stunned. Shocked that Robert Blessing was dead. After all, he was the man who met me on the road when Stately Jenkins died. He was the one who gathered the men of the town to help bury my husband. And it was Robert Blessing who rounded up the women to cook me meals and mourn at the wake. Robert was a good man. A kind man. A concerned man. Gentle. Pleasant.

I felt my chin quiver. Emotion swept over me like a cloud of dust over the ground.

It took me back that he was dead. I watched as that breeze twisted wilted flowers around the tombstones, and I wondered, where had the time gone? When Stately died, it was like I just went into my own self. Just survivin. I carried on with the farm till my eyes got so bad I couldn't do it no more. That was when I quit hitchin Stately's mare to the wagon and goin into town for supplies. Things just went to pot after that. When that old mare kicked the bucket, it was Robert who dragged the beast off and then showed up one day with Belle. He traded my corn and potatoes for meat, salt, and flour to get me through the winters.

I eyed the young Blessing. I rubbed my chin and pondered him. "I don't recall Robert havin no youngin, but now that I look, you remind me of Robert." I pulled him close to get a good look.

"Thank you, ma'am. That honors me. My daddy was a good man. Raised me to walk in the ways of the Lord."

"That's good." I nodded.

"My daddy is the reason I took to preachin at the church over there."

"That's right nice. I'm sure he would be proud. Can you walk me over to his restin place? Robert was good to me and Stately. Real good. I'd like to pay my respects."

Del took one arm and Robert Jr. took the other, and they helped me off the porch.

"I'm afraid my feet don't move like they used to," I said. "This hump on my back makes me look at the ground more than what's in front of me."

"It's fine. Take your time," Robert said.

"Well, if you look at me, you can see time ain't rightly my friend." I stopped and went to laughing. "Seems I'm the oldest one in these parts. That makes me old as dirt?" I punched Delano.

"Miss Minerva, you are as beautiful today as I am sure you were when Stately Jenkins fell in love with you." Del pushed open the iron gate to the graveyard. It cried like a wildcat.

It was almost beyond me why this man never married despite the woman that turned him away. Why that girl in Lexington would want more than this good man befuddled me. Del was a keeper. He was raised right. Polite. Kind. And woo-ee, he was a charmer. Maybe she could not understand faithfulness, or maybe her eyes were just bigger than the prize in the barn. I'm guessin he never found another love cause there wasn't another as good. Reckon I understood that more than most. Either way, I'd have been proud to call him my son.

"This way, Mrs. Jenkins." Robert Jr. pointed toward the poplar tree. "This is where we laid Daddy to rest. Momma too. They were good parents."

I couldn't recollect a Mrs. Blessing, but then it come to me. She'd helped me when Stately died. Shy sort. Right sweet.

I stopped and looked at the tombstone. The letters carved deep into the rock seem to be fading. Just like my Stately's marker. We were always told when something was carved in stone it would last forever. But I was seein now with the eyes of my heart that they ain't nothin eternal. Just temporal, as the pastor used to preach. Time even wears away stone. Eventually there ain't a sign of what was carved.

"Preacher. Do you mind if I call you Preacher?" I asked.

"Preacher is fine."

"Good, you can call me Minerva."

He nodded, and a smile come across his lips, sinkin a dimple in his cheeks.

"I think I used to believe there was an eternity with the good Lord. But as I stand here and see that even Robert Blessing's name is wearin off his headstone, I'm comin to wonder if there really is eternity at all. Seems nothin lasts forever." I scrubbed my knuckle over the fading name on the stone. "Do you believe, Preacher?"

He dug the toe of his boot into the dirt and twisted, rippin a dandelion out of the ground. "That's a good question. So if you will oblige me, I'll give you two answers."

"Good lands a Goshen, are you gonna preach?" I asked.

Del broke into laughter, then shushed me.

"No sermon, I promise," the preacher said. "But the answer is yes. I do believe in eternity. Can I stand here and prove it to you? Ain't sure who could. All I can do is share with you how much I believe and hope that it's enough for you to believe too. Does that make sense, Miss Minerva?"

I shook my head as I bent down to pat Robert's stone again. "And your second answer?"

He bent and picked up the dandelion, then opened my hand and placed the yellow bloom in my palm. "You watched me dig that flower outta the ground with my toe. I gave you the bloom. By this time next week there will be a new bloom startin in this very place. It's because I didn't dig the root up. I think of eternity like that root. It can get kicked around and folks can quit believing, but the hard facts are, that root's gonna spring up a new flower. And it will year after year after year. Into eternity."

I pressed my fingers to my lips and then pushed them on top of Robert Blessing's stone. "I'm sorry you're in the cold ground. Can't say I ain't far behind you. You were good to me, and that will live for an eternity." I put my hand out and took hold of the preacher's arm, then pulled him close. Poochin my lips out, I give him a tiny peck on the cheek. "I'll have to ponder over eternity with the good book whence I get back to the cabin. I will say this, I am eternally grateful for the good your pa did."

I turned and started toward the wagon. Both men grabbed my elbows. I gently pulled away.

"If you both don't mind, I need a few minutes. I'll be fine." As I walked away, I could feel their eyes on me. They had to be wonderin what was runnin through my head. Still, I kept on walkin.

I heard Del ask the preacher if any strangers had been in town other than him. He proceeded to tell the preacher about what had happened at the cabin. By then, I was outta earshot and glad that I couldn't hear any more conversation. I imagined Del told the preacher I was seein and hearin things. Maybe he told him I was so old and decrepit that my mind was goin. He mighta warned the preacher I had several "iron-clad" friends and to be careful if he was to decide to come callin. I didn't need to hear the things I already knew.

I stopped by Belle and reached my arm around her neck. A flood of sadness washed over me, and tears poured down my cheeks. Over the years, I'd shed one or two tears, but I'd never broke into a hard sob—not since Stately Jenkins died.

It was beyond me why Robert Blessing's dyin hurt me so deep. I reckon it was his kindness toward me, his carin that my needs were met. He was a good soul to me. It broke my heart that I was so taken by my own grief I never noticed why he stopped delivering goods to me. Maybe I thought he was sick or too old to make the rough trip. But death—that never crossed my mind. I took off them spectacles and rubbed my eyes right hard. My fingers grew wet with tears.

I was beginning to see more about myself than I cared to see. I'd locked myself away. Me. Not Stately. After he died, it was me who put a chain around my legs and hooked it to a stake in the ground on that mountain. I chose to stay hidden away, and I chose to blame that on Stately Jenkins. Seems hurt and sadness can do a number on a body, and I'd fallen straight into that snare.

I commenced weeping harder. I'd always thought I was a good person—not perfect, but good. Yet I never knew that the one person who was so good to me after Stately died had passed himself. I never noticed. How selfish of me. All I concerned myself with over the years since Stately Jenkins died was that blessed ole secret. I never took nothin or nobody else into account. I was so blinded by my own pain that I never took note of those who cared about me.

I never asked for that secret of Stately's. Never wanted to bear it, but I let it hold me tight. I allowed it to become my curse and, oddly enough, the one thing that give me a will to go on. When I didn't think I could take another step, that blessed ole secret picked my foot up and set it down. In the middle of my grief, I promised to keep a secret that I shouldn't have. When I did, life passed me by—and it was all by choice! In my anger, I let it take what life I had away.

Seems this dyin woman had more reality to take in than she was ready to admit. Now I wonder just how long a body keeps a secret to a dead man.

Good Father, is it too late for an old woman who thought she was good to find mercy? Is it too late to believe in eternity?

The tears wouldn't stop comin. There I was, layin my head on Belle's neck, blubberin like a baby. Swipin tears and snot on my sleeve, which only meant I'd have to wash my dress sooner than two days. Lawsey mercy.

The men stopped a bit behind me, and Del cleared his throat. There seemed no end to the man's manners.

"Miss Minerva. You ready to go home?" He waited until I answered.

I dried my cheeks and wiped my spectacles. I straightened my shoulders as best I could, then turned. A smile stretched across my face. "Ready and willin. And Preacher, you come by the cabin. I make a mean chicken and dumplins. It's been my pleasure." I reached toward the step of the wagon, and both men lifted this bag of bones onto the seat. "It's a beautiful summer day, ain't it?" I said. "Beautiful."

The preacher patted my knee. "It's my pleasure, Miss Minerva. Thank you for the kind words over my daddy."

I dipped my chin and winked.

Del jutted his chest out like a prancin rooster as he come around the wagon and crawled in. "I'm glad you came with me. Did us both some good."

"You get all your business took care of?"

"I did. Robert Jr. will let me know when my boss sends my pay, and then I'll buy us a little extra bacon for breakfast."

"Bacon? Sausage. Sausage is better."

Del bumped my shoulder and whispered, "Bacon."

"I done told you, my hearin is fine. I heard you whisper bacon."

He whistled and hollered for Satchel, and when the hound jumped and missed the wagon, Del crawled down and lifted him in. "See, Miss Minerva? This old dog can't see any better than you." With that, he let out a war whoop of a laugh as he swung his leg over the step and into the wagon. He ruffled Satchel's ears and scratched his chin. "Old is hard, isn't it, boy?"

I crossed my arms and leaned against the wagon bench. The hum of the wheels turnin sounded like a song. Del didn't say much. I reckon he was givin me my time.

We headed up the mountain, and I noticed the deep green of the evergreens. I took in a breath, and the scent of pine filled my senses. The birds set on the branches of the oak trees, and their song was like a choir singin in harmony. Through the trees, I could see the sun slowly restin itself on the summit. There was hardly anything prettier than the yellow hue that glistened over the mountain at dusk. I rubbed my eyes, dreadin the day my sight would leave me altogether.

We'd be home before dark, and before we turned onto the path to the cabin, I glanced once more at the sun twinklin off the river, whose rollin rapids washed away anything that dared to set on its current.

"You smell that pine?" I asked.

Del took in a breath. "Uh-huh. It's nice, isn't it?"

"Indeed."

Just as we come upon the end of the garden, Satchel leaped to his feet and let out a howl that scared the tarnation outta me and Del. The hound like to have scratched the tar outta my legs, getting outta the wagon over me.

Del pulled the wagon to a halt and reached under the seat for my revolver. He glanced at me and pulled back the hammer. "I brought it just in case."

Satchel tore toward the cabin, lettin out howls that would wake the dead. Del tossed the reins in my lap and jumped outta the wagon. "Stay here!" He pointed betwixt my eyes. He beelined it toward my porch, then around the back of the cabin.

Things grew quiet. Too quiet. Since I ain't never been good at doin what I was told, I slapped the reins against Belle's back, and the wagon groaned over the clods of dirt. I pulled Belle to a stop in front of the house and hollered, "Delano! Delano Rankin?"

I rolled to my stomach and dropped my legs over the edge of the wagon. Just as my feet hit the ground, I heard the blast of my revolver.

"Lordy mercy," I shouted. The gun fired again, and terror shot through me as though the bullet had hit me square in the heart. "I can't lose nobody else."

FOURTEEN

MY HEART SKIPPED, and I lost my breath. My shoes felt like someone had tied rocks to them.

"Delano, answer me!" I screamed. I hobbled from the wagon to the porch and worked to catch my breath and my balance. My chest heaved, and my lungs burned for air. "Good Father, help me. I can hardly walk or breathe," I muttered.

I took hold of the porch rail, got my footin, then commenced easing my way around the cabin. The smell of sweet pine was replaced by the scent of a spent bullet from my revolver. I pressed my hands on my knees to help me pull my body up the slight grade of the ground toward the back of the house. Satchel stood howlin at the path toward the barn.

"You have fresh meat in sight, dog? Go get it." I slapped my hands against my hips, and it felt like daggers stabbin my legs. "Go on! Go get it, dog."

That was all Satchel needed. My approval for him to take after whatever grabbed his attention.

I pushed my fingers into the crevices between the logs of my cabin. Del had done a good job patchin the gaps, but he hadn't worked his way around the back of the cabin yet. Holdin to the side of the house, I was able to pull myself up the small bank to the back.

"Del, you all right?" I hollered. I found him sittin on the flat rock by the pump, rubbin his head. "Lordy mercy. What happened? Did somebody hit you?"

He rested his head on his folded arms. His knees were bent and his back hunkered.

"Del, are you all right? Answer me." I shook him by the shoulders.

"Yes, ma'am. I'm fine." He rolled to his knees and stood. In the glow of the lantern, I could see blood tricklin down his face. "Let's go in the cabin. We'll talk inside." He took my arm to steady me, despite his own feet bein unsteady.

I was terrified. Scared witless. All I needed was this young man to die tryin to help me.

"Miss Minerva, before we get inside, you need to know that someone has ransacked your place."

"I told you!" I shouted. "I knew it and you didn't believe me earlier. Maybe you believe me now. There was somebody in my home."

"Calm down. I never disagreed there was anyone in your house. I told you. I just couldn't figure out how they managed it."

"What do you suppose they wanted? Outside of you, they ain't hardly been a soul up in these parts for months," I said.

"That's what bothers me. You didn't have trouble till I came along. That tells me there is someone else who knows about that gold, and they've come looking for it."

"There ain't no gold," I snapped. "There ain't nothin here but a run-down homestead." I felt sick to my stomach. Exactly what had Stately Jenkins got me into from the grave? I didn't like misleadin Del, not bein truthful about Stately's secret, but I'd promised my husband. Promised the man I loved to keep his blessed old secret. Right or wrong, I made a promise.

Del pressed his hand on my shoulder. "Miss Minerva, I'm growing weary of defending every word I speak. At some point, you have to trust me."

My mouth shut tight, and I couldn't think of a thing to say. The man was right. If I was gonna let him be a part of my life, which he was becoming with all his kindness and work, then I was goin to have to trust him.

We climbed the steps into the cabin. Again Del was right. Someone had tore through what little belongins I had. Del lit the other lamps through the cabin and helped me to my rocker. The lamps on the tables only dimly lit the inside of the cabin, but with each flame coming to life and Del stokin the fireplace, it become clear there was little left in its place.

Daddy's Bible was flung to the wall and lay half-opened. The back was bent backward with the papers and notes strewed alongside. My quilts were tore from their spot in the pantry, and the feather mattress laid tilted off the edge of the bed frame Daddy had built me. I didn't have much from my life in Lexington, but I had that bed and Daddy's Bible. Seemed whoever ripped through my place had no regard for the sentimental. The tin cups and plates were thrown on the table, and the washbasin was tossed toward the screen door. And that door, the one that whined and creaked, hung sideways.

"Lordy mercy, who woulda tore up an old woman's place like this? Who?" I stood and grabbed a rag from the basin, then snagged Delano's sleeve. "Sit down. Let me clean you up whilst you tell me what happened."

Del sat on the hearth. I wrapped the rag around two fingers and then dipped it in the bucket of water by the hearth.

"Seems our person dumped everthin but the water. Shows he wasn't the tidy sort." I smiled.

A knot went to raisin above Del's left eye. "I saw a light in the house," he said. "That's when I ran up the hill. Satchel beat me to the cabin. I suppose his barking like a wild animal spooked the stranger. The man took off around the house, Satchel on his heels. I ran close behind, but as I rounded the house, I caught my foot on that rope. Sent me sailing to the ground, and when I hit—"

"My 'friend' went off by accident," I said.

"Yes, ma'am. I hit my head on the rock by the pump."

"Well, Del. It takes a real man to admit he tripped and fell instead of spoutin out some gosh-awful lie about bein hit from behind. Leastways you're all right, shy of a little hurt pride." I swiped the blood from his cheek.

He pressed his hand over mine as I dabbed his forehead. "I'm sorry, Miss Minerva. I would have never come here asking questions had I dreamed it would put you in danger."

"Don't be silly. Life is filled with twists and turns. This twist just yanked us a little off the path. Hold that rag tight and let me find a piece of cheesecloth to tie around that gash. We need to stop that bleedin sooner than later."

It took me a few minutes, between bein slow walkin and dodgin my belongins on the floor, to get to the pantry and tear off a strip of cloth. I had some black salve I could dab on it before I tied it around his head. The salve would pull out any dirt or small things that might have stuck in the skin. I folded the small square of cloth and smeared the salve on it, then took hold of Del's fingers and pushed the cloth to the cut.

"Keep that there. That ought to hold." I wrapped the cheesecloth around his head and tied it snug.

Del stood and staggered.

"Maybe you oughta just stand there." I inched around the crooked mattress, rested my hip against it, and pushed. It didn't budge, so I eased my knotted fingers around the edge and tugged. It slipped onto the slats. "Come on, son. Lay down and rest a minute." I put my arm around his waist and eased him toward the bed. "Ain't this somethin. I'm steadyin you this go-around. Life's full of little oddities." I chuckled.

"I'll be fine. I'll just sit over here."

I shoved him onto the feather mattress. "You'll do as you're told. Hear me?"

He nodded and stretched out on the mattress.

I pulled a quilt over him and propped his head with a pillow. It took me a minute, but I tugged my rocker next to the bed. "I'm right glad you dragged my rocker back into the cabin yesterday. Come in handy tonight. You rest. I'll keep watch."

Del had laid my revolver on the hearth. I picked it up and spun the chamber, peerin into the holes to be sure there was bullets. When it met my approval, I laid it in the seat of the rocker.

"You think you could drink a hot cup of coffee?" I asked.

Del nodded a weak yes and laid his arm across his eyes.

"I imagine you got a nasty headache. A good cup of coffee will ease that hurt. I'll drop you a leaf or two of peppermint in the brew. That always eases the pain."

I stood the night table to its feet and replaced the crocheted doily I'd made along with the pewter candle holder, a years-old weddin gift. The candle was rolled against the hearth, so I placed it neatly in the holder.

I dropped another log on the fire and pulled the pot over the flame. Coffee was scarce and pricey. It would be weeks before neighbors would bring me more supplies. I was grateful the bandit had the good sense to just look in the coffee can and not dump it. He'd at least left the can upright. I picked it up, scoopin what little had dumped onto the hearth into my hand. It was just enough to make a pot. I measured another scoop into the strainer for good measure and dropped two peppermint leaves into the pot. The water had already commenced to roll, and the smell of coffee mixed with peppermint made my mouth water.

"Won't be but a minute," I said. Del grunted.

I wiped two cups clean with my apron and planted myself on the hearth to wait. The fire warmed my fragile frame, and I felt the ache of my joints ease for a minute. As I set there eyein this sweet stranger, it came to me that he'd come to be right close to me. This stranger that had been nosin around lookin for Stately Jenkins's secret had laid that search to the side and stepped up to help an old woman. It was clear that this child—this man—

was a man of his word. He held the integrity of my daddy, and I suddenly believed what he told me when he said, "It's not about the treasure. It's about the story. The people who are impacted." I reckon he was tellin me the truth.

Satchel come scratchin at the door. I stood though the pain in my knees was about more than I could take and walked through the kitchen to let him in. The screen hung crooked, and the bottom of the door scratched the wooden plank floor. We'd have to fix that come mornin. Satchel run his head under my palm and licked my fingers.

"You're a good dog. I hope you caught yourself some fresh meat tonight." I gently patted my leg and called him to the table. Biscuits was strewed across the tablecloth. I broke one in half and handed it to him. "Good boy. I'd have married you if you'd been born human. Leastways you're faithful." I scratched the hound's chin. I brushed my hand down his back, and a wet spot caught my attention. When I glanced at my fingers, I saw blood.

"Have mercy. Are you hurt?" I pulled Satchel close and went to fingerin through his coat. A hole the size of two fingers pierced his saggin skin. It looked like this stranger had took a knife to my dog.

I felt my anger rise to the surface, and I scooted out onto the porch. Cuppin my hands around my mouth, I shouted, "You can push your way into an old woman's cabin. You can wreak havoc. But don't you never touch my dog again. You hear me? Never again." My voice echoed across the mountain pass. Anyone close would have heard the warnin carry across the gap.

It took me a spell, but I cleaned up Satchel and wrapped his wound. "Lucky for you, your skin is as saggy as mine. It saved your life."

The dog licked my hands. I pulled his face close, and we touched nose to nose. "Go lay down now. Go on. Get you some rest. Thank the good Lord that hole only got your skin and nothin below that."

The coffee boiled, so I poured one cup. Del had done dozed off and I saw no need to rouse him. Satchel jumped onto the mattress and curled next to him.

"Wait a minute. You know I don't allow varmints on my bed," I said. The dog whined. "You did good tonight. I reckon you earned a spot. Just don't get used to it."

The hound took in a breath and moaned. I could tell he was hurtin. He walked in a circle makin his spot right, then laid against Del's side again. Del's hand come up and rested over Satchel. The two looked pretty friendly. There was something comfortin in knowin Satchel was at home with Del.

I set my cup on the small night table and used both hands to guide my stiff hips into the rocker. My toes stretched toward the floor and managed to push the rungs on the rocker into a slow, lullin motion. I blew the steam that twisted and spun upward from the tin cup, then gingerly tapped the cup against my lips, testin if I could take a sup. It come to me in that moment, as I watched this young man's chest rise and fall, that I'd called him son.

Stately Jenkins would never hear of givin me a youngin. He rarely laid with me for fear I'd come with child. But I loved him despite. I loved him with all my bein. I give him my best for years. Funny how that old sayin "Love is blind" falls true. I loved Stately with all my heart, but I'd turned a blind eye to his actions. I wondered, as I thought over the last couple of months and the kindness this stranger had showed me, just how much I'd missed by bein blinded by love. I remembered I'd longed for that love to be returned. It never was. Still, I looked past it and blamed myself. It was my fault Stately didn't love me as a husband should. I must not have been a good wife.

It was the simple things I missed. Stately had been a good provider, or leastways we didn't do without the necessities. He'd hunted, gardened, farmed. But the more I saw the goodness in this young man, the less I saw in Stately. He was never mean to me a

112

day in his life, but there was always somethin that separated us. I'm seein now her name was Melba Bishop.

I propped my feet against the hearth, and as I rocked downward once, my toes touched something. I bent over and glanced at the floor. My dish. There it laid, broke in half on the floor. This wasn't no white rock. It was my dish.

FIFTEEN

SLEEPIN IN A ROCKER ain't all it's cut out to be. I'd forgot the way it cricked your neck if you dozed off. It had been years since I'd slept sittin up. I stretched my arms over my head and clasped my fingers together. Pain shot through my knuckles where they was swelled from arthritis.

"Lordy mercy," I whispered, rubbin my fingers gingerly. The searin ache brought tears to my eyes. But I kept quiet. That young man needed to rest. He took quite the warp to his head when he fell.

Look at that, Stately Jenkins. That rope that keeps me safe purt near killed Delano.

I rolled my head from side to side, tryin my best to stretch out the leaders in my neck. It took me a bit, but I managed to make my way to the coffeepot and pour another swig of the stout brew. It was still warm, and that peppermint smell filled the cabin. Made my jaws sting and my mouth water. Though I wasn't hungry, the thoughts of a buttered biscuit dipped in warm coffee just enough to make it soggy sounded right good.

I peered across the room at Del and thought back over the last couple of days. It tore at me to keep that secret. What good was it? In fact, *what* was it? All I ever knew was there was a handful of gold in that box. The more I dwelt on that silly thing, the more I wondered if there was any gold at all. A body woulda thought if

114

there was gold, Stately woulda loosened his white knuckles enough to spend some. What good was it buried? Every time I blurted that out to Del, it made good sense that there wasn't no gold worth an iota in that box.

I looked around the cabin. Bare necessities. Three plates. Four bowls. Flour bowl. Sugar bowl. Grease jar. Slim pickins for years of marriage. I never was one who insisted on bangles and gifts, but a new skirt would have been nice ever few years. A ribbon for my hair when I was young . . . that woulda brought some joy. Made me feel like a proper lady. But . . .

I rubbed my fingers over my mouth, only to feel the years laid deep in my skin. Crevices and bumps trailed the edge of my chin, and a tiny hair next to my dimple stuck out. I was old. Lordy mercy, when did I get old? Somewhere along the way, the wrinkles replaced the soft and tender skin on my cheeks. I just never knew when. I reckon that's what age does. It just sorta sneaks in and takes over, unbeknownst to us. It takes somebody young workin circles around us to even notice that what seemed commonplace was old age.

I walked to the window and stared out over the garden. A chill run over me, and I realized it was almost dawn. It's always coldest just before dawn. It was strange to me that over the last few months, I'd commenced to tie up loose ends. I'd done told Stately when I visited his grave that I'd probably rot where I fell when I died, since there wasn't a soul up here to find me. Then comes Del.

I tried to keep clean clothes on and wipe my boots down at night just in case. I would never want to be found dead, all nasty and dirty. Over time, I'd quit herdin the cows into the barn or the goats into the pen. I figured they'd need to forage if I dropped dead at night. They'd need to be outta their holdin pens. And I'd wrote a few words inside Daddy's Bible in case I passed. It was a harsh reality that I'd die and it would be weeks before anybody noticed I was gone. That was why I prayed the good Lord wouldn't let me die alone, and why I cleaned up good at night. If I died in bed, at least I was laid out proper.

There was a time I thought I'd be buried by Stately. After all, I'd lived well over half my life with him. But lately, I was finding bein buried next to a coldhearted man was no different than bein laid to rest in the cold, hard ground alone. I did love Stately, and I think that was what was breakin my heart the most. Comin to the truth that he might not have loved me like I thought. A tear slipped down my cheek.

I slapped my hand over my mouth. That was a thought I'd never imagined would come from me. I loved Stately Jenkins. It was important to me that I keep remindin myself of that fact. For even the good book says that love covers a multitude of sins. But since Delano Rankin showed up and commenced to show me some attention and kindness, I'd come to question a love that mighta been lopsided. I was too old for this to injure my feelins like it did. Still, it hurt.

Del groaned, and I twisted toward the bed. Layin my palm on his forehead, I thought he felt a bit tepid.

"Del, you feelin all right?" I brushed his dark hair away from the bloodstained cheesecloth.

His eyes cracked open, and he moaned. "I feel like I was hit by a wood plank." He raised to his elbows, and I took a cup of water from the night table to give him a sup.

"Don't gulp," I said.

"I know, it'll make my head hurt." He grasped the cup and guided my shakin hand toward his mouth.

"Well, that's the spring water that'll freeze you like a winter river. But all I need is for you to get choked. Wouldn't that be peachy?"

"When the sun comes up, we're moving that rope before you get tangled up in it. What hurt me might just kill you." Del rubbed his head.

"Rope's been there for years. I know it's there. Don't need it moved."

"Are you ever willin to be accommodating?" He chuckled.

"I guess not. I got things where I know they belong. That satisfies me." I jutted my chest out like a proud rooster. "Besides, I reckon I've offered you a place to stay, ain't I? That's pretty accommodatin." I propped a pillow behind his shoulders so he could sit. "Don't guess you got a look at who was in my cabin? He sure wreaked havoc on a place that only housed an old woman and a dog."

Del nodded. "He was already around back. Even the lantern didn't give me enough light to make out who it was."

"Think he'll be back?" I edged around the bed and to the hearth where my broken dish laid.

"Best guess is yes. I do think he'll be back. Doesn't look like he found what he was looking for. So we need to be ready." Del wiggled to get comfortable on the feather mattress. "Miss Minerva, don't get all up in arms, but I need to ask you a question."

I rolled my eyes. "Ask."

"Are you tellin me everything? I mean, seriously. No more beating around the bush. You should know after a few months of working like a dog around here, I'm not after gold. But if there is something on this farm you aren't telling me about, and someone thinks I might have knowledge of it, neither of us is safe."

I twisted on the hearth and cleared my throat. My gut told me I needed to tell Del about Stately's little box. But I'd promised. I'd promised the man I loved. And a promise has meanin. Leastways, to me it does.

I nodded my head to keep from openin my mouth. My stomach turned. Standin, I handed the two pieces of the broken dish to Del. "Is this . . ."

"My dish. The one in the garden."

Del worked to fit the pieces together. "Does it have a special meaning?"

"It did. Now it's just an example of a broken dream." I walked to the washbasin and rewet the rag I'd used to clean his head.

"Aw, don't say that, Miss Minerva. Your mother gave this to you, right?"

"She did. It was her momma's, and hers before."

"Oh my. A family heirloom. Maybe I can send it to Lexington and see if a potter can repair it." Del was doin his best to figure out this mess.

"Stop it, Del. You can't fix everything for me. I appreciate your kindness, but you can't fix what is broke in my life. You can't fix that I loved a man who hid me in the backwoods of Kentucky. You can't fix everything on this farm that is fallin apart. You can't fix none of it." I yanked the dish from his hands. All my anger—years' worth—boiled to the surface. "There ain't nothing a body would want on this run-down chunk of mud. And there ain't nothin in this house worth a penny to anybody but me." I leaned back and flung one piece of the dish. It hurled across the room and smashed against the wall. "There ain't nothin."

I hung my head and walked onto the porch. I'd never felt so used up as I did right that minute. The sun peered through the treetops. Lavender and pink streaked across the sky, and a morning breeze nipped at my skirt tail. To one side of the garden stood a doe and her fawn, their ears perked at the sound of my footsteps on the wooden slats of the porch. I took in a gulp of air, and it tasted like honeysuckle smeared on toast.

I lifted my fist toward the sky and shook it toward the good Lord. "Did You bring me ninety-four years on this earth to run the reality of my life with Stately Jenkins past me? Did You? Couldn't You just take me and leave me to believe my life was good? I didn't need to know there was more to Stately than I thought. Did You think I didn't know he had feelins for that Bishop woman? I ain't stupid, You know. Can't You just take me now? End this life with a whiff of a breeze."

The trees rustled as if to whisper to me. *You're wrong, Minerva*

Jane Jenkins. That's not My plan at all. I wanted to believe the good Lord was speakin to me, but my anger had other ideas.

Melba Bishop had held somethin over Stately's head. I ain't sure what, but I had plans of figurin it out. The good Lord wouldn't go ahead and take me, so He left me no choice but to start diggin into Stately's business. I'd make my way out to the shed after breakfast. I'd open Stately's leather-covered chest that he'd kept tucked away under a stack of mess. Why, shoot. I might just dig up that box next to his grave.

My anger just kept climbin. If I needed to, I'd dig through every pocket, every slip of paper, every piece of belongin that Stately Jenkins had owned. I'd find out what Melba Bishop had held over him. As poor as they are, my eyes would open, and I'd look back over the things I shut them to years ago. There's a reason Stately drug me up this mountain. There's a reason he brung me and not Melba.

I'd about decided to lay down and die. Figured my time was close.

I snagged the second half of Momma's dish from inside and raised it toward the sky. It glistened in the morning sun. My fingers rubbed over the rough, broken edges. There was no fixin what was broke. No matter what Delano Rankin thought he could fix, he couldn't fix this secret. He couldn't fix the pain pushin down on me. Del couldn't take back a promise that haunted me, and he couldn't convince me that it was right to break it despite what it's done to me. Even if it was killin me.

I pressed the piece of the porcelain dish to my cheek, and sweet memories of the day Momma give it to me flooded my mind.

"Minerva Jane, one day you can use this dish to rest your weddin bands in at night. Just like I do." Momma opened my hands and laid the pretty dish into my palms.

I won't ever forget my words to Momma. "I'll take good care of it. I promise."

That promise was broke now. My hand shook, partially from

just bein old, partially from the rush of emotion. I eyed my fingers, bent at the knuckles. The band that was there had worn thin, but even in its weakness it had worn away a dent in my finger. One that pushed the skin up, refusing to let the band slip over my knuckle. I never took the band off. So Momma's dish had sat empty over the years, and in my hand laid a broken promise. I thought nothin of breaking a promise to Momma, but a promise to Stately . . .

I drew back and threw the piece of dish off the porch into the dirt. Sometimes a promise gets broke, and they ain't a thing you can do about it.

Sixteen

"WHAT ARE YOU DOIN outta bed?" I growled at Del as he stood starin at me.

"I . . . I . . . just thought I'd check on you." He leaned against the door. I could see he was light-headed.

"You fool. Sit down. Ain't you got a lick of sense? You took a right smart of a hit to your head. Enough to send you a little crazy. Sit down in that rocker, and don't you get up again for a spell."

Del inched real slow into the seat.

I eased my fingers close to his wound to swipe a drip of blood. "Do us both a favor. Sit there till you ain't dizzy no more. If you fall, there ain't nothin I can do to get you up."

"I was just worried about you. And what was that you threw over the railing?"

"That dish Momma give me. It was shattered. No good." I sighed.

"I'm sorry it was broken. I know it meant a lot to you."

"Well, at my age, possessions ain't worth a hill a beans. Not unless you plan on buryin them with me. Once I'm dead and gone, I sure ain't gonna care if they're in the ground or not."

That box of Stately's come to mind. I'd buried it with him. Seems my own doins had come back to bite me.

121

I lifted my finger and pressed it into Del's chest. "You sit right here. You hear me?"

"Where are you going?" Del took hold of my wrist.

I gently twisted my hand and pulled free. "I got some business to take care of. Ain't none of your concern. You just rest."

I figured I had the ability to change my mind, and I was doin it. I needed to go to the shack. It hadn't been opened in years, and it was time I dusted off the spiderwebs.

I pointed at Del and give him the stink eye. He leaned back in the rocker. The knot on the side of his head had started to ease, and the cut closed up enough that there was no more bleedin.

After I warmed his coffee and set it next to him along with a biscuit, I left him alone and let him rest. I took Satchel and headed out to the shack down toward the barn. It wasn't that far to the building, but it took a spell when your feet were heavy and your legs were slow.

It grated at me that there was somebody messin in my home. To know there was someone meddlin in my business was enough. But knowin they'd made their way into my cabin, openin every drawer and cabinet, handlin everything I owned . . . Mm-mm. There was something not right about somebody havin the gall to handle what unmentionables I had in my cabinet. It made me feel . . . stripped naked, for lack of better words.

I picked up a stick thick enough to lean on as me and Satchel walked to the shack. Stately had begun layin a path of flat river rock from the house to the shack. He had an idea it would help me find my way back and forth to the smokehouse and shack. I reckon his thoughts were good. I always knew once my feet hit that path of flat rocks, I was goin the right way. When I had real bad days with my eyes, the path helped.

I tapped the stick in front of my feet until I heard it hit the rocks. A sense of calm come over me—a confidence that I wouldn't get lost. Even with the spectacles, my eyesight was growin weaker and weaker. If I judged my days left on this earth by how well I could see, the number would be right slim.

A cottontail come outta its hole and scampered across the field, takin the old hound's attention. Satchel took after the critter, howlin and wailin, all the time snappin at it. I sorta wished the old dog would catch the rabbit. It woulda been a nice reward for his years of huntin so someone else could gain the prize.

I stopped near a bale of hay left from the cuttin. The Amos boys were always lookin for hay, and I needed the field cut. It benefited us both. I worked myself against the bale and leaned back on my arms to rest. There was a time that troddin down this field was just a short jaunt. These days it felt like miles.

A summer breeze formed a small tornado of hay that twisted up from the ground. I closed my eyes and raised my face toward the sun, letting the warmth draw out the soreness in my neck. This was the time of summer that I loved. Mornings that still let the dew hang in the air and afternoons that made for good bread bakin.

I stared at that shack. It was built sturdy. Stately had never shied from building something to last. I smiled. He did take pride in his work.

Digging that walkin stick betwixt the stones, I pulled myself up and gazed across the mountain. Doddling around wasn't going to ease my curiosity any more, so I continued on my path to the building. A body couldn't help but love the smoky mist that rose over the valleys or the smell of honeysuckle or lilacs that hung on the breeze. It was the bitter loneliness I hated.

I'd told myself Stately loved me. He didn't. I'd convinced myself he took good care of me. He didn't. He kept me like a singin bird in a cage. Cruelty don't always take the form of black and blue. After all these years, it was time I faced the truth. I pressed my hand against my chest, tryin to stop the ache that throbbed where my heart was stuck.

"Hellooo!" A voice from down the way echoed up the hill.

Satchel let out a whoop that give me a start. I shaded my eyes from the mornin sun, tryin to see who the person was.

"Hellooo! Lookin for Delano Rankin. Is this where he stays?"

I didn't budge. I stood there ponderin whether to answer. The dark outline of a man came into focus. He was tall. His shoulders were broad, and his arms hung long against his sides.

"Ma'am? I have a letter for Delano Rankin. He live here?"

It struck me odd that Del had sent a wire only yesterday, and now he was getting a letter. I was never a momma, but for some reason it was instinct to be a hair protective over Del. He was, after all, hurt for his efforts of protectin me.

"Ma'am. Delano Rankin stay here?" The man huffed his way up the bank where I was.

"Maybe. Maybe not. Where's it from?" I pressed my hands on my hips.

He stared at me like he didn't understand.

"You need me to slow my words down?" I asked.

"Uh, no, ma'am. I was just trying to decide whether to leave the letter."

"I reckon you got yourself a dilemma, then, don't ya?"

"Yes, ma'am. I suppose I do." He stumbled over his words.

Satchel sniffed around the man's feet and decided he didn't like what he smelled. The beast let out a round of howls that woulda put any wolf to shame. The man took a step back. I could see the fear in his eyes.

"Awww, there ain't nothin to worry over. He's a hound. Barkin is what he does." I slapped my leg with my palm. "Satchel, get from here. Leave the man alone."

The dog took a breath and let out one more gosh-awful bark, then trotted toward the barn.

"Miss Minerva, you all right?"

I twisted toward the house. Del stood leanin over the rail of the porch, rubbin his head. Seemed that noggin of his was harder than we thought. He was up and movin without much trouble. I waved to let him know I was fine.

"Colton! That you?" Del shaded his eyes from the mornin sun. "Coltoonn!"

124

The man clapped his hands together and then started toward the porch. "It is me. I thought you might have been taken hostage on this mountain. You've been gone from Lexington for over two months."

Del rubbed his head again and started down the stairs. The two grasped arms at the elbows and bumped shoulders.

"I see you met Satchel. And Miss Minerva."

I commenced making my way back to the house. My curiosity was getting the best of me.

"I did meet them. Can't say I had a warm welcome from either."

"You just haven't had the time to catch hold of Miss Minerva's wit. She's really quite the charm." Del went to laughin.

Quite the charm. Them wasn't words I'd ever heard used about me before. I wasn't sure if it was nice or snide, but it raised my hackles.

"She's really a unique lady. Lots of fodder for good articles for the paper."

My anger commenced to crawl. "I ain't deaf, you know. I've told you this a hundred times. I can't see worth a dang, but I hear just fine."

Del came a few steps closer and took me by the arm. "Colton Morris, I'd like you to meet Minerva Jane Jenkins."

"Colton Morris? Ain't he the typesetter?" I eyed the man.

"You remembered." Delano rubbed my back. "That's right. Colton is the typesetter. We work together at the paper."

"It's my pleasure." The man took a few steps toward me and then stuck out his hand.

I crossed my arms, ponderin whether to shake his hand or not.

"Go on, Miss Minerva. You can shake his hand. He won't bite," Del reassured me.

I inched my hand toward Colton, and he took hold of my fingers. I figured he wasn't worth a strong handshake, so I give him a weak shake. I smiled, right proud of myself. "You're the one who found them papers about my Stately?"

125

Colton glanced toward Del as if to ask if it was all right to say so. Del nodded.

"Uh, yes, ma'am. I found the papers on a trip up north. Thought the story, though in bits and pieces, deserved a little more attention. After all, a box of gold. Wouldn't that be a treasure to hold?"

I looked right hard at him. "Wouldn't it though? Exceptin they ain't no gold here to hold."

Del pulled me closer to him. "Miss Minerva doesn't have any knowledge of the gold. She was pretty surprised to find out we had the warrant papers."

I felt the hair on my arms stand and pulled away from Del. "I don't need you tellin anybody what I know or don't know." I put my finger in his face. "What I know ain't your property. It's mine. Shellin out my business ain't open for discussion." I turned right quick to Colton. "And you! I'll tell you the same thing I told Delano. Look at my house. Does this look like the house of a man who hoarded and hid gold? Of all the stupid notions. I ain't never in my life had to prove what was obvious so many times."

"Miss Minerva," Del said, "don't get upset. Colton didn't mean anything by his remark. He was tryin to be polite."

"I'm sure he was. Polite, my foot. You look at my house, sir. You look and tell me if this looks like the house of a man who had gold. What in tarnation good is it to hide gold and not spend it for your benefit?" I felt my anger raise a notch. "And besides, even if Stately Jenkins did hide gold, he's been dead for years. You think I'd not dig it up and spend it to feed and clothe myself? Stupid idiot."

"Miss Minerva, calm down. There is no reason to get upset," Del said in a soft voice.

"I don't need calmed." I lifted my hand and pointed to my chest. I took hold of my blouse and rubbed my heart. "What I need is for every one of you to get off my mountain. Go back where you come from. I never had no trouble till you showed up." I stumbled to the side, and Del grabbed me to steady me.

The words had slipped outta my mouth like they were greased. I knew they were wrong, but I couldn't stop them. Del stood speechless, and his friend wasn't sure what to think of my vengeance. I'd done come this far. What was the harm in finishing my rage?

My mind went to spinnin. There wasn't a soul alive who could understand the pain this promise I made was heapin over me. When I was growin up, a promise was a body's word. It meant somethin. I was good for my word, despite Stately Jenkins. What made me angry is that it took me this many years to see what he did to me. This memory of Melba—it was hauntin me. Eatin at my innards. Makin me question all I'd known for years. How could any man that loved his wife guilt her into makin a promise that was a lie? Worse yet, it was his wrong, not mine. I shouldn't be the caretaker of a secret that digs at my very soul.

I wanted to be left alone. Even though I hated loneliness, right this minute I suffered, and loneliness seemed to be the thing that understood my plight. My anger at Stately Jenkins boiled over, and Del was right in the line of fire.

"You know where the barn is. Take your friend to your own hole in the wall. Leave me alone," I shouted. "Leave me be. Let my life end in peace."

I turned from the shack and commenced to walkin to the house and mumblin. I was too upset to open that shack right now. Tomorrow. What was one more day?

"Good Father, how much longer? How much more are You tryin to teach me? Can't You see? I'm hard of seein. I ain't hard of understandin. If I tell Stately's secret, what does that make me? Less than honorable? Less than truthful? What does it make me?"

SEVENTEEN

I STOMPED the best an old woman could stomp up the hill to the cabin. I felt the tears roll. Since Del had come, I'd cried more than I'd cried in my life. I liked this young man, but I ain't right sure I liked the memories he dragged to the surface.

I took hold of the bucket by the porch and limped to the pump. I slammed it under the faucet. It was just seconds before the icy mountain water gushed over my palms, and I splashed it on my face. My chest ached again. Enough that I stumbled to the cabin and leaned against it. I couldn't tell if this ache in my heart was the hurt and frustration I felt or if it was the beginnins of the end. It didn't matter much. At my age, things were gonna end one way or another. I just wanted answers before the grass started to grow over my bones.

The vines had worked their way up to the house. I took the heel of my boot and dug at them, snappin them at the root.

"Stately Jenkins, if you don't kill me one way, you'll kill me another." I laid my head against the rough wood on the cabin and sobbed like a miffed youngin. I couldn't dig my heel fast enough into the plants. Every thud of my boot brought a wail.

"Miss Minerva?" Del peered around the edge of the cabin. "You all right?"

I swiped my eyes on my sleeve. "I'm fine, Del. I mean, I'm . . .

Look, I know my heart is givin out. Dyin ain't somethin I'm afraid of, but I sure don't look forward to it. And I reckon I owe your friend an apology. I lost my temper unjustly. A person does odd things when they face their demise."

Del eased against the cabin and gently bumped up next to me. "Miss Minerva, it didn't take much my first few days here to see you counting your days. And I've heard you say more than once that you'd probably drop dead and never be buried."

"Awww, that's just an old woman yappin." I leaned harder against the cabin and rubbed my chest, hopin to ease the ache. I eyed Del right hard. "Del, let's stop with the cat-and-mouse game. Be honest. What is it you really want? I done told you I got nothin here worth a penny. Why are you here? Why are you still here? There ain't nothin here for you unless you keep hopin I'll cough up a stash of gold. There's nothin here but a dyin old lady."

Del stared at his feet, and I could tell he had a reason. I might be an old woman, but my instincts were right. He was after Stately's gold. All this kindness was just to soften me up.

"I sent Colton back to town," he said. "I figured he could find a room with the pastor."

"You what?" I felt my legs growin weak. "You sent him away?"

"Come on, let's go inside. We need to talk."

I'm wise enough to know when a body says they want to talk, it usually means things ain't right. "Lordy mercy. What now?" I asked. Del chuckled.

We got in the cabin, and Del helped me to the knee-high stool by the table. I grunted as my backside slipped onto the seat. He poured me a cup of coffee. Though the warmth of the tin cup soakin into my stiff knuckles eased the pain, it didn't stop my hands from shakin.

Del set himself on the other stool. He rubbed his chin like he was thinkin right hard. "Minerva Jane Jenkins, I have some news for you. It won't be easy to take in, but just give it a few minutes. Don't interrupt. Let me speak."

"Oh, mercy. It was you that come in my house, wasn't it?" I took my gaze from him.

"What?"

"You were the one that broke my dish then tried to make me think I was losin my mind. Well, I ain't doin this. You hear me? I ain't doin this."

"Minerva?" Del went to his knees.

"You took me to the river to soften an old lady's heart. You took me to town to win me over. You said you wanted to know about the people in my life. You said you wasn't after gold. I shoulda knowed you were a liar. Stately wasn't always the best in the world, but it was to protect me when he brought me here." I buried my head in my hands. "Oh, Stately Jenkins, how could you dare die on me?"

"Minerva, everyone isn't out to take from you. I've already told you I believe you about the gold. I thought we could be friends. Is there any harm in only being your friend?" Del cupped my hand in his. "Is it so hard for you to believe that all I want from you is to spend time with you? I like you. I *want* to be here."

I stopped my tears and snubbed. My brow furrowed, and I cocked my head to one side. I ain't sure what disbelief looks like on a person's face, but I felt it on mine. I gently lifted my hand and rested the wrinkled, bent fingers around his cheek. "Ain't nobody ever said nothin like that to me before."

Del smiled and eased on down to sit at my feet. "You've been alone far too long. You and your loneliness only think people are out to take away from you. I see a woman filled with kindness and sass. If I had a grandmother, I would want her to be you. I never had that. So ask me anything. Ask me what you need to ask me to convince yourself I am only here for an old woman I admire and . . . well . . . I've grown to love."

My heart ached for a whole new reason. This time it was a good ache. The kind that warms you from the inside out. The kind that makes a body feel loved.

"Go on. Ask me anything." Del focused his eyes on mine. "Anything." He patted my knee. "I'm an open book."

"All right. Why did you really come here?" I come close to his eyes. Eyes never lie. They are the door to the soul, and though folks can be mean to a certain extent, their eyes always tell the truth about what is deep inside.

He took in a deep breath. "Well . . ." He hung his head. "I wanted to see for myself."

"See what?" I asked.

"First, I wanted to know if Stately Jenkins was real. And if he was, would he be capable of stealing. That was the story I sought out for the paper. Miss Minerva, there is a lot of controversy around the Bishop family in Lexington. Freelaw and his nephew Travis were known in the area for . . . well, let's say, unscrupulous doings. They managed to stay one step ahead of the law in Lexington, and with their wealth, they could afford to buy their way into any freedom they saw fit."

I rested my elbow on the table and then twisted on the stool to get comfortable. "That so?" Daddy had always told me to stay far away from the Bishops, but I never understood why. Maybe now I'd find out. "What's this got to do with my Stately?"

"The warrants looked like someone had tampered with them. Or at least I thought they did. Something didn't seem right. There were things missing that shouldn't have been."

"You mean, a lie?" I come forward and gasped. "You let me believe they was real." I felt my anger crawl again.

"No, Minerva, I never said if they were real or not. I said Colton found paperwork. I just didn't tell you I thought it looked fake. I needed an honest answer from you. And I could tell by your expression you had no idea about the warrants."

My nose flared. "That don't make it right, what you did. You deceived me." I felt a bit ashamed fussin at the man about bein truthful when I knew I was no better. But I was keepin a secret, so that made it right—or did it?

Del stared at the floor. "It wasn't a hundred percent truthful. You're right. I'm sorry. But it also was necessary to find the truth."

"Truth. And what truth was you lookin for? Care to smack me in the face again?" I snapped.

"It wasn't a real surprise to find the warrants weren't real. But if a person didn't know that, and they thought they might be accused of stealing something from one of the wealthiest families in Lexington, then they might find their only option would be to run."

"You think Stately knew something about the Bishops that caused him fear?" I asked.

"I do. But I don't think it had to do with gold."

That took me back. "Then what was you lookin for, Del?"

"My mother used to tell me that lies are like webs spun by a spider. The more you lie, the more the web tightens until you have pinned yourself in the middle. When you're tangled in the sticky mess and can't move, the spider takes his prey."

"Your momma was wise," I said. And a greater truth couldn't have been spoken. The longer Del stayed on the homestead, the more my promise become a web of deceit. I'd made a promise, and that was different than a lie. It was my word, despite how I thought Stately was wrong to ask me to keep a secret that wasn't mine to keep. That promise felt just as deceitful.

"You ain't answered my question," I said. "What are you looking for, Del?"

He twisted on the floor and bent his head side to side, crackin his neck. "Family. I'm looking for family."

I busted out laughing. "I reckon you got the surprise of your life. You ain't found nothin here but an old woman whose husband never give her any offspring. All you got from me is an empty shell of a woman. One who is figurin out she ain't never had anything to start with."

Del couldn't have come here for any two people more alone in this world than Stately and me. Stately never had no family. His momma died when he was six, and she never had any other children. His daddy died of dysentery, workin the railroad. With my momma and daddy gone and my momma's sisters havin died long before I left Lexington, there was no family.

My stomach turned as the realization of just how alone I was in this world hit me. I'd outlived all my family. The only friend I really had died years ago. I was the matriarch of absolutely nothin.

There are people in this world who have hordes of family. But when you wake up one day and look across the sky, the deep blue of God's eyes, and you realize there's nothin, it hits you hard in the gut.

Somewhere between being a girl in Lexington and turnin into this wrinkled-up old woman, I'd lost years. I'd lost them and didn't know it.

Del crawled to his feet. He shoved his hands deep into his pockets and commenced to pace.

"If I wasn't such an old ninny, I'd swear you had more on your mind than you're spoutin," I said.

He took the coffeepot and filled my cup again. "You should drink that before it chills. The pot is cooling down. Unless you want me brewing a new batch, you should finish this cup off." He hung the pot on the hook and then rested his elbow on the mantel. "Miss Minerva, what if there was an inkling of a family?"

I let out another laugh. "Well, if that was possible, I reckon I'd have to entertain that fact. But as I said, I ain't got no family, and neither does Stately."

"Brackston Rankin was my father."

"I don't reckon I know no Rankins other than you. What are you tryin to say? Because you're confusin me."

"Miss Minerva, my grandmother was Melba Bishop."

I lost my breath. My mouth went dry like someone had poked it full of cotton. That news hit me hard, and I could hardly breathe.

It took me a minute to take in that Melba was Del's grandmother, but I had to accept somethin I'd never admitted to myself.

I despised her. Then it come to me—why would I expect less? Despisin her was fair, or I tried to tell myself it was.

"And best I can tell, my grandfather was Stately Jenkins." Del's voice drew me back into reality.

My heart sunk, and every bit of the air in my chest was sucked outta me. I didn't have no fight in me. Suddenly, things made sense. What I knew in my heart but refused to believe was true.

"Melba married Freelaw Bishop, and just a few months later, a child that was conceived wrongly was born. That infant was Brackston—my father."

"Now, wait a minute," I squawked. "There's two last names here. Bishop and Rankin. Three if you add my Stately into the web. Somethin ain't right."

"I know, it's hard to get everything straight. Melba was married to Freelaw Bishop, but he was later killed. Murdered. And that was part of what looked wrong on those papers Colton found. How could Freelaw press charges against Stately and his friend if he was dead? That's what started me on the search for the truth. The charges couldn't have been real."

"Where's the Rankin name come into this mess?" I growled.

Del scratched his head and leaned up on his elbows. "Walton Rankin began to court Melba after Freelaw died. A while later, maybe a year or so, he married her. He took Brackston Bishop, changed his name, and made the child his own. The child was never known as anything other than Brackston Rankin."

Everything I'd believed but pushed to the side had come to light. Pictures flipped through my mind until they stopped on that day I stood by the river and watched Melba kiss my husband and give him a box.

I took in a breath and did my best to act as if I didn't understand. I wanted to hear it from Delano. I wanted the words to drop from his lips. That would be the only way I would believe it was true.

"Melba ain't no kin to me," I fired back.

"No, ma'am, she isn't. But she knew Stately Jenkins, and she gave birth to his child. Brackston Rankin, my daddy."

He dug around in his pocket and pulled out his wallet. Inside was a yellowed and wrinkled folded paper. The folds were so deep they hid a few of the letters. He gingerly handed it to me. *Birth Certificate for the State of Kentucky.* The hand-drawn letters had smeared slightly over the years, but the names were clear. *Mother: Melba Bishop. Father: Stately Jenkins.*

"The child Melba led Freelaw Bishop to believe was his was really Stately Jenkins's son. I believe Melba was trying to protect Stately, knowing Freelaw would kill him if he knew about the child."

I stared at the paper, and Momma's words about a web of lies made sense. And oh, what a web of lies it was. I suddenly saw that the lust and greed of people forced lie after lie to cover the mess up, and I was the innocent victim. I was used.

I shook my head. "No! This ain't right. It can't be," I cried.

"Miss Minerva, this is my daddy's birth certificate. The papers don't lie."

EIGHTEEN

I SAT AT THE TABLE, and for the first time in my life, there were no words to be had. There was no need to make my way out to the shack. No reason to dig any further for what Melba held over my husband's head. Stately Jenkins had took the faithful love of a young girl and deceived her.

I never knew there were so many ways a body's heart could ache. But I'd just found a new way. The paper waved with the shakin of my hand. A sickness rolled in my stomach. I pulled my lip inward and bit down. There are times when a body is so taken back that a response ain't possible. They ain't no words. No movement. Nothin that can loosen the chain that binds you to the ground.

There was no pain in my chest anymore. No feelin in my hands. No reason I needed to take another breath. There was nothin.

I stood and laid the paper on the table, then slapped my leg and clicked my lips. "Satchel. Come on, boy." He'd found his way into the house and laid by the hearth. Now he come to his feet and pushed his head under my hand. "Come on, dog. Let's go."

"Minerva?" Del spoke.

I held my hand up to stop his words, then pushed open the screen door.

Satchel eased down the steps, letting me lean against his body as balance, and once we got on hard ground, I went to walkin. I walked down the pitted path, steppin in holes and twistin my ankles, but I kept on. And when my feet touched the stone pathway Stately had built to help me find my way, I stepped off into the pitted grass of the field, never once takin to fall. I made my way to the rough road that trailed down to the river, and when I stopped, it was under the last clusters of wisteria by the river.

I bent over, then eased myself onto the grassy bank. A tender breeze brushed my face and twisted the loose hair around it. I gazed up into the trees, and the rustle of the leaves spoke sweet phrases from the good Lord.

You ain't alone. Ain't never been alone. I've always been right here.

I wondered if that was my own thinkin or if the good Lord really spoke to my soul, for the emptiness I felt compared to nothing since the day we threw dirt over Stately. The day Stately Jenkins died, I'd made a promise. It took my life from me. I chose to pull away from the world, but my promise was what I blamed for stoppin me from ever goin back to Lexington and even makin an attempt at startin a new life. I was stuck between a promise and a lie.

High up in the pines the limbs swayed, their branches reachin up to the heavens. I wondered why, at this very moment, I couldn't catch a cloud and sail on into heaven. Why in the name of everything good did the Lord see fit for me to lay here and feel this pain? Was He punishin me for making a promise to Stately I shoulda never made? Was He smackin me on the hand for not tellin Del about the box, despite how small it was? Or was the good Lord remindin me that I should put no other gods before Him? Had I done that? Had Stately become a god to me?

The white droppins from a blue jay landed on my shoulder, and in the midst of my tears I laughed. "Fool bird. You coulda turned your backside the other way." I took a leaf and scraped away the white muck.

As I rolled to my side, the tall bluegrass of the Kentucky mountains wrapped around me like a silky blanket. It felt as though the good Lord was remindin me again He was with me.

There's a smell to the bluegrass. I'd nearly forgotten it. Sweet like honey. Tart like persimmon. I closed my eyes and took in the scent. My body let loose, and I felt my eyes grow heavy. The river sang a tender lullaby, and I wondered if this was heaven. When I died, would God Almighty lay my body in a field of sweet bluegrass and poppies? Would I hear the birds peep and the groundhogs mumble? Would I open my eyes and see the golden color of the fall maples and feel the soft touch of the spruce?

All I wanted at this very moment in time was to go home. To freely give up my soul and let it soar on the wind with the eagle. I wanted to look down from the heavens and feel the wind on my face as I lifted up and over ever mountain peak. I wanted to walk and not grow faint. The anguish was almost too much.

I felt the arms of a strong man slip under my knees and head. He rolled my body into his grasp and carried me home. I never opened my eyes. I only hoped it was the arms of the good Lord, for my soul was spent.

NINETEEN

WHEN I WOKE, Satchel had plastered himself at the foot of my bed. I raised up on my elbows and peered at him. His chin laid firmly on my ankle, and his front legs was stuffed under his chest. When I spoke to him, he just rolled them big brown eyes toward me and lifted his brow as if to say, "You're wakin up now?"

I bent my knees to set up, but the hound crawled across my legs, pressin them deep into the down mattress. He whined, then scooted his backside against my legs. I reached down and scraped his haunches with my fingernails. "You're a good boy. But you ain't supposed to be on my bed."

He looked backward over his shoulder and laid his head over the other side of my legs.

"I ain't never seen a dog lay in such a twisted-up way. I need you to move." I pulled hard to release a captured leg from under him. My legs ached and they were still swelled. The weight of that animal wasn't helpin me.

It took me a minute, but I finally got Satchel off me and my bed. Every step I took, he was right on my heels. The beast knew. I reckon the good Lord blessed man's best friend with a way to decipher a person's feelins. Satchel knew I was broken, and he had no intention of leavin my side. A faithful hound indeed. He lapped at my hand, beggin for me to rub his ears.

"Rotten hound," I said.

I had no idea what time of day it was, only that the sun hung on the west side of the house and my stomach grumbled a lot, so I figured I'd missed dinner and was headin up to supper.

"Del. You here?" I eased into the kitchen. I uncovered a loaf of bread and pulled a knife off the shelf to cut myself a slice. When I looked out the window, I saw Del and his buddy cutting back vines.

"Ain't that nice of you?" I whispered. As quick as the words left my mouth, it come to me what they was doin.

"Lordy mercy. Stately's grave!" I dropped the knife and hobbled my way outside and around the cabin.

I wasn't sure what to say without soundin like I was hidin something, but I took a stab at it. "That knot on your head makin you a little vengeful over a vine?" I chuckled.

"Miss Minerva." Del dropped his hatchet and come to my side. He took my shoulders and pulled me close. My arms hung straight to my side like they were frozen. "That's a hug," he mumbled.

"I know what it is. I ain't—"

"Stupid. I know. You're just old." He grinned.

"That's right." I eyed my vines. "How much of my vines do you plan to cut back? I like my plants." I felt a twinge in my stomach, which I figured was the good Lord proddin me for that white lie. "Well, I don't love them. But Stately grafted and planted them. I'd mind you to leave the most, please."

"Mr. Jenkins grafted these? They're tougher than gristle." Colton leaned against his pickaxe.

I smiled. "He was paid a little money by the US government to plant some. Seemed it had to do with something about holdin the ground in place."

Del butted in. "Erosion. I read about that. It was a plant that came from the Orient. But how did he graft it if it came from the government?"

I rested my hands on my hips. I hated them long, growin stems, coverin everthing in sight, but still, they were there because of Stately. It was a small part of him.

"Stately was a smart man. He took them ole, hard vines that grow wild from the trees and grafted them together. They took to growin and covered that bank in no time. It's thick so it keeps out the mountain lions."

"Mountain lions?" Colton's face turned pale.

"Yep, there's times you can hear them up on the ridge, screamin. Sounds like a woman hollerin for her life." I winked at Del.

Colton inched away from the vines whilst Del went to laughin. "I don't think he gets your humor," Del said.

"I reckon he don't. But humor or not, I'd be obliged if you'd stop trimmin them vines back. Looks like you cut the vines off the path and off the pump. It looks right nice. I appreciate your work. That's enough. Stop now. The both of you come on in the house."

"Mountain lions?" Colton asked.

I couldn't pass up the chance, so I held up my hands like a bear and growled. The man nearly fell over his pick.

Del let out a guffaw that got him choked. "What a pushover. Do you suppose we could rustle up enough tomatoes, bacon, and lettuce to cover a slice of that homemade bread you made? Looks like Colton needs a bite to eat."

I nodded. Del slipped his arm around me and helped me back inside the house.

"My legs are getting weaker," I said.

"Naw, they're just tired."

"My chest hurts a lot."

"It's been a morning filled with hard news. It'll ease."

"I ain't sure I wanna go on." I stopped and pressed my fingers around Del's face.

"You're a tough woman. You can go on. It's what you do." Del nudged me forward.

"I ain't got nothin left to live for." Tears filled my eyes.

"You got me, and for the record, you worry too much. The summer heat is getting to you."

Colton took a tomato and sliced it into a bowl.

"Stop right there," I shouted. "I hope you don't plan to touch my clean vegetables with them nasty hands."

Del grinned and tossed a rag to Colton. "Washbasin is over there."

I leaned against the table. "Don't you think for one minute that I ain't watchin you scrub them fingers too."

"Yes, ma'am." Colton went to washin his hands, and I reached for the bowl of lettuce from the cupboard. I pulled out several leaves and laid them on tin plates whilst Del sliced the bread.

"They's bacon in the skillet from breakfast," I said.

"Always is," Del said. He pulled a chair from under the table and motioned me to sit. "Miss Minerva here always cooks extra bacon in the mornings. She says it's good with anything."

I nodded. "I can see I taught you somethin." I looked at Del out of the corner of my eye.

"Yes, ma'am. You have." With the food on the table, Del took my hand and bowed his head.

Colton sat at the table starin at the two of us, so I reached over and bent his head. "We pray before we take a bite. Understand?"

"I understand."

I took the man's hand and closed my eyes. "Good Father, there is much to be thankful for and much to be sorted out. I thank You for the blessins of the day and for the food. I trust for the smarts to make wise decisions. Amen." I took a slice of bread and passed the plate to Colton. "Take a piece."

He hesitated like he had no idea what we was doin.

"Lordy mercy, boy. Ain't you never had bacon, lettuce, and tomato on bread?" I stabbed a slice of tomato and slapped it on his bread, then added the bacon and lettuce.

He stared at the meal.

142

I put a knife in one of his hands and a fork in the other. "You know how to cut meat?"

He nodded.

"Then you cut this the same. Now, do I need to chew for you?"

Del snickered. "Miss Minerva, the city isn't anything like the mountains. You have to bear with us . . . with Colton."

I grunted and shoved a bite in my mouth.

It was quiet for a few minutes while the two men cut and chewed. I could see it only took a couple of bites before Colton developed a real taste for bacon and tomatoes.

There was an awkward silence at the table. I could tell Del was waitin for me to respond to his news, but there wasn't nothin to respond to. I had to take in what I already knew in my heart. There were years of dishonesty to slosh through, and I wasn't referrin to the gold. My stomach twisted and gurgled. I was hungry, but pain filled my gut.

Del's eyes kept walkin across my face like a spider huntin for its prey. I slapped my knife on the table. "What do you want me to say, Del?" I stood and carried my plate to the basin.

"Excuse me?" Del twisted uncomfortably in his seat.

I turned and rested against the cupboard. "Don't set there like you got no mind of what's goin on. You're the one who brought me the news. What do you expect from me?"

He cut into his bacon and turned his eyes the other direction.

"Don't look away. Don't you think I deserve an answer? I've give my whole life to being a good wife to Stately Jenkins. I mighta fussed with him a little through the years, but truth is, I never disrespected him, and I honored him. Still do. I loved Stately. I reckon I'll never know why he married me, seein as he had bigger eyes for Melba." I wiped my hands on my apron. "Whatta ya think, Colton? You reckon an old woman will spill the beans now? Her body is broke. Her heart is broke. I reckon her spirit is broke too. So you tell me, whatta you want from an old woman?"

Colton scooted away from the table and excused himself. He shrugged. That action spoke to me. He couldn't be trusted.

"I'll head on into town. I'll be back in the morning." He nodded and thanked me for the meal, then slipped out the screen door.

"Well, that was right cowardly of him. Refusin to answer my questions." I poured my cup to the top with hot coffee.

"I'm sorry. My intentions were never to hurt you." Del slid his chair away from the table.

"That right? Then why did you see the need to tell me such a tale?"

"For one, you asked. But mostly because I care about you. I wanted to know who I was. You asked, for Pete's sake."

I glared hard at him.

"Stately's name was never spoken in our house, and Mother never mentioned him," Del said. "He was like a blank page in a book. Erased."

"So you come lookin for a grandmother?" I snapped. "Did you think you'd find a wealthy woman in her prime, ready to welcome you in with open arms?"

"No, I . . . I . . ."

I slammed my hand against the table. "You what, Del? You what? It wasn't enough to be nice to me. To act like I might mean something just because of who I am—Minerva Jane Jenkins. You had to drudge up memories from the past. Let me taste the bile little by little before it made me so sick I vomited."

"That's not true and you know it isn't. I care about you. Why do you think I stayed around?" His voice raised a notch.

"I don't know, Del. Why did you stay around? I sure as whiz didn't ask you to stay. I never asked you to do a blessed thing around this place. That was all you. You."

I felt the tears rise again, but I swallered them back. I wasn't about to let this man take what was left of my dignity and pride. No sir.

"I'm sorry, Miss Minerva. I truly never meant any harm. I just wanted to know you. I wanted the gentleness of truth."

"No, Del, you wanted to know if Stately Jenkins hid a box of gold, and you deceived an old woman tryin your best to have what you wanted. Well, I done told you. There ain't nothin here."

"I see that. Please listen to me. Let me try to explain more."

"Ain't nothin left to explain. If you're worried about me sendin you away, then stop. My days are numbered. You stay. Maybe you'll see fit to bury my bones. And since we are family, when I'm gone, you take this place. Make it your own. Won't do me no good when I'm dead. I'm happy to sign a paper to give it to you."

"Minerva. Please."

I held my hand up to hush him. "No, Delano Rankin. This is where it ends!" I slammed my coffee on the table and shoved open the screen door. It wiggled on the hinge. "Now that you own a cabin, you might wanna fix your door before it falls off."

TWENTY

I PUTTERED AROUND THE GARDEN, pullin what was left of the summer beans. The vines were turnin brown, so I pulled them out of the ground as I picked off the remainder. I filled my apron pocket three or four times, makin trips to the gate to dump the beans into a bucket.

Satchel's nose went straight into the pail. The old hound always did like fresh-picked beans.

"Get outta my bucket. You behave and I might leave you some in your bowl. Now, get from here." He tucked his tail and fell in behind me.

I walked the rows, mutterin, occasionally lettin a curse word slip when I mentioned Stately Jenkins. There was one thing for certain, I no longer had a desire to know what Melba held over Stately's head. Now I knew it was a child. And whether Stately had decided to leave on his own or whether Melba sent him away didn't matter no more. I was ninety-four years old with one foot in the grave and no desire to see Stately in eternity. The man I thought was in heaven was, in my eyes, judged and steamin in hell.

I went to pullin up tater vines. There was no need to dig the remainder. I'd be gone in a bit. Leavin them in the ground would make them sprout in spring, and that ole bear would have something to gnaw on. If this blasted hound managed to live through winter, then he'd have some food.

"You hear that, Satchel? You remember to dig here in the spring for fresh taters."

"You're determined to die, aren't you?" The voice came from behind me, givin me a start. Del took the hoe from the fence and chopped off the tater vines.

"Yes, sir. I am."

"Why?"

I busted into laughter. "Why? Right stupid question, don't you think?"

Del stopped in front of me. "No, it's not. You're mad at me. I understand that. I should have told you the first day, but, Minerva, it wouldn't have prevented you from being hurt. I was hoping to find out there was no Stately Jenkins. I was hoping there was no family here to connect this to. I wanted my life to be regular, without much incident. But then, here you were. And there was Stately Jenkins. Nobody was any more surprised than me."

I put my finger in his face. "You lied to me."

"No, I didn't. I came for a story. I told you it was not about the gold, it was about the people. You remember that, don't you? I never anticipated someone would try to break into your home. I never expected your dish to be broken or your home to be ransacked."

I stood pointin my finger for the longest time, and then I realized he was right. "You see that rosebush down by the shack?"

Del looked that direction. He lifted his hand to shade his eyes. "Which one? There's several. Which color?"

"There ain't several. There's one." I cupped my hands around my eyes. "It's one bush. It blooms several colors. Depends on the weather. Sometimes it blooms them all out at once. Red, yellow, pink, purple, white. You won't see another one like it." I motioned him to follow.

"I thought it was more than one bush."

"Nope. I grafted them roses together. Stately was always graftin somethin. Most of the time it failed, but every time he come from town, he'd bring me a single rose that he'd pick along the road. I'd keep it in water till the bloom went to drop, then I cut the end at a diagonal. I'd slit the top layer of skin off a small spot on the bush and tie that stem to the bush."

We'd made our way to the bush.

"See what happened." I tenderly pulled the colored blooms to my nose and smelled them. "Them grafts took and commenced to grow, then bloom. This was the one thing me and Stately Jenkins had in common. Graftin. And I cherished it. We worked together to create something beautiful."

Del touched a bloom. "It is beautiful. Looks like Stately cared a lot for you."

"I ain't so sure anymore. But I know every year since I buried him, this here bush has bloomed the most gorgeous flowers. These roses remind me of a time that I lived to love. Now it seems I just live."

"I'm sorry. I truly never meant to hurt you. I would have never intentionally made you mad at me." Del leaned against his hoe.

"You are right. I am mad, but I ain't mad at you. I'm mad at myself for refusin to accept what I knew. I figured if I was a good wife, Stately would fall in love with me. For years, I told myself his coldness was because I wasn't doin things like a wife should. But I knew the truth. You see, I stood out on the bank of the river and watched Melba kiss my husband goodbye."

"You knew about the affair?" Del took a step back.

"I was a young girl. Fourteen. Just married. Raised to be a good wife and trust your husband regardless. You might say I chose to trust my husband. That meant ignorin what was obvious. I rested in the fact that at night, it was me and him by the fireplace. Not him and Melba. Besides, Stately never spoke of her. Never mentioned a thing about why or how. He just loaded me up in a wagon and moved me away from Lexington."

"You knew?" Del asked again.

"Not for sure. I never had nobody tell me. But I knew in my heart. And I shoulda listened. I shoulda pressed him for peace about what ate at me. Instead, I trusted him."

"I'm sorry." Del put his arm around me.

"Awww, they ain't nothin to be sorry over. You wasn't a thought in your momma's mind when this happened. But if I was to say anything good come from Stately Jenkins, then I'd say his seed come down the line to make a right nice young man." I patted his hand.

"So, you aren't going to send me away?" Del asked.

"No. You can stay. You'll have to be obligin to forgive me in my shock. All these surprises make an old mind struggle to understand. Then there's the question of how come. When I grow ill with you, it ain't necessarily you. It's what I'm learnin about Stately and about me."

"I understand. It has been a lot to take in." Del smiled.

"You best stay around. Besides, I need to write my will. I might need some help from a reporter." I rubbed his arm.

"Will you be all right to get back to the cabin? I'll finish mending this lower fence."

I looked in his eyes, and for a minute, I could see the green eyes of Stately Jenkins. Despite the hurt in my heart, I loved Stately. He was a handsome man, and though Melba might have had him in her bed, I had him in my life. Even if it was one-sided. Maybe Stately's secret had seeded another and another. This might just be the beginnin of his lies.

I stepped over the clumps of grown-up grass and made my way to the shack. Twistin the wood slab that held the shack door shut, I leaned hard and pushed it open. The wooden door creaked. The smell of hay and musty wood filled my nose. Stately was never one to move things around, so I took a flint from the shelf it had rested on for years, cracked it twice, and lit the old oil lantern. In the corner behind some jars was the worn leather trunk we'd brought with us from Lexington.

I brushed my way through cobwebs and inch-thick dust, webs catchin on the lantern. The flame singed and burned what hit it. I pushed back a few old hoes and a shovel along with some meat hooks Stately had hung from the rafters. The years had rusted the pointed hand-forged plow. Hammered dings still showed in the reddish color of the plowshare. Leather reins hung neatly wrapped over one handle of the plow while the other handle lay broken and leaned against the beam that held the clevis.

"Lordy mercy. It's been years since I've been in this shack." I rubbed my fingers over the point of the cutting edge. The rusty metal nicked the flesh on my finger. "Darned old plow," I growled and moved past.

Wooden boxes filled with hand tools and horses' bits lay to one side, and as I reached the leather trunk, Stately's work boots, dried with mud, sat in the corner. How I remembered those boots. Stately had gone two winters with holes in the sides of them. We bartered with Robert to get a new pair. I would never forget pickin a wagonload of corn and seein Stately off as he drove it down the mountain to Robert. Then his comin home with them new leather boots.

I eased myself down onto the wooden floor, hopin that the slats were strong enough to hold what little weight I pressed on them. I leaned forward and blew the dust from the boots' leather ties. A cloud of dirt bellowed into the air, forcin me to cough. But when the dust settled, I wiped my hand over the tanned hide. Memories flooded back. A pair of dirty socks in need of mendin was stuffed inside the boots. I pulled the boots into my hands and squeezed them against my chest. Memories were all there was.

After a spell, I set the boots down and crawled next to the wooden chest. Momma had called it my hope chest, and I remembered when Daddy had slid the trunk onto the wagon.

150

"Minerva, there are some essentials here," he said. "You'll need them for your trip. And your momma added some special things she wanted you to take with you. I'd like to think that this isn't goodbye forever, but a poppa knows that when his girl marries, forever can happen right fast." He kissed my forehead.

I felt tears raise. "Yes sir." I sniffed.

"Your momma and I have raised you right. You know what it means to be honest, a person of your word, a good wife. You've been taught. You just remember, you are and always will be the light of my day." Daddy pulled me close. His bear-sized hand pressed my head against his chest.

Momma dabbed her eyes with a tiny handkerchief she'd embroidered roses on the corner of. "Goodbye, my love." She kissed my cheek long and hard.

I'd not thought of them memories for years. I'd tried to put them behind me. Every time they come to mind, I'd find myself longin for my parents.

Decades of memories played in my head. Some joyful, like the first kiss I got from Stately the day we were married. He was timid and a little backward, but so was I. Just two youngins unsure how to move ahead.

I pulled the leather straps on the chest and unlatched them, all the time watchin for critters. The leather was stiff but still made well enough that it had not begun to fall apart. The lid creaked open.

I'd not opened this since Stately died. He'd took this chest as his own, and though it was mine, I didn't mind he used it. Last time I pushed open the lid was to put his three shirts and two pairs of trousers inside. Even to that point, I'd never paid any mind to what else was in the trunk.

I pulled out the smidge of worn and tattered clothing. Under that was a small box with Stately's wallet and his pocketknife. There was a fifty-cent piece—the most money I'd seen in years—and to one side a book with a pen and dried-up ink in a bottle. I eased my fingers under the book and lifted it. LEDGER was printed on the cover. When I gingerly opened it, torn pages dropped to the floor, each filled with line after line of words.

I lifted one and unfolded it.

Dearest M,

It has been some time since we have corresponded. I hope this finds you in good health.

There is little to be said when the years and the miles rush betwixt us, but it is important to know that I have never forgotten your face, your words, or your tears on the day I took my bride and left. I will never forget. Leavin was the right thing to do for you and me, but for the woman I took as my bride, it will never be right. Enclosed you will find $2.00. It's all I have. Use it for the child.

Regards—S. Jenkins

I pressed my fingers against my mouth to stifle the sob. There was no money in the letter. Perhaps Stately decided it was best not to send it.

I turned to another page.

Dearest M,

I cannot express my loneliness. How I miss you. How I long to see your faces . . .

"Faces. Whose faces?"

Dearest Melba . . .

There were more half-written pages, but I couldn't bring myself to sort through the pile on the floor. I rested my elbow on the trunk's edge and pushed my hair away from my forehead. *Why, good Father? Why now? I've pleaded for You to just take me rather than let me read these sorts of things. You know I'll keep goin till*

I get my answers, cause I ain't got the wherewithal to stop. This woman has waited too many years to know. I've cried out for Your mercy. Just take me! What in the name of all that is good does lettin me live through this pain bring?

I slammed the trunk shut and heaved myself to my feet, turnin to reach for the lamp. It was gone.

"What on earth? I coulda swore I set that lamp on the box behind me." I took a step back and heard a *ting*. A flame went to risin along the floor. I must have kicked over the lamp.

Smoke commenced to rise, and my lungs went to burnin. I swatted at the white haze, tryin to find my way out, but there was no light by the door. No way to see clear. I was on my knees, tryin to crawl along the wall, but nothin seemed familiar. Between the thick smoke and my poor eyesight, I couldn't see to the door.

Then it come to me. My time was here. My time to die had come, and I wasn't afraid. I eased back to the trunk and pulled open the lid. I grabbed the ledger, pulled it tight to my chest, then just laid down on the floor. I laid there, balled up like a baby, and waited for the smoke and flames to take me.

I was ready as I'd ever be.

TWENTY-ONE

"MINERVA JANE JENKINS! Where are you? Minerva . . ."

The voices must have been them angels searchin for me in the smoke.

"Where's she at?" The panicked voice sounded familiar but distant. "I can't get the door open. Help me."

"Minerva, are you in there? Minerva!"

I could hardly hold my head up, much less catch a breath of air. The smoke circled me like the white Appalachian mornin clouds floatin along the ridge.

"Move back, I got the axe."

I heard bangin on the door of the shack, but if the truth be known, I figured the good Lord was waitin with His arms open wide on the other side.

Just leave me be.

Maybe He'd turned His face toward me and decided to show me mercy. Just walk me on to the other side. I was ready, but instinct took over and I pulled my apron over my face to try and cipher out some of the smoke.

It's funny. We beg and plead for the good Lord to take us home, end our sufferin. Yet when we face the curtain between the clouds and heaven's door, the urge to live grabs us by the ankles and keeps yankin us back. Here I laid on the floor of this old shack, my spirit as broken as the slats, yet I felt the chains of my earthly body holdin me tight. I shook my foot, tryin to break free, but that earthly part wouldn't loosen its grip. Somethin kept me bound to a life that I was tired of living. Takin my own life was never a thought I'd took hold of—I was too much of a coward. But with my life danglin betwixt heaven and earth, I did wish my ninety-four years would come to a stop.

All I'd known for half a century was that the love I'd felt was for Stately Jenkins. My eyes mighta been closed to his real soul, but the one I saw had satisfied me. And now it was like the rug was yanked from under my feet. All I'd believed, all I'd known down deep, rose to the surface, belly up. I was drained. Taken apart. Shattered. If anything, that secret weighed heavier than ever. Would I spit it out to seek retribution or revenge, or would I be what my daddy said I was? Honest, a person of my word. Upright.

It became harder and harder to get air in my lungs. The taste of smoke dried my tongue. My heart raced and my soul battled betwixt living and dead.

"Minerva, where are you?" Del's voice come louder. "Miss Minerva—Mamaw Minerva. Please answer me. I can't find you. If you don't answer, I'll die here with you."

Mamaw Minerva? The child called me Mamaw. The terror in his voice was real, and his cries echoed clean into my soul. Del called me . . . Mamaw. I tried to lift myself to my elbows, but all I could do was cough and gag. I did my best to cough hard.

"Mrs. Jenkins, hold on. We're comin." Robert Jr.'s voice bellowed over the roar of the flames. "Daddy buried Stately. Please don't make me bury you."

I coughed again, and when I did, a hand grabbed my wrist. Then another. I felt my body rake over the rough floor of the shack, takin hide and all.

"Get some water. There's a cup and a bowl by the gate of the garden. The spring starts there." Del screamed the orders to the pastor. "Miss Minerva, come on. Take a good, clean breath. Please,

Mamaw Minerva." Del's voice quivered as he gently patted my face.

My eyes cracked open and slowly focused as best they could. I eyed the young man who'd come to have a place in my heart. Liftin my hand, I licked my finger, then rubbed the soot off his chin. "You got black on your face," I groaned.

Del laughed. He swiped my face and pulled me to his chest. Both arms wrapped tight around me. His body twisted from side to side as he whispered, "Thank You, Lord. Thank You."

My face was smashed into his chest. Catchin a breath right this second was just about as hard as breathin in that smoke. "Del. Smoke is bad enough. But you're squeezing what little air I got outta me."

He pushed me away and laughed even harder. "I thought you were gone. Scared the life outta me."

I coughed again and spit. Robert come to his knees with the bowl of water. He scooped a small sip into the cup and tipped it to my lips. I don't think I'll ever forget that sip of cold mountain water. I could feel it puttin out the flames in my throat and lungs as it went down. The taste washed away the nastiness of the smoke.

Memories of wadin waist-deep in the river come back to me. How my skin raised chill bumps and then grew numb from the iciness of the river. Ever few days I'd make my way down to the river, strip off my skirt, and wade into the water. I remember turnin toward the rush of the river and buryin my head under, scrubbing my hair. I flung my head and the long locks of ash-blond hair sprayed water into the air. My hair landed against my back, leavin a small trail of rainbow in the air. What a sweet memory. What a sweet, sweet time.

It come to me that Stately would slip to the edge of the wisteria and peer at me as I washed. I never let on like I knew he was there, but I wished for—longed for—him to ease into the rush of the river with me and take me as his own. It remained a dream, for Stately only watched from a distance.

I wondered why he kept so far away. He'd tinker with my hair as we sat on the porch in the evenins. He'd gently cup my face in his hands and kiss my cheek. He'd even gaze into my eyes for what felt like an eternity, but he never come close. He never, more than a handful of times, took me to his bed, and I wondered why. Was I not good enough?

What I know now was somethin I was glad I didn't know then—that his tenderness was an apology of sorts. A way to say he was sorry for not lovin me like he loved her. I was an escape. An excuse.

He might have cared for me, but his heart was in Lexington. And now I know his reasonin for keepin me at a distance. He was honorable in a twisted sort of way. He never gave himself to me because he'd done give himself to Melba.

"Miss Minerva. You all right? Do you know what happened?" Robert Jr. asked.

I raised up and straightened my legs. My knees throbbed. "I took the lantern to the back of the shack. I was sure I set it on one of the wood boxes that was waist-high. I heard a *ting* like somethin tippin over, then the flames took hold right fast. I couldn't find the door. I was sure I left the latch twisted to hold it open." I rubbed my face. "Lordy mercy. I know I set that lantern on a box."

Del helped me to my feet. "It doesn't matter, Miss Minerva. What matters is that you are alive. You got the pastor here to thank for that. I was in the lower field."

"When I went to the house, you didn't answer," Robert said. "That's when I saw the smoke. I was scared you was hurt. Or worse."

"How did the door get latched from the inside?" Del brushed my skirt down, then wrapped his arm around my waist to steady me.

I stopped dead in my tracks. "What? Locked from the inside? What do you mean?"

"We couldn't get the door open. Took an axe breaking it in," Del said.

"I done told you, I twisted that wood latch to the side so it would hold open the door. I didn't know there was one on the inside."

"Maybe it was just up higher, out of your line of sight. It may have just slipped over the door when it closed."

"It didn't slip over anything. I turned the latch sideways to hold the door open. I needed the outside light to find the lantern and strike it."

"It ain't important, Mrs. Jenkins. What is important is you're all right," Robert said.

But it wasn't all right. I saw Del eye Robert like somethin was not right. I could see they didn't believe me.

I yanked my arms away from Del. "I'm tellin you, I know what I did. I know. And what's more, I didn't kick that lantern over, fer I set it on a wooden box. They had to be somebody in that shack."

Del scrubbed his fingers over his chin. "Let's say someone was hiding inside that building who didn't want to be seen. How would they have gotten out if the door was latched from the inside?"

I put my hand on my hip and huffed. "You fool. The window. There's a window in the back of the shack. There had to be some-body in that shack with me. I'm tellin you the truth."

"Minerva, it's fine. We believe you. Simmer down. Let's just count it lucky we had some rain during the night. It wet things enough to make the shed burn slower. Because of that, we could get you out. Had that shed been completely dry . . ." Del gently rubbed my back. "Well, we might not have been able to save you."

"He's right, Mrs. Jenkins," Robert said. "Things are fine. We believe you. I know you're a woman of your word."

And there it was again. A reminder that I wasn't a woman of my word, and it angered me. It rung right funny to me that two men could say they believed me but try to convince themselves I was wrong.

We turned toward the shack. It was becoming nothin but a pile of smolderin wood. The timber mighta been damp from the rain, but it was old and dry. It only took minutes for it to become a pile of ash.

"My trunk. Daddy gave me that trunk. I imagine it's gone. Along with what was left of Stately Jenkins's belongins." I sighed.

The men twisted me away from the shack. Del handed me the ledger. "This was squeezed tight in your fingers. I figured it must be important, so I made sure to grab it from you."

I gently wrapped my fingers around the leather-bound book, tattered and worn, then pulled it close. A tear squeezed from my eye. "Thank you." My knuckles tightened around the book. Was it important? Did it really matter? It was just one more slap in the face.

"Let's get you to the cabin. This does you no good, starin at what was." Robert tugged at my elbow. "Come on now. Watch your step."

We headed to the cabin. I stumbled, but the men kept me from fallin.

"My trunk. Lawsey mercy. My trunk. It was all I had of Daddy's besides his Bible. Seems lately anything that has any value to my heart is bein destroyed." I sniffed, then commenced to cough right hard. We stopped walkin till I caught my breath. "First it was my dish Momma give me, and now this. Daddy's trunk." I dropped the ledger into my apron. *Then there's this.*

"I'll come back tomorrow and bring a few men from town," Robert said. "We'll sift through the ruins and see if we can find anything left. The rain we'd had wet things enough to keep the flames low, while we kept haulin water from the spring to douse it. Maybe that helped save a few things inside the shed as well. Will that be all right with you? My wife can gather some of the women too. They can help you around the cabin."

I nodded. The last time someone brought men to the mountain to help, it was Robert's father comin to bury my Stately. Strange turn that now his son was helpin me.

"Pastor?" I asked.

"Yes? What can I do?"

"What brought you up here? Hadn't been for you, I'd be dead. What brought you up here?"

"I come to deliver Del's telegram."

"I suppose you was a godsend. I'm obliged."

"I think I was a godsend. I nearly waited until tomorrow."

"You know what I find humorous, Pastor?" I nudged his arm.

"What's that?"

"I keep prayin for the good Lord to take me home. My body is tired. I'm old. Broken. And twice, someone has come to my side. Saved me. You reckon three times is the charm?"

TWENTY-TWO

TWO DAYS PASSED and I barely remembered the time. Robert and Del worked the better part of them days, alongside the men from town, cleanin up and burnin what needed to be finished off. That Colton showed up too. My trust toward him was slim to none, but his hands was kept busy workin, so there was little mischief he could get into. I reckon my mistrust told me he was huntin for more than anything that survived that fire. The way he meticulously sifted through the mess proved that to me.

Robert's wife, Cherry, and a few women from their church in town worked like beavers to get my cabin put back together from when it was ransacked.

"Miss Minerva," Cherry said, "I am much obliged that you would let us come in and help you clean up what someone tore apart."

I stared at her. How could a man as kind as Robert Jr. find a woman just as good? "There ain't no need for you to be obliging. It's an old woman who finally give into the reality that she's not so spry no more."

Cherry set next to me on the down mattress. She wrapped her fingers around my hand and gently squeezed. "None of us can escape growin older. It is just part of life. I remember when my hands were smooth, and now I look at them and see folds formin around veins. It's life, Miss Minerva. Just life. And now that we know you're up here on this mountain, we can see to it you ain't left alone."

Her words took me back. Now that they knew I was here? I swallowed hard, tryin to take them words in. I was reminded of the life I'd forged for myself. It was me that quit goin to town after my Stately died. It was me that separated myself from others. I couldn't even blame that part on the secret Stately made me keep. It was *me* that made me a lonely old woman. It was a choice, though one I wasn't aware I was makin. Grief does that.

My heart ached. All these years wasted, wallowin in my own pity.

"Miss Minerva? You all right?" Cherry asked.

Her sweet voice pulled me back from my thoughts.

"The ladies have brought you enough fixins to keep you and Del fed for a month. There's green beans, beets, corn on the cob, flour. And of course, Robert and me will be by to check in on you every little whipstitch." She patted my knee.

I was overwhelmed by the kindness of the townspeople. Overwhelmed and shamed all at the same time.

"Now, we got all your belongins tidied up," Cherry said. "Put back where it looks like they needed to go, but you move things around if we got it wrong. Two of the women brought you a couple of new blouses and two right pretty skirts."

I'd never had anyone *care* about my needs. They brought me clothes? I was moved by their love. But then, when I think back on the good book, we are told to love our neighbors. I reckon these women were doin just that.

"I . . . I'm sure it will be fine. I'm touched." It was all I could do to fight back the tears. "I'll never know why a body would want to ransack an old woman's house. I got nothin worth havin."

"Well, don't you worry. Del and Robert have talked to the sheriff, and he'll make his way by here just every so often. You'll be safe. Now, you stretch out on your bed. Rest. You've had a pretty rough week."

I thanked Cherry and the ladies from town again, then rolled to one side. My lungs still felt the burn of smoke from the fire. My window was cracked open, so I reckon Cherry wanted me to have some fresh air—that, or she was tryin to clear out the stench of old that lingered in the cabin. I was never a nasty person. My momma taught me cleanliness was next to godliness, so my house was right tidy. But there's something that happens when you get old. A body just . . . smells old. A mixture of bad milk and dirt, I reckon.

A tender breeze seeped through the window, and I could see Del and Robert on the porch talkin to the sheriff.

"I'm not comfortable leaving her alone. Her eyes are growing weaker by the day and her legs aren't steady. Not to mention that she's daydreaming a lot." Del rubbed his chin.

"Is her mind still good?" Pastor Robert asked.

"I'm still on the fence with that. There was no doubt someone ransacked this house. But that whole incident with the fire . . . When the boys found the window she claimed someone would have climbed out of, it seemed too small for a grown man to get out."

The sheriff leaned his back against the window. "Reckon what happened in that shack?"

"I think she couldn't see well," Del said, "and in the process, she probably twisted that block of wood to hold the door open, not realizing it wasn't turned in the right direction. It's easy enough to happen even if your eyes are good. It's old and worn. It doesn't hang right anymore. It could have spun around, latching on her. I'm guessing the *ting* she heard was the tipping of the lantern." He twisted against the side of the window. "It would have been easy for the tail of her skirt to catch the rusty handle. I mean, these are things that could happen to anyone, not just an elderly woman. But something isn't right and I can't put my finger on it. It's obvious someone is trying to get to Miss Minerva. But they're sly and good at making her seem a little off. I want to believe her. I just can't put the pieces together."

I rolled the other way. Turned my back to the window as my anger seeped to the surface. Now wasn't the time to grow mad. Not after everything these folks had done to help over the last few days. They were thinkin I was nuttier than a tree full of hoardin squirrels, and I wasn't no sucha thing. I know what I saw. I know what I know, and I didn't kick that lantern over. There was some-body in that shed with me.

Or was there? Even I was startin to question things.

I felt the anger fill my chest, and when it reached my head it turned to sobs. "I ain't never said I was a young thing with a perfect mind. I've said all along I was an old woman. But I know what I saw and heard."

Cherry stuck her head around the door facin. "You say some-thing, Miss Minerva?"

"I said I ain't never let on like I was a young chicken. I've always said I was an old woman. I ain't got good sight, but I ain't stupid. I know what I know." I dropped my legs over the edge of the bed and tried to stand. My knees give with me, and Cherry jumped to grab me before I hit the floor. She eased me into a chair.

"Of course you're not stupid. Why would you say that?"

"I hear 'em talkin on the porch. I know what they're thinkin."

Cherry took my shoulders in her hands and twisted me toward her. "You listen to me. There ain't a soul here who thinks you're crazy. But I'm gonna share some words that might sting. You just need to know they are meant with love."

Love? I wasn't sure what love was anymore. I'd lived fifty-plus years thinkin I was loved, only to find out at the end of my life it was nothin but a lie. Why would I question her words was meant with love? Reckon I had reason?

"Miss Minerva, you are right. Age has caught up with you, and so has the years of loneliness. You've been up here on this moun-tain with only a handful of folks walkin the river who might know you're here. You ain't crazy. But like your body is tirin out, so is your memory. You ain't crazy. You hear me? Your age is catchin up to you. It's time you stopped livin in the past and come join us in the present and the future. Let a body do for you. This is how it should be. The men don't think you're losing your mind. They are tryin to work through the things that have happened." She brushed her fingers along my cheek. "They want you safe, and that means askin hard questions. So let them things roll off like water on a duck's back and know they ain't meant to do you harm. They're meant to cipher through."

She was right—the words stung. She didn't say nothin I didn't already know.

"My body is tired, and I reckon so is my mind," I said. "Things might not fall into place like they used to."

Cherry stroked my arm, pushing the wrinkled skin to one side.

I commenced to laugh. "That skin looks like a wadded-up burlap sack, don't it?" A giggle slipped out and then a big belly laugh. Cherry went to giggling, and before I knew it, we were both swipin tears of laughter.

"Your age might have caught you, but your humor is still sharp." Cherry dabbed her eyes. "Will you be fine here tonight? Cause you're welcome to come to town and spend the night in our guest room."

"She'll be fine. She's got me. I'll take good care of her." Del eased through the door and squatted at my feet. "She's my grandmother. I'll see to it she is taken care of."

My laughin stopped as I felt the warmth of something I can't say I'd felt since I was a youngin. It was tender. Sweet. Gentle to the heart. It was . . . the feel of family.

I lifted my hand to Del's face. "You called me your grandmother. But I ain't your grandmother. I ain't blood."

"Blood doesn't make a relationship. Kindness, caring, love makes a family. You don't have to be blood to be the perfect fit."

I couldn't think much past that moment. I wanted it to last a spell. I'd known they was something familiar about Del. Them eyes. He had Stately's eyes. Same square chin. Same loyalty. So was

I to accept this gift or should I brush it off? And what about that secret Stately Jenkins wanted me to keep? I had some ponderin to do. Some strong thinkin. And as nice as all these folks was being, Del included, it was a lot to take in. A lot to figure over. A lot to wonder if I was deserving of it.

"I need some time to myself," I said. "You reckon y'all could just give me some breathin room? They's been a lot happenin over the last few days, and I need to do some cipherin and sortin."

Cherry leaned down and hugged me right gentle. "You rest. I'll be sure supper is ready when you wake."

I nodded. Del laid a quilt I'd stitched years ago over my legs. He leaned against my ear and whispered, "Family is all about those who love, not those who give birth. I'll be in the other room or on the porch. I'm not going anywhere."

Cherry's words about my age were like eatin a dry biscuit. You could chew, but it sucked ever bit of the spit outta your mouth. Tryin to swallow it was purt near impossible. But as much as I wanted to be mad, the love I felt seemed to smother the embers of anger.

There was never a time in all my years I'd felt so torn. I was comin to terms with years of my Stately's lyin to me. The curtains of what I thought was love was really burlap—hard and scratchy.

It come to me that when you close your eyes to what is right in front of you long enough, sooner or later it vanishes beneath the lie that is. A body can close out any memory, rewrite anything that happens. If they close their eyes to the truth long enough, it goes away. Or leastways, we think it does.

I remember Daddy speakin from the good book, quotin what the Lord said. "I am the way, the truth, and the life." And I always wondered exactly what was so special about Scripture that made Daddy quote it so often. I reckon it might be comin to me now.

Me and Stately married when I was fourteen—maybe it was fifteen. Reckon that was one of them things that "old" took from my memory. I was a child, and he wasn't much more than one himself. Youngins don't know squat—leastways not what they think they know—but I know now that when I saw Melba kiss my Stately across the river, my gut was tellin me the truth. He didn't love me. He loved Melba. He loved her enough that he laid with her and give her a child. But me . . . I was a casualty of a lie. I was the scapegoat, the way out, and I was made to believe it was all right as long as I was a good wife. A good woman. It was me that rescued Stately from livin his lie with Melba, but it was Stately that convinced me it was the right thing to do.

I imagine the hardest biscuit for me to swallow ain't my getting old or even dyin. It's spendin my life believin I was second-best and now findin out it was true.

TWENTY-THREE

I ROLLED TO MY SIDE and wiggled deep into the down mattress. The scrap fabric I'd used to stitch the blanket that covered my feet was heavy and comfortin. I brushed a tear that trickled down my cheek and puddled in a wrinkle.

It was so much to take in, and I commenced to question why the Lord was waitin until I was old and feeble, teeterin betwixt heaven and earth, to let this news seep out. Maybe this was that time when we get closure on our life. Sort through the things of the past before we move into eternity with a clean slate.

My hurt wasn't over Del. I reckon if any good was to come from this, it would be that the sweet man come into my life at a time I needed someone with me. The pain, the agony that haunted me, was wonderin why Stately bothered to marry me. Why didn't he just walk away and leave a young woman to live her life in truth, instead of takin everything from her and leavin her alone to hold a secret? I was stuck between bein angry and bein devastated. All I could do was run this whole ordeal over and over and over in my mind.

All them years of livin with a man that I felt I was lucky to have but never good enough to deserve. All them years—wasted. Not a dern thing to show for it.

The thoughts just kept rehashin in my mind, and every time

they started over, the knife in my back dug in a little deeper, cut a little further. I couldn't stop thinkin about the deception. I reckon it took replayin it again and again for me to accept it. Come to believe it. Come to live with it.

I let out a wail, then buried my face into my pillow. "Lord, just take me. Please take me. I can't bear this pain no more. Quit makin me relive this."

A peck come to my door facin, and I twisted to see who'd heard me cry out like an infant.

"Miss Minerva, it's Colton," a whisper come.

I turned back toward the window. "What do you want?"

"May I come in?"

"Ain't like there's a door blockin your way," I snapped.

Colton come around to the side of the bed and pulled a chair next to me. The legs squealed like a shot varmint. I pulled my hand over my ear and frowned.

Colton leaned close and patted my shoulder. "I'm sorry about your finding out about Del like this. And I'm really sorry you were trapped in that shed when it caught on fire." He held up the ledger, and my eyes opened wide.

"Where'd you get that?" I set up straight in the bed and reached for it. He pulled it away. "I said, where'd you get that?"

"It was layin on the hearth. I hope you don't mind, but I thumbed through it." He smiled a right cockeyed grin.

"Give it here. Ain't none of your business." I grabbed for the book again, but he kept it at a distance. "Just what do you want, Colton? I knew when you walked in this door you were crooked. What do you want from an old woman?"

He licked his thumb and pushed open several pages. "Seems Mr. Jenkins wasn't the man you thought he was. What a shame. You seemed like an awful faithful wife."

I drew back and slapped him across the face. His bristled chin felt like prickly pine.

"Well. You might be old, but spry isn't out of your abilities."

His voice reminded me of being taunted in the schoolyard as a youngin. *Bully!* The memory scraped at my soul. I drew back again, and as my hand moved toward his face, he caught my wrist midair.

"Slapping a guest. That's not how we behave." His words hissed like a snake.

I dropped my legs over the edge of the bed and stood. Yankin my hand away, I pushed past him. "I got no intention of askin you again. What do you want?"

"Del never believed there was gold hidden on this mountain. He's what we call at the paper 'too trusting.' A sucker. I happen to believe there's gold up here, and now that we found you, I think you can lead me right to it."

If there's one thing about a mountain woman that a body from the big city needs to know, it's that there ain't no amount of threats gonna budge her. If anything, her heels will dig in and the fight will seep out like a slow poison.

I got right in Colton's face. "You ain't right bright, are you, boy?"

I reached for the ledger, and Colton tucked it behind his back. My nostrils flared and my eye began to twitch. Anger was lit in my feet and the heat was crawlin up my legs. I bit my bottom lip and turned toward the night table by my bed. Inchin closer to the stand, I leaned against it. My hands behind me, I wrapped my fingers around the knob and gently eased open the drawer.

"I reckon you think you're somethin, don't you?" I said. "You find one paper and you think that makes you the be-all, end-all of knowledge. Right sad, Colton. Right sad." My fingers crawled around the drawer, searchin. I could only hope the women put my "friend" back where it belonged when they straightened up the room. "I don't know what you got in your craw outside of greed, but I woulda thought you had common sense enough to see there ain't no riches around this run-down place. And that ledger—it's my Stately's letters. I ain't sure what you think you hold in your hand that is so precious. Letters to the woman he loved, never sent. That shows nothin but a man who lived a lie about the woman he loved. And if you think it's painful, it is. Is that what you want from me? To tell you I'm broken and hurt?"

Colton stood and held the book out. "There's more here than broken-heart letters."

I felt my revolver and gingerly took hold. Fittin my thumb over the hammer, I pulled the gun out of the drawer and pointed it at Colton. My thumb shook, but I pulled the hammer back. "I see my friend here wiped that greedy smile off your face. Now, I might be old. I might even be a little crazy. But there is one thing for sure, there ain't been a person alive who can take what belongs to me away. And there's been even less who have threatened me and been able to get by with it. So right now, you're gonna lay my Stately's book on the bed, and then you're gonna take your greedy rear and get off my property." I motioned with my gun for him to lay my book down.

"Miss Minerva! What are you doing?" Del shouted as he come into the room.

"Get that gun from her. All I was doing was bringing her this book that was on the floor." Colton dropped the book on the bed. "She came after me like I was stealing everything she had."

"Minerva, let go of the gun." Del took hold of my hands and loosened the gun from my fingers.

"He ain't tellin you the truth. He threatened me. Said there was more in Stately's book than old letters, and that I knew where the gold was. And I was goin to tell him."

Colton eased past me. "I knew she was hard-pressed to see, but her mind isn't right. I was only trying to help her."

I pushed past Del. I drew my arm back once more, let my fist fly, and split Colton's lip. "Get outta my house, you thief. Get out."

Colton pressed his fingers against his lip and swiped a drop of blood. "I'll be in town if you need me."

"Stay in town. Don't you never set foot on my property again. Get the—"

"Minerva! That's enough." Del spun me and wrapped his arms around me. "Calm down."

I pulled my leg back and kicked like a mule, strikin Del in the shin. "You let me go, and you do it now."

The harder he held me, the fiercer my anger grew, until I bent around and bit a chunk from his arm. Del squawked and turned me loose.

I pushed my hair away from my face, slobber drippin from the corner of my mouth. "Now ain't the time to console me. Don't you lay another hand on me, or I will . . ."

"You will what, Minerva? What will you do?" Del stomped his foot and rubbed his arm.

I stared him straight in the eye, then walked to the bed and took Stately's ledger. I tucked it in my apron and made my way to the door.

"Aren't you going to tell me what exactly happened here?" Del asked.

I walked past him. My face felt hotter than a flat rock on an August day. "Don't matter. Besides, you done decided what happened when you let that snake go free." All I could do was point at him as I walked away. "Don't you bring that thief on my property again. You understand?"

With that, I walked outside and down to the rock path. I tapped my toes on the ground until I felt the rocks.

The black smoke had finally cleared, but the smell of burnt wood still filled the mountainside and occasional embers still floated into the clouds. Three or four men worked pullin out what odds and ends managed to survive the flames in the shed.

I waved my hand to the men, and one worked his way to me.

"John Rowe." He tipped his hat. His face was covered in soot, and streaks lined his forehead from the sweat that trailed from his curly hair. "I'm a mess, ma'am, but I can help you so you don't trip. Just take my arm."

I grasped hold of his elbow, then slipped my arm through his. "I'm obliged that you are takin the time to help out."

"My pleasure. That's what neighbors are for. Me and my wife, Lydia, live about three miles upriver. Never knew this place was here. The path up was grown over. But I'm glad to help out. Gladder you ain't hurt."

"No, I ain't hurt, short of my pride. In your pullin out things, did you find a trunk? Did my trunk get by without getting burned? It was a gift from my daddy when I left Lexington."

The man shook his head, then hollered at the others, "Y'all seen a trunk in all that burn?"

They shook their heads, letting us know there was nothing.

"We did find this." John Rowe turned me loose and walked a few steps to a blackened heap. "Found these plates. Small wonder they didn't smash when the roof fell in." He spit on his sleeve and swiped away the soot, then shined the plate on his hip.

I slowly took hold of it. The plate glimmered in the sun. White porcelain with hand-painted flowers. "There were three of these Momma bought when I was a little girl. She hung them over my bed."

"We found all three. Seems you have that memory saved. Will you be all right?" he asked. "You need me to help you somewhere else?"

I nodded. "If you find any of the trunk . . ."

"Yes, ma'am. I'll bring it straight to you."

"Thank you much, John Rowe." I slipped the dish into his hand. "Whatta you say, you take them dishes to Miss Lydia as a thank-you. I bet she can serve you up a piece of cooked trout on one."

He eyed the dish. "I couldn't. These is your childhood memories."

"John Rowe, I got one foot in the grave and one hand diggin the hole deeper. You take that and make some sweet memories with Miss Lydia." I pressed it against his chest. "Take it. Take all three. It would mean a lot to me."

A sideways grin brushed across his lips, and he lifted his hat to me.

"I'll be fine. I'm just gonna walk a spell should Del or the pastor come lookin."

"Yes, ma'am."

I brushed my hand over his arm and commenced to walk. I remembered a shortcut path through the trees that wound its way down to the river, so I took my time moseying through a stand of pines. I'd forgotten the beauty of the woods. Their quiet serenity. The peacefulness. When I come out on the other end of the shortcut, I set down by the river and wrapped my arms around my knees.

"Look at that. I can still wrap my arms around my knees," I shouted, then went to laughin. Big, hard, belly laughs until I fell backward in the tall, soft grass.

A tender breeze blew over me, raisin a chill in my bones. I took in a deep breath and pushed my spectacles tight on my face. The limbs of the pines hovered over me, fannin me like I was some queen in a storybook. A blue jay landed on the ground next to me and cocked his head to one side as if to say, "What are you doin?"

Odd as it was, my eyes cleared, and I could almost count the needles on the pines. High above me, a rounded nest teetered on a limb. I spread my arms open in the grass and took in the bittersweet mixture of lavender, honeysuckle, and fresh water.

"This is where I want to die."

Twenty-Four

THE BREEZE TICKLED MY NOSE, forcin me to scratch at my face. There was no reason to open my eyes. I was content layin in that grass by the river. Sweet memories of fishin danced through my head. It was a time I was happy, or I thought I was anyhow. I could see myself windin a worm on my hook and tossin the string into the water, then the wash of the river snagging hold and carryin it downstream. I could even smell the freshness of the mornin air by the water.

But as I looked around my memory, it was just as I thought. No Stately. Just me. Alone.

If I could do things over, I'd have made me some trips back to Lexington to see Momma and Daddy. Growin old alone is horrible. I would have made new friends after Stately died. But them is just wishes—I-wish-I-wouldas.

I wiggled in the grass as the sweet memory went sour. It was always just me. I dropped my arm over my face, tryin to erase the memories, but they just hung on like honey on a bear's paw. The more I thought about my time on this mountain, the more I could see—I could count on one hand—the times Stately had joined me. It's enough to fib to yourself, to believe what a body wants to believe. But it's worse to believe what someone else wants you to believe, especially when your gut is naggin at you.

And my gut nagged for half my life. Nag, nag, nag. I'd pushed it to the side. Ignored it. Believed what Stately wanted me to believe. But why? Why couldn't I be my own person?

I remembered Mamaw Whaley settin me on her lap whilst she rocked on her big front porch in Lexington. She'd wrap her arms around me and start her sermon with "Mini." A smile crossed my lips. Mini was her way of shortenin Minerva.

"Mini," she'd say. "Every woman has certain duties she performs as a wife and momma, but just cause she performs them duties don't make her any less a person. You always follow what you know to be right and understand you might look up and find yourself walkin down a road alone. So be it. The good Lord walked alone at times too. You stay true to the person you are. Even if you are by yourself."

Lawsey mercy, I'd forgotten them times. And I suppose I'd done what Mamaw Whaley told me—leastways partly. I stood by my Stately cause my gut told me that's what a wife does. Seems I was obeyin duty, not what my gut was really sayin. Had I done everything Mamaw Whaley said, I'd have believed my own heart years ago that Stately was a liar and that he, in his cloak of sweetness and good looks, had convinced me of what I knew not to be true.

"He never loved me. Never," I whispered.

I tried to wipe the memories away, but they stuck hard to my heart. How could I have lived a lie the bigger part of my life? "I know how. Love."

I just kept rehashin that question. I'd stumbled over it for days—doin everything in my power to justify, convince, rant, or stomp my way to acceptance.

There was nothin I could do about the days that washed away with the flow of the river. They were gone, tossed and swirled in the eddies of rushing water.

"Minerva." A voice come from behind me. The sound of my name was like the hiss of a rattler.

"I told you not to come back here. Apparently, you don't understand simple words." I slowly pushed myself to my elbows and then set up. "Colton, you're beatin a dead horse. Now, get from here."

I heard his footsteps come closer and then the click of a pistol hammer. I never turned. Never budged. Never looked at the coward. I just gazed toward the river.

"It's time you take me to where Stately buried that box." Colton stood over me.

"Or if I don't, you'll shoot me?" I went to laughin. I laughed so hard it made me break into a cough. "Please, Colton. Please. Shoot me. Put a bullet right through my chest. I've been beggin to die for months. Come on. Shoot me."

I heard the hammer release. "You aren't worth killin. I'll just share all I know with your new buddy, Del. He'll be interested to know about Stately." He huffed.

"I know. I reckon the good Lord's been sayin I wasn't worth takin home for months since He has yet to snuff out my life. And your threats ain't nothin to me. But you know what, Colton?" I pointed downriver. "There's a stand of cattails that way. I remember Stately spendin a lot of time down in them cattails. If I was gonna guess where he'd bury a box of gold, I'd start there."

I heard Colton turn away and his foot click into the stirrup of his horse's saddle.

"Wait!" I hollered.

"What?" he snapped.

"Ain't you gonna kill me?"

If a body could hear a sneer, then I heard Colton's.

"You know cattails is in the mud, right?" I asked.

I tried to warn Colton. But I reckon greed is stronger than common sense. He'd find out I only told him half the truth. The cattails are in the mud, but Stately's box bein there—that was just a suggestion. It might be a good place to start a treasure hunt.

For the second time, I pulled my knees up and wrapped my

arms around them. "I'm getting good at this, Lord." I clasped my hands together and wiggled my fingers.

I don't know how long I set there on the riverbank ponderin, but it was a good while because before I knew it, folks was lookin for me. I could hear them squallin my name along the ridge.

I rolled to my knees and pain shot through me. There ain't nothin that hurts much worse than knees three times the size they ought to be. It took me a minute, but I managed to crawl to my feet and start back up the darkenin path.

It surprised me that I remembered this trail from the house to the river, and it surprised me even more that the path was still wore enough in the ground that I could find my way down it. I picked up a stick about as tall as me and as big around as my wrist and used it to help me climb my way back up the hill. It wasn't steep but it was long, and anything for me to walk very far was painful.

"Miss Miinnneerrvvaa!"

Minerva. Minerva. My name echoed across the plateau. Should I answer? By now, I was just gettin sassy.

"Whatta you want? I'm comin!" I shouted, and I shouted it right nasty and hateful.

"Thank goodness! There you are." Robert Blessing come slippin down the bank toward me. "I was scared to death. The boys said you headed down this way. I was afraid . . ."

He caught my eye, and for a moment, I saw Robert Sr. My heart warmed.

"Afraid you'd find me dead, Pastor? We ain't that lucky, now, are we?" I said.

"Miss Minerva, I know you've had a hard week. And I can see things ain't goin the way we think they ought to go. But you have a purpose. And you have folks who care about you now."

I busted in on him. "Pastor, you said it right. I got folks that care about me *now*. It ain't that I don't appreciate you and Miss Cherry. It ain't that I don't want to get to know a newfound grandson like Del. But I'm at the end of my life. 'Now' don't mean a hill of beans."

The pastor stopped dead in front of me. His eyes never parted from mine. I could see the wagon wheels turnin in his head as he thought through the perfect words to say.

"You know what? You're right. You're at the end of your life. Wouldn't we all be fortunate enough to live ninety-four years? Most of us die long before we see sixty."

"That's right. About time somebody figured out the curse of old age," I growled.

"The thing is, most of us ain't as strong as you, Minerva. Most folks don't have the wherewithal to manage years alone on this mountain. You're a pretty unique woman, managin all these years on your own. You must be proud that you hid yourself up here all alone for so long that folks down in town thought you'd died. Ain't you proud?"

He kept drivin in his point—I was alone.

"I know, you're a might proud woman. Feelin sorry for yourself ain't something I pictured coming outta you. Now a fine young man has claimed you as his mamaw, but you don't need a grandson. I don't blame you." The pastor turned and took a few steps ahead of me. He didn't offer to help me, even when I stumbled over a rock. Instead, he pointed to the ground and told me there was more where that come from. "Watch your step."

It come clear to me what the pastor was doin. Besides callin me out for being stubborn, he shamed me for refusin the love of those who offered it. I felt more than shamed. I felt sad, hurt, unfixable.

As Robert walked ahead of me, I begun to see how bitter I was and just how mean I was bein.

"Robert," I hollered. "Robert Blessing, come back here."

He stopped and turned. "Yes, ma'am?"

"You made your point. You got some time to hear my sins?"

Robert sat down right where he was, took off his hat, and waited for me to make my way up the hill.

Once I got to where he was seated, I tapped his legs outta my way with my walkin stick. "You didn't offer to help me up the bank. Can you manage to scoot over? I reckon you've punished me enough."

Robert stood and took my arm. "Let's sit on that downed tree. I believe it'll be easier on both our backsides." He chuckled.

So it was. Robert and me set on that tree trunk for the better part of the afternoon. I poured out my soul to the pastor, from the time I saw Melba kiss Stately, to never havin children, to findin out Del was Stately's grandchild. It was more like I vomited it all out and the pastor listened.

"I got one last question for you, Robert. Pastor Robert," I said.

"Robert is fine, Miss Minerva. There ain't many folks who call me Pastor except on Sunday. Through the week, I'm just the general store owner. What's your question?"

"How long does a body keep a promise?"

Robert stood and paced. He scrubbed his knuckles over his chin. "That's a hard one. I reckon it all depends on the circumstance."

"But a promise is a person's word. And we're only as good as our word. Ain't that right?"

"I might agree with that on some level. I mean, if folks can't trust you when you tell them you'll do something, then you aren't very dependable. But that's where us mountain folk get a little twisted in our thoughts."

"Twisted?" I leaned forward to listen.

"Yes, ma'am. We tend to hide behind our word. If a body can't be what we think they outta be, then we say they ain't a person of their word."

"That might be right." Robert made a point. We use our word as an excuse when we don't meet up to the expectations of others.

"Truth is, Miss Minerva, I don't know a person alive who can meet the expectations of everybody. Ain't a one of us able to be all others think we should be. So when someone disappoints us, it's easier to say they broke their word rather than admit they couldn't be what we imagined they should be." Robert pushed his hat back on his head and dabbed sweat with his sleeve.

"Well, ain't you the wise one?" I muttered. "But you ain't answered my question. How long does a body keep a promise?"

"Like I said, it depends on the circumstance. You wouldn't keep a promise to a child if you knew that child would be hurt down the road. You might say you'd keep the promise to find out what was ailin the youngin, but then your common sense would take over if you saw that the youngin might be in danger. Circumstance plays a part. The only promises that have been kept over time are the ones from the good Lord. And I reckon when you're the Lord, you have the strength and knowledge to be able to keep a promise, despite the trials that come."

Robert held out his hand and I took hold. He helped me stand, then threaded my arm through his.

"I'll help you to the cabin if you'll let me." He smiled.

I could see this man was genuine. His kindness and honesty was the real thing. But despite his goodness and his wise words, I still had to wrestle with this blessed old promise Stately Jenkins made me keep. I didn't know for sure what was in that box or even know what his secret was. But despite his goodness and wise words, I was left to wrestle with a promise I was unsure of. It was Stately's secret. Not mine.

Twenty-Five

THE YELLOW GLOW OF THE FIRE lit the room enough for me to see the coffeepot hangin on the hook. The sun was makin its way behind the house and stars were showin themselves early. Del had moved my rocker from the porch and carried out the old straight-back chair. He fretted its cane bottom would give and I'd fall through. Having the extra rocker inside was nice.

I eased outta the chair and patted my hand across the small side table until my fingers wrapped around the tin cup, then I reached and poured me a swig of coffee. There was nothin like the fresh scent of hot coffee. Can't say I ever really liked the taste early on, but Stately liked a strong cup ever mornin, and I learned to like the taste. The difference was, I liked to drink it all through the day, hot or cold.

Follow suit. Huh. Seems all I've ever done is follow. Ain't never took the lead on nothin. Not that it mattered anymore. When you're facin the grave, there ain't a lot you can do to change the past.

I leaned back in my rocker and took a sip of coffee. Nothin these days had much taste, but my tongue worked well enough to know it wasn't right big on the flavor swishin over it. I swallowed hard and set the cup down.

I slipped my hand in my apron, pulled out Stately's ledger, and flipped through a few pages. It was hard to see in the dim light of the fireplace, so I got up and set myself down on the hearth. It was warm outside. Hot, in fact, for Del spent a good amount of time swiping sweat. But my old bones and thin skin got no flesh underneath to hold in the heat. The warmth of the fire felt good against my bones.

I twisted toward the glow and squinted hard to read what was on the pages. Pages of lists, things he needed to collect when he went to town, even a page of cipherin he'd done on a field of hay he'd sold off. I kept flippin, and I come upon a white crocheted bookmarker. I never was much at crochet. My skills with a needle and thread were better, so I knew that bookmarker never come by way of my hands. I picked it off the page, and a long string pulled from betwixt the pages with a note attached.

> *From here to there and there to here. Wherever you travel I will follow in your heart.*
>
> *~Melba*

My chest ached. When did she slip this into Stately's hand? What did she say when she gave it to him? Was this the goodbye gift? Why? Why would Stately do this? When had he seen her to get this?

Question after question filled my head—the whys and hows that would never be answered. They would always be silent. Buried with his secret. Truth be known, maybe this was his secret. It was comin to me that the secret in that box wasn't gold but all of Stately's sins.

I turned another page, and a letter lay neatly pressed between. I picked up the white page, now yellowed with years, and gently unfolded it.

> *My dear Stately,*
> *   Every time my husband holds our son, I long for the arms he's cradled in to be yours. A son. Yes, a son. He has his father's eyes . . .*

I dropped the letter in my lap and stared into the fire. I didn't think there was any more hurt to be felt, but there it was, plain as day. And it just kept comin like rushes of wind before a storm. Like sheets of hard rain shoved over me. Memories flooded back. Back to the day I held a dyin man in my arms. Back to my cryin over the one I loved. Back to his last words—"Promise to keep the box a secret."

Before I could stop myself, I lit the extra lantern and headed to the porch. After inchin down the steps, I made my way around the house. The sun was barely holdin its own against the darkness fallin over the mountain. I never stumbled once. Wasn't sure why. Maybe it was that my eyes were clearer than they'd ever been before, or maybe it was a drivin hurt. Either way, I grabbed the hatchet by the pump and ducked under the overhangin leaves of them vines.

"If you want to eat me now, have at it." I kicked at the vines and fumbled my way through the thick and darkness right to where I'd buried Stately years ago. "I want you to look what you've done to me. Look at me. Open your eyes under that packed-down dirt and look at me!" I rared back with the hatchet and slammed it against the stone bearin his name. "How's that feel, Stately Jenkins? How's it feel to have a hatchet driven into the rock that sets over you?" And I hauled off and struck it again, this time breakin off a corner.

I went to my knees and walked my fingers over the dirt till I found that piece of stone. Then I commenced to dig at the ground until I hit the top of that blessed old box. It took me a few minutes, but I managed to yank it from its grave. I took that piece of broke headstone, dropped it in the hole, and then covered the hole. After crawlin to my feet, I took the lantern and made my way back to the cabin.

I realized when I come from outta that stand of vines that I'd not tied my rope around my waist. It came to me in that moment that my fear wasn't in the vines that covered Stately's restin place, but it was in displeasin him. My whole adult life had been spent tryin to please a man that could have cared less about me. I believed what he made me *feel*—that maybe I couldn't do for myself, that I had to depend on him. I had the know-how but missed the confidence to believe I could stand on my own. That is, until I was forced to be on my own.

For an instant, I felt free of a weight I'd carried for years. A fear that I wasn't good enough.

I'd walked on eggshells for years. Tiptoed around anything I thought would upset Stately or allow him to think I could stand on my own, and yet, there was nothin to fear. Stately might never have loved me and he might have been a stern old cuss, but he never once raised his voice to me, never once raised an angry hand to me. Why, then? Why had I feared him?

I made it to the pump and grabbed hold of the handle. "Dear Lord, I'm askin You to prime this pump. I ain't got the umph to do it."

I set the box under the faucet, took both hands, and wrapped them tight around the handle. It squealed and squeaked as I pulled it upward, and when I pressed down, icy water shot out over the box.

Thank You, Lord. I pumped twice, and all the water I needed to rinse off the box washed over it. I swung the lantern slowly over the box, tryin my best to see if the dirt was cleared. When I felt like I'd cleaned the mess off, I carried it inside and set it by the fire.

I plopped down in that rocker, my heart raced, and I breathed like I'd run a race. The pain in my chest wrestled with the pain and stiffness of my knees and fingers. My head rested against the back of the chair, and I knew right that minute that my days was short. Real short. I didn't have a lot of time left to make things right.

I pressed my foot against the box and shoved it against the rocks on the fireplace, then I laid a crocheted doily over it and set Daddy's Bible on top. The ledger lay on my bed where I'd tossed it earlier. I shoved it off the bed and onto the floor and inched as best as I could into the bed.

If I lived till mornin, I'd add a few lines to Stately's ledger. If not . . . well, then I kept his secret until death did us part.

I set up straight in bed and rubbed my eyes. The fire burned as bluish embers. Tiny pops and crackles reminded me the flames hungered to be fed. I eased out of bed. The weight of my body on my feet brought a throbbin ache. Del had filled the wood bucket the night before, so I took hold of a piece of applewood and dropped it on the smolderin ashes. The bark caught quick, and the flames gnawed at the hardwood like a dog on a bone. That applewood gave off the scent of fresh green apples and made me have a hankerin for an apple pie. I closed my eyes and took in a deep breath. A breeze slipped through the open window, and the sweet scent of apples left me for . . . bacon?

I limped to the window and there was Del. He'd done built a fire out from the porch, and he was cookin.

I pushed the window up more. "You got my iron skillet over that fire?"

He waved. That scutter had my good iron skillet over that open fire. I wasn't much at a lot of things, but cookin was my gift, and I learned years ago a good iron skillet needs to be seasoned and used on a solid grate. Momma and Daddy had given me an iron skillet, and Daddy had the blacksmith make me a solid grate to put over the flame. It was the best gift, outside of that chest, that they'd given me. I kept that skillet greased with lard, and water never once filled it. I wiped it clean.

"Del! That's my iron skillet. You're goin to ruin it," I shouted. All I heard was a belly laugh.

"Come on down. Breakfast is ready. The girls gave us some good eggs today."

"Lawsey mercy, he's done ruined a perfectly good skillet. But I'll give him one for the smell of breakfast."

I slid my feet into my shoes and pulled my dress over my night-gown, then tied my apron around my waist. When I glanced on the floor, I saw that ledger. *Let it lay. It ends here.* And I made my way outside.

Del met me on the porch and helped me down the stairs. "If you've ruined my skillet . . ." I warned.

He went to laughin. "I got the grate. See!"

I peered over the rocks around the fire, and sure enough, Del had laid the grate over two rocks and set my skillet atop.

"Well, I believe you just saved your rear."

Del leaned over and kissed my cheek. My hand flew up and covered the spot. It was a sweet kiss. One that was filled with . . . love. I couldn't recall a time I'd ever felt that kind of kiss before. All them years married, and the times Stately kissed me was on the top of my hand or my forehead. And to think, I thought he was a gentleman.

"Del, I got somethin to show you after a while. What sort of plans you got goin today?"

He run his finger along the edge of his chin. "Well, I was going to finish plugging the holes around your house. I want you warm through the winter."

I rolled my eyes. "You're right sweet, but you know the only place I'll be this comin winter is in the ground."

"Stop it. I don't like to hear you talk like that. You'll be fine. I'll see to it. And I thought it might be nice if in the fall, we made a trip to Lexington. I've thought a lot about it. What do you think?"

Lexington. He wanted to take me to Lexington. I shook my head. "Like I said, Del. I won't be doin no travelin by then."

"But I want you to meet—"

"Del, stop it. I ain't in no shape to make a long trip to Lex-ington. I can barely get in and out of the cabin. So before I drop dead, I want to show you something. You willing to go with me?"

He nodded and scraped the last of his egg onto the ground for Satchel.

"And I don't feed my dog from the table," I grumbled. "Well, I don't feed him much from the table."

"No table. It's outside. Besides, look at those sad eyes." Del patted the hound's head.

"Mooch. That's what he is." I took a bite of egg, and it felt like it grew to the size of my fist in my mouth. Eatin anything made my stomach churn, but I chewed and swallowed so as not to hurt Del's feelins. Eatin was gettin harder, and the harder it got, the less I swallowed and the thinner I was gettin.

"Come on, Miss Minerva. Try a bite of bacon. It's really good. Miss Cherry brought us a big plateful."

It smelled good as it could and I did my best to take a bite, but my stomach went to turnin and all I could do was spit it on the ground. "I'm sorry, Del. I just ain't got the stomach today."

He rubbed my shoulder and took my plate. "Maybe at lunch, bacon, lettuce, and a tomato slice on bread."

"Maybe," I said, tryin to make him feel better.

"What do you want to show me today?" Del smiled.

"I'm gonna take you to see your grandfather's grave."

He stopped short. The smile left his face. "Really?"

"There's things I need to tell you, and it starts with Melba."

Del helped me to the porch, where we sat and talked.

"Now, I know you like that Colton, but you need to hear me out," I said. "That man is rotten. And I don't know how he found out about some of the things he knows, but he's done took and ripped my heart out of my chest."

"What? Colton? What did he do?" Del took my hands.

"Well, outside of lyin to you yesterday, tryin to make me look like I was crazy—"

"You were holding a gun to his head!" Del squawked.

"You listen to me. He run me down at the river. Threatened

me. Threatened to tell you all about me. Tried to make me look like I was lyin.'"

Del sat stunned at my words. I could tell by his face he didn't know what to believe. So I just kept pushin at him.

"He took that ledger of Stately's, and he read through it. He let on like I knew what was in the book, but I didn't. So before we go a step farther, you need to know that the first I'd heard of Stately havin a youngin was when you told me. And it broke my heart."

"I'm sorry. I didn't come here to hurt you." Del brought my hands to his lips and kissed them. There it was again. A kiss that come from love.

"I didn't know nothin about a child. I only knew that the day we left Lexington, I saw Melba kiss Stately from across the river. I reckon I knew in my heart then that he didn't love me, but I didn't want to believe it. After all, he brought me here. He left her behind. He must have chosen me. Right?"

Del stared at the porch floor. "I . . . I . . ."

"You don't owe me no more apologies." I squeezed his hands tight. "All you need to do is hear me out. And when the time comes, walk an old woman to her grave. That would be the answer to my prayer. I've said before, I don't want to die alone." A pain shot through my chest, and the sunlight begin to fade to dark. "I don't want to die alone."

TWENTY-SIX

"MINERVA. Mamaw Minerva. Are you all right?"

My eyes opened as Del gently patted me on the face.

"Let me get you some water."

"I don't want no water." I pushed him away and stumbled to stand. "I want to make things right before I die. Are you comin with me or not?"

Del wrapped his arms around me and eased me down the porch steps. I pointed around the house, and we headed that direction.

"Can't we do this after a while?" Del asked. "You need to rest."

"I need to do what I need to do! Surely this old heart can withstand a little confession," I grumbled.

Once we reached the edge of the vines, I took a deep breath. It gnawed at me whether to tell Del about Stately's box. There was a part of me that held a sourness in my soul over Stately's secrets. One that wanted to lash out and get even at him for ruinin my life—makin me an old woman that hung on to the lie that her husband loved her. Oh, I could taste the bitterness in my gullet. But the good side of me, the side that the good Lord held firm to, kept whisperin in my ear, "Turn the other cheek." I know turnin the other cheek took a mite more gumption than I thought I could muster up.

"Where are we going?" Del rested his arm around my waist.

190

I lifted my hand and raised a crooked finger toward the stand of vines. "In there."

"Are you sure?"

"Sure as a cat has fur." I could see the doubt in his eyes. All I could do was straighten as best I could and walk headlong into the vines.

"Those vines are thick," he said.

"Grab the hatchet by the pump."

Del reached for the hatchet, but it wasn't there. It hit me then that I'd left it layin by Stately's gravestone.

"No hatchet, Miss Minerva."

"Fiddlesticks. Just follow me and watch your step."

We pushed our way through the thickness of the vines. They wound and twisted over the trees and along the ground like some monster strainin to free itself from its cage. They were so thick, the sun barely cut through the leaves. And when a body found an inch of blue sky peekin through the thickness, the vines seemed to choke the tar outta ya.

"I hate these things. Stately planted them years ago. You cut 'em back today and by nightfall they've stretched further than they were when you cut them. I'd swear they were born in the bowels of hell just to crawl out and snag you by the foot, then drag you into the pit of flames. Maybe you just thought that tumble you took a while back was my rope. Most likely it was these beasts that snagged your foot."

"That's not a thought I wanted to have in my head." Del chuckled.

"Well, it's true." I stopped to catch my breath, and my chest heaved up and down like the bellows by the fire. "Shew, lordy mercy. This walk gets harder ever time."

"You make this walk often?" Del asked.

"Often enough." I took hold of a vine and yanked it, pulling it loose from an overhangin branch. When it toppled, there in front of us was Stately Jenkins. "Here he is. Your granddaddy. The old cuss ain't moved in years."

Del took to chortlin like a little girl. I eyed him, tryin to figure what he found so funny. He coughed and swiped his mouth, tryin to stop his laughin, till I'd finally had enough.

"What in tarnation is so funny? Ain't you got no reverence for the dead?"

"I don't know. Maybe it was how you said the old cuss ain't moved in years. I suppose that is obvious." Del put both hands on his knees and laughed out loud.

All his chortling come over me like a yawn. You see a body yawn and you can't help but do the same. I tried not to be a party to his foolishness, but his laughter spread, and before I knew it, everything was funny.

"This ain't how I expected to introduce you to your grand-daddy. This bein his grave and all. I'm sure he'd rather have met you face-to-face." I brushed my fingers over the tombstone. "I figured Stately might bargain with the devil for a chance to meet his grandson."

"I might be worth the bargain." Del grabbed his sides and roared.

It took me a second, since things are slower sinkin in these days, till I grabbed aholt of his humor. I snorted as the laughter crawled up my throat. We laughed a good spell at Stately's expense, and I had to admit, makin light of him eased my stomach.

I slid my bent fingers under the vines wrapped around Stately's marker and pulled them away. The hatchet stood on its end next to the stone. "There's that hatchet. Think you can use that to cut away the rest of these vines?"

"Of course. Whatever you want." Del looked at me as if to ask if he'd gone too far.

I bowed my head and shook it, and before I knew it, I was hee-hawin long, hard guffaws. "Lordy mercy. I ain't laughed like this since the day you come to the farm. It seems right out of place to be makin such light of your dead granddaddy. But truth be known, it feels good."

Del wrapped both arms around me and pulled me tight. He squeezed me gently and kissed the top of my head. In that moment, I felt somethin. I felt loved to the bone.

It was an odd feelin. One that filled me like a cup at the pump. My heart let loose, and it was filled with genuine love. It wasn't just any kind of love . . . it was the love of a child.

I'd never held a youngin. Stately had never give me that opportunity, but now my arms was filled with a live, breathin youngin. He mighta been grown up, but right in that moment, he was mine and I felt loved. I felt compassion. I felt . . . filled.

We cleaned off Stately's gravestone, and Del never once asked me no questions about a box of gold. He never hinted. Never pushed. Instead, he gently pulled away the vines and talked about all he'd learned on the farm. He spoke of how well Stately had built the barn and how every notched log fit perfectly together, and how amazed he was I'd managed to keep the place up as best I could. I swallowed hard when Del said I was the strongest woman he'd ever met. The ache in my heart softened, and I felt a warmth through the pain.

"Mr. Jenkins was a very organized man," Del said. "Everything in its place."

"And a place for everything. That was him. He done things orderly. I was always one to just get it done. But Stately would do and redo until every line was perfect. You shoulda seen him plowin rows in the field. I can't count the times he'd make a pass with his workhorse, then go right back over and cover it cause it wasn't straight to his squinted eye."

"He must have been a fine man in your eyes," Del said.

I hesitated. "Well, I thought he was. Fine, that is. Appears I was wrong. If you're ready, I need to sit a spell."

"Yes, ma'am." Del hung the hatchet off his pocket and commenced to help me back to the cabin.

I wondered while we'd stood over Stately's grave if Del saw the soft soil where I'd dug up the box, but betwixt the vines and the heavy coverin of leaves, he'd never noticed. We dodged and swerved through the stand of trees and vines till we got back to the well pump. Del hung the hatchet back in its place and primed the pump. Water spilled out, and I held my palm open to grab a sup of the cool water.

"Miss Minerva, may I ask a question?"

"My, my. You said 'may I.' It must be a doozy. Especially since you ain't never hesitated to ask your questions before."

"Why all the vines? Didn't you want to see your husband's grave?" Del motioned me toward the cabin.

I had to think on that one. And this time it had nothin to do with the box or Stately's secret. Why had I let them vines overtake things? In sight of a minute, it come clear to me.

"I suppose it's admittin to the lie I believed. I thought I was the apple of Stately's eye. Suppose my mind knew the truth. His heart was in Lexington with Melba and his youngin. I guess keepin them vines and letting them stretch everywhere covered the truth I didn't want to admit. You know, outta sight, outta mind." We walked around the cabin.

"Think we might sit on the porch and look through that ledger together?" Del asked. "Maybe we can answer your questions. I just think there was more here than Mr. Jenkins having a second love."

And rightfully so. I had no intentions of tellin Stately's secret, but if Del found it on his own, that was a different matter altogether.

TWENTY-SEVEN

DEL PULLED MY ROCKER CLOSE to the window, and once I was settled in my seat, he placed a cup of cold water and a slice of bread next to me.

"Try to nibble on the bread. I've not seen you eat in two days. I'm gonna head down to the lower field and finish patching that fence to keep the cow in. I'll pull some tomatoes and you can show me how to make that tomato soup that you've bragged so." Del leaned over and kissed my cheek. "I won't be far. Oh, and look." He lifted a rope that hung inside the window. "I found a bell in the barn. Thought it would be a great way for you to call me. So if you need me"—he pulled the rope, and the bell rang—"just pull. Heck of a lot better than shooting a gun, heh?" He grinned, and them dimples sunk deep in his cheeks.

"Like them flat feet of yours can move you faster than green grass through a goose." I chuckled.

"Now, Minerva. Be nice." Del went to laughin and shakin the back of his drawers like he was that goose I was talkin about. "We can look at your ledger after supper. That all right? You need to rest for now."

I had to smile, for Del was just a youngin aimin to please. Give him a little praise and he'd smile and be off to work up somethin else to make you proud. It was kind—sweet of him. And truth

195

be known, it made me feel better to know he could hear me if I needed him.

Stately had brung that bell up on one of his visits from town. His intention was to hang it so I could call out for him. The fool died before he got it hung.

I watched as Del trotted down the hill to the lower field, and I felt somethin rise inside me. Gettin out of the rocker, I slowly eased to my knees. As bad as they were, I hadn't knelt in years, but I folded my fingers together and rested my forehead on the chair.

"Good Father, You're a mighty good Lord, ain't You? I've prayed for years not to die alone, and I might be stubborn, but I'm smart enough to know that You have given me that person. It sure as whiz wasn't what I expected—to find out Stately was a father and then Del was his grandson. And what of Melba? What of the woman who took my husband?" A tear dripped off my nose. "It don't ease the hurt, but—"

"Isn't that just the sweetest." A voice come from behind me.

"Colton?" I opened my eyes to find him standin next to me. "I knew you wasn't to be trusted. You make a right nasty habit of sneakin up on a body. Is that your pride? Scarin an old lady?" I tried to stand, but I just didn't have the strength. "Aw, bull. Help me up?" I squawked.

He let out a laugh and slid his arms under mine, then lifted. It felt like every muscle in my body tore loose from the bone.

"Never mind bein gentle." I eased into my rocker by the window. "Every time I'm alone, here you come. That's the thanks I get for feedin you from my table. What in heaven's name do you want now? Oh, wait. You want to know where the gold is."

Colton smacked the top of my hand. Had it been anybody else, it would have been a kind pat, but him . . . it was a nasty smack. I pulled my hand away and rubbed the paper-thin skin that had begun to redden.

"You should give me what I want," he said. "I'm tired of your rabbit trails. There wasn't anything in those cattails."

196

"You know what? You're right. So here's what you do. You take your happy backside around my house and work your way back through them vines. Don't worry if you think there ain't nothin in them vines, cause if you keep walkin and dodging them devils, you're gonna find Stately Jenkins's grave. He never left me no gold, but I'm guessin if he had any, it would be buried with him. He spent a lot of time back in them vines. I never followed him back there. I'd wager everthing I have that if there's a mound of gold, it'll be buried in his grave."

"That wasn't so hard, now, was it?" Colton smiled right big. "You better be telling the truth."

"Well, one man's truth is another's lie." I chuckled. "You want this gold, you ain't got no option but to believe my truth. I done told you I ain't got no gold. But since you ain't bright enough to believe me, I'll send you to the source. You meet up with Stately on your own. They say if you hold your mouth just right, the dead will speak. Go see what he says."

"We'll see, old woman. We'll see." The words hissed out of his mouth as he stormed out.

My momma used to tell me there were people who could talk outta both sides of their mouth at the same time. This Colton—he was one of them people. He could lie one minute, so perfect that a body would never suspect a thing, and the next, he was sweet as pumpkin pie. Those kind of men are dangerous. Greedy. Vindictive.

I leaned back in my rocker, twistin to one side, and eyed the box on the hearth. "Plain sight," I said under my breath. "Plain sight. Don't reckon you can fix stupid." I covered my mouth and chuckled.

I pushed the rocker, and it gently bumped over the uneven slatted floor. My eyes gazed through the window at the blue sky and beautiful mountain peaks. Stately had laid our little cabin out so that the window looked over the mountain pass. If it wasn't enough to set on the porch and admire the rise and fall of mountain peaks on the horizon, you could stand inside and look through the window. I remember him sayin it was good to see the rain comin before it got here. And you could. If you watched on a day that clouds bumped and pushed together, you could see the darkness grow tight over the mountains. You could see streaks of lightnin form and stretch across the sky, and you could smell the rain as its scent carried on the wind. Before a hard storm come, you could watch the cows fold their legs under them and lay on the ground. The goats huddled in a bunch, nudgin the wee ones to the middle for protection. Birds flocked and their cries carried across the holler till they lit in the trees and snugged themselves together, puffin their feathers.

It was a good thing Stately had faced this house toward the east, for I certainly did enjoy years' worth of lovely sunrises and views that would take your breath away with each season. To think, Stately did that for me. Maybe that was his way of makin things up to me—givin me the golden rays of mornin sweepin over the mountain.

We spent many evenins, fingers threaded together, sayin little but dreamin over the mountains that lay in the distance. That's why acceptin this mess was hard. We had moments—times when things seemed sweet.

For a minute, I remembered how those quiet times sitting together with my husband brought me joy. Real joy. I could have swore I heard the good Lord speak to my heart. *Ain't a man alive that's perfect*. I reckon that gnawed at me, for in the midst of my heartache over Stately's lie, here was this moment of joy.

I don't know how long I sat lookin out that window before I finally pulled myself outta that rocker and walked to the porch. I didn't have it in me to walk down the steps, and though I needed to find my seat in the outhouse, I wondered how terrible it would be to just hike my dress over the edge of the porch. I giggled.

"What a thought. What a terrible but funny thought. Let's go, legs."

I inched my way to the outhouse. It's funny, the things we find when we least expect it, but as I relieved myself, I run my fingers over a childlike carvin on the wall. Stately had carved a corny heart and two initials—"M + S." He never could spell Minerva. Writin the M was just easier, or so I thought. Now I wondered. Minerva or Melba?

My fingers slipped over the dug-out heart and initials. Once again, a sweet thought come to me. The day I found that carvin on the wall, there was a small pickin of daisies layin by the seat.

It come to me that Stately, as gruff as he was, held a tender spot for me. I felt the good Lord whisper to me again. *Things ain't always what they seem.* Maybe these sweet moments were Stately's tryin to ease his guilt. Maybe not. I felt a twinge in my heart and then a stabbing hurt.

I cleaned myself up and rinsed my hands in the bucket of water that hung on a handle on the side of the outhouse. It wasn't that far to the house. Only steps, but when a step felt like a hundred, I knew it would take me a spell to get back to the cabin and up them three steps to the porch. Every step sent a stab of pain to my heart, and I wondered just how close the end was.

The sun had made its way from straight up to hangin in the west, and I wondered when Del would be back. I hoped soon, for I had this hankerin in my gut that something wasn't right. Colton wasn't about to let go, and when he figured out there was nothin buried in that hole but Stately, he'd be on a rampage. I wished Del was back already, for I hated facin the devil alone.

Ain't been many times my gut has been wrong, and today was no different. As I climbed the last stair to the porch, Colton come stompin around the house.

"You think you're funny, don't you? You think I won't find the gold, don't you?"

I spun around to see him standing at the foot of the steps, holdin a bag. "Lawsey mercy, what do you have in that bag?" I asked. Had he actually found something I didn't know about? "What did you find? The gold?"

"I didn't find anything of value. I dug all around that tomb-stone. Nothing!" he shouted.

"I told you so. But you don't believe me. There ain't no gold. Lordy mercy, man, don't you understand that?"

"Oh, I understand. I understand so much that I kept digging, and I finally decided to dig in front of the stone."

My heart sunk. "In front! You dug Stately's grave?"

Before I could say another word, Colton wheeled that bag off his shoulder and dumped it at the foot of the steps. Bones dropped into a pile. Bones and pieces of tattered cloth.

I gasped. "Lord forgive him. Is that my Stately's bones?"

"How long has it been since you've seen him? Fifty years? How's he look?" Colton kicked the bones until he found the skull and held it up. "How's he look?"

I took a few steps back, and my hand pressed against the win-dowsill. There was the rope that hung from the bell. I grabbed it and yanked. The bell rang across the mountain. Over and over, I pulled the rope. All the while Colton, in a rage, stomped the bones, shouting and cursin me.

"Stop it. Colton, please stop."

But he kept stompin.

A horse come to a halt, and there was Robert Blessing. "What are you doin?" he squalled. I never imagined the preacher could have such timin, but then the Lord's timin ain't nothing to mess with.

My chest tightened. Pain wrapped around my heart like a lynchin rope. If I died right this minute, I'd die knowin the truth about Colton had come to light.

Robert jumped off his horse, put his head down, and took to runnin right at Colton. I pulled the rope to the bell again, and it wasn't long before I saw Del tearin up the hill. It only took minutes before the three of them men rolled and tumbled all over the place.

All my hollerin didn't do an ounce of good, but when I glanced down, I saw my hatchet. Del had set it by the door earlier when he notched some wood. Me and Stately used to hang a board on the barn and toss that hatchet to see who could hit it. We'd count the number of times we'd aim at that board and hit it. I remember Stately sayin, "It don't count if it don't stick," at the times I tossed that hatchet and it bounced off the wood.

Some things a body never forgets once they learn how to do them. I learned how to throw a hatchet that day with Stately. Now I picked it up, tightened my fingers around the handle, and drew back.

Before I knew it, that instinct kicked in. My heart pumped harder than it ever did priming the water pump. It took all my might, but I closed one eye, aimed, and flung that hatchet. It landed square at the feet of Colton.

"Stop it!" I shouted. "Next time it'll be a knife, and I won't be aimin at your feet."

Colton froze. Robert pulled Colton's arms behind him while Del grabbed twine I kept between the porch rails for the tomatoes. They bound Colton tight.

I stumbled through the door and to my rocker. I gasped, tryin to catch my breath. Then I heard it again. That quiet voice.

It's over. A secret never saves a soul. Never.

I buried my face in my hands. Long, hard sobs fell from my lips. I wasn't sure what the good Lord was tellin me, but over the course of the day He'd reminded me of times with Stately that I'd forgotten in my grief. In my anger. In my hurt. All this whilst I mourned the loss of my love not once but—thanks to Colton—twice. I begin to forget the pain and realize what I had. I begin to see deeper than Stately Jenkins's secret.

It had to stop. *This is where it ends!*

TWENTY-EIGHT

I SPENT A LOT OF TIME starin out the window these days. Walkin was just too hard. The sun had done climbed over the house to call it a day. As I watched the night sky crawl across the mountain, the birds of the day settled and quieted. The crickets and toads wound up their calls. Them crickets seemed to never quit, their chirps risin and fallin like a preacher's voice from the pulpit.

I closed my eyes, and darkness come alive. It sang its own song.

"Minerva, you all right?" Del squatted next to my rocker.

I could hardly speak, for every word that come from my mouth felt as though I made a hard run up the mountain. I nodded and pressed my palm to his cheek, rubbin my thumb across his lips. "You have Stately's eyes. I never thought I'd see them again."

"I take that as a compliment. You want me to help you to the bed?" He leaned into my hand, tilted his head, and gently kissed my palm.

I shook my head and wrapped his hand in mine. "There is something I want you to do, though. If you will. Let's set on the porch where we can talk."

"Anything. You know that." He moved from a squat to his knees. "What do you need?"

"I know that there ain't much in a name, but it would warm my heart if you'd call me your mamaw. Just make that my name. No more Minerva or Mrs. Jenkins. Is that too much to ask?"

Tears pooled in his eyes. He stood, took my hands, and lifted me from the rocker. Wrapping his arms around me, he buried his face in my neck. I felt the warmth of his tears against my neck.

"There is nothing more in this world I would rather do. You are the reason I set out to find Stately Jenkins. You were the surprise story in this adventure." He eased me to the porch and helped me rest against the railin. "When Colton found those papers about the gold being stolen, something didn't sound right. My folks never talked much about my grandmother Melba. In fact, Daddy rarely brought her up other than to say she disgraced the family. The one time I questioned him, he said exactly what you said. Melba was . . . well . . . a woman of the night. She made her living inviting or tricking men into her home. Despite her husband."

I looked him square in the eyes. "That so? My momma was right." I shook my head.

"If she said Melba was a woman of the evening, then she was right. Daddy was ashamed because he was always called a bastard child. I suppose he lived with that ridicule all his life. That's why I questioned whether those papers Colton found were right. Melba spent so much time trying to make her wealth that when she became pregnant with Stately's child, she had to save face by making out that the child belonged to her husband. My guess is Freelaw never saw the birth certificate. That wouldn't have been unusual. If he had seen it, he would have killed her if he thought she'd been unfaithful—maybe even killed Stately too. Apparently, she truly loved Stately."

My heart sank. "My guess is she tried to convince Stately the youngin was Freelaw's. That didn't work, so she sent Stately away to keep him safe."

"That's the best I can tell." Del rubbed his fingers over mine. "If she wanted her lie to work, if she wanted Stately safe, then she had to charge someone with the deed. Who better than her husband—allow him to believe the child was his. Though Melba was married, she never let on like it. At least that's my theory. I think Stately went along with the lie to protect Melba and himself."

I knew the answer to my question, but my heart wasn't ready to accept it. I leaned forward and asked, "Is Stately the daddy or not?" I commenced coughing hard.

Del rubbed my back till I stopped hackin. "She put his name on the records. Stately is my grandfather, a kind man who loved a mistress he wanted to protect. But, like I said, the details died with them both. The details really don't matter. What does matter is I found you and there's no other person in the world who can take your place in my heart, Mamaw."

"If you'll get my ledger book, I'll show you somethin that might help clear the mud." I sighed.

Del made his way into the cabin and brought the ledger from the nightstand. I flipped through the pages till I found the letter from Melba. I handed him the worn and tattered paper—the one I'd found while sortin through the ledger.

My dear Stately,
  Every time my husband holds our son, I long for the arms he's cradled in to be yours. A son. Yes, a son. He has his father's eyes . . .

I dabbed the mornin dew from my brow. "I never wanted to believe Stately would be unfaithful to me, but there ain't no changin that you look like him. I've spent days comin to grips with his unfaithfulness. I ain't an easy bird to convince. But you, child, have Stately's eyes. Trust me. Seems like my Stately was your granddaddy. And you're right. We won't never know the truth behind the actions, but I can tell you, it has broken my spirit. The only good to come from all this . . . is you. You're sweet to protect me." I smiled, grateful for this sweet kindness in the midst of the pain. I patted Del's arm. "Think I'll go inside and warm up some coffee." There was some ponderin to do, and I needed a minute to sort through.

At that moment, my years of longin for a child dissolved like sugar in water. I could see that Stately was a good man in his own sort of way. Though I'll never understand why he married a woman he didn't love, I will say he did his best to make it up to me. The truth shall set you free, and I had to agree. It hurt, but there was somethin freeing about knowin the truth.

For a moment, I had to wonder if the real secret Stately wanted me to keep was what he knew that I knew. He'd turned that day at the river and our eyes met. He couldn't deny that I knew the truth, but I never spoke of it. Was that the secret? It had to be. His sin was his secret, not what was in the box. And them horrible, hurtful things I've been pullin up from the past—well, they didn't seem so important anymore. Truth opens your eyes.

I stopped just inside the cabin door. "Stately knew we'd never be back to Lexington," I said. "He knew he'd never see Melba again. Did he ever love me? We'll never know for sure. It'll always be an assumption, and you know what assumin does, don't you?" I coughed again.

Del wrapped his hand around mine. "That's my thought. Albeit right or wrong, we'll never know. Colton took hold of those papers and began trying to track down Stately. When he found you, I knew I had to meet you. I knew there would be a story—not about gold but about my family. And if it was a lie, then I could lay it to rest with my own daddy. The truth would bring me to you."

"Let me think a minute." Satchel followed me inside, and the screen closed behind me.

I wasn't sure if my good hearin was slackin or if my mind was slippin. But it was gettin harder to think things through. All this news, stacked on top of Colton's rampage, had about done me in, but my heart was commencin to soften and my anger eased toward Stately Jenkins.

A wagon come up the path. Its lantern swung to and fro from a pole as the sound of two horses clopped over the rocky road.

Del opened the screen door to let Satchel out to do his yappin. He lit a stick from the coals and laid it on the lantern wick. "There's us a little light. Let's see who the cat dragged up the hill."

"Hoooo-weeee!" A voice rung out in the darkness.

"It's the pastor. He's back." Del walked off the porch to greet him.

Robert's voice echoed through the darkness.

"What are you doing back here, Robert?" Del held his light high so Robert could see to come up the steps.

"I was worried. The thoughts of the day gnawed at me. I wanted to be sure Miss Minerva was doin all right."

"She's well as could be expected. It's not every day someone digs up the bones of a loved one and throws them at your feet." Del shook his head. "I'm still stunned Colton would do such a thing. I knew he was on the hunt for gold, but his antics—I pushed them off as Miss Minerva's mind clouding. I was wrong and I feel terrible."

"There was no way you could have known. Colton is a sneaky sort. I guess he figured if he tried to plant those thoughts, Minerva would slip up and tell whatever he wanted her to tell."

"You oughta feel bad." I pushed open the door and eased out of the cabin. Del and Robert rushed up the steps to help me into a chair. I chuckled. "I must look pretty decrepit for the both of you to come runnin."

Robert tipped his hat. "I just wanted to check in on you. It's been a right unusual day."

"It has indeed. Just so you know, I forgive you both for thinkin my mind was on a slick downslide. Look, now, both of you pay attention. I know what's comin for me. I've been tellin you this for weeks. My days is endin, and there surely ain't nothin left to surprise me after these last few weeks. I just have to take it in. Come to peace with it."

"What will come of Colton?" Del asked.

"He's locked up in the jail," Robert said. "The sheriff managed to get some news, though. Speakin of your mind bein on the downslide."

I smacked his arm. "Give me the news."

"Seems those few incidents you had was Colton all along. He thought if he could make you look as though your mind was slippin, then it would make it easier to scare you into showin him the treasure. He was the one who broke in and busted your white dish. He knew you couldn't see good, and he broke that dish and was countin on that messin with you. And the fire—you were right. You didn't kick over that lantern. Colton admitted to lockin you in and crawlin out the back window. Though it befuddles me how he wiggled through such a small window. He lit the fire from the wood under the shed. His sides were all scratched up from squeezing through a too-small window."

I bent back and roared laughin. "Woo-ee! I knew it! You'll believe me next round, now, won't you?"

"Why didn't the dog bark that night Miss Minerva thought there was someone in the house? He never leaves her side." Del pushed his hands into his pockets.

"Seems like even the dog gives up barkin for a good piece of raw meat."

I lifted my arms into the air. "Finally, the truth."

"Seems not." Del went to laughin.

"I'm guessin Colton won't find a comfortable bed where he's headed," Robert said. "You plan on lettin your newspaper know?"

Del nodded. "I got no choice. I'll jot down a wire for you to send tomorrow."

"I'm glad this story is over for you, Miss Minerva. It was takin its toll, wasn't it, ma'am?"

"I'm the better for the wear. But, you know, stories don't end. They's always more that crops up," I said.

Robert tipped his hat again, then leaned over and kissed my

cheek. "I'll head back down the mountain. I know now why daddy thought so much of you, Miss Minerva."

"Yeah, yeah. I'm sure he was cuckold in his judgment too." I squeezed Robert's hand. I motioned to Del, and he helped me to my feet. "I guess I'm ready for bed."

It took a few minutes for me to ready myself for bed, and Del was kind to help me shed the dirty clothes for a clean nightshirt. He offered me as much privacy as he could, considerin I could hardly lift my arms over my head.

I laid back, and Del pulled Momma's blanket over me.

"Del?"

"Yes, ma'am."

"Why don't you sleep on that feather mattress in the back room? Beats the devil outta a straw one in the barn."

He smiled and nodded.

I rolled to my side and gazed out the window. The night sky didn't seem black but a grey hue. I raised my hand and traced the dippers until I found the North Star. I hoped the good Lord in His mercy let Stately Jenkins look down on me so I could tell him I forgive him for whatever happened with Melba. He didn't need the forgiveness, but I needed to give it. I needed to find peace.

Del was right. We'd never really know the truth, and I reckon this was a side of Stately I didn't know.

I reached to the side of my bed, picked up that leather ledger, and commenced to thumb through it. I couldn't see in the dark. When the mountain closed its eyes, that pretty much shut mine down too. I run my fingers over the pages and imagined there were things written there about my life with Stately. Though I knew better in my heart.

We still had some things to hash out about this secret he'd made me take on, but tonight wasn't the time. I didn't feel like tonight was my last night.

I dropped my legs over the edge of the bed and inched my way to the hearth. Under Daddy's Bible was that blessed ole box. My curiosity was reelin, but I remember Momma sayin curiosity killed the cat. I moved the Bible and run my fingers over the smooth box still a bit dirty from being buried next to Stately. Would this haunt me to my grave?

I tapped the box with my nails and gently laid the Bible back on top. Turnin to head back to bed, I knocked my elbow on the top of the rocker. For a moment, every curse word I could think of raced through my mind, but not one left my lips. I sat on the bed and tried to rub my knees, but touchin them was like stabbing a knife in my back.

"Lord, what more is there for me to do? Can't You just take me? Ain't it time for me to take flight?" I guess the good Lord wanted an old woman to let go of everything before she dies. A clean break. I remember Daddy sayin, "What is temporal ain't worth nothin, but what is eternal is. Reach for the eternal." Took me till Stately died to understand just what that meant. Now my blindin eyes saw. Now I understood.

I could see how over the last few weeks the good Lord was answerin my prayers. Them things I'd prayed for and wondered about for years after Stately's death, He was bringin to light. I never had no youngin, and then here come Del. I never understood Stately's standoffishness, and then here comes the reason with Melba. I never wanted to die alone, and then again, there was an answered prayer—Del and Robert. It was comfortin to know my body wouldn't turn to dust where it fell. There'd be somebody here to put me to rest. It was more of a comfort to know that havin faith in somethin you couldn't see was proved right. I supposed that was the good Lord. I had faith even when I couldn't see, and here He proved Himself.

I laid back on my pillow and stared out at the stars again. My eye drew a weak line to the North Star. "You know that star ain't in the Big Dipper. It's in the little one. Folks lose their way cause they miss that when they look for the North Star."

Stately taught me that when we took the wagon into town and

came home after dark. That was back before the road was worn. "If you're ever out at night, Nerva, and you get yourself turned around, just look up," he said. "Find that North Star, and you'll find your way ever time. Remember the star ain't in the Big Dipper. It's in the little one."

I believe it's true that a body has the opportunity to make their life right before they leave this earth, and I still have some things to make right. But for now, I'll just look at that bright star of the north and point myself in that direction.

TWENTY-NINE

"MINERVA—I MEAN, MAMAW? You awake?" Del pecked on the wall by the rocker. "Morning's passing you by, and your coffee is ready."

I rubbed my eyes and stretched. "Lordy mercy, it must be mid-mornin. The sun ain't shinin through the window and lightin up the fireplace. Why'd you let me sleep this long?" I strained to sit. My bones ached, and my feet looked the size of a mushmelon.

Del took my arm and helped me to my chair. I leaned forward and pulled the chamber pot close. "I'd thank you for my privacy."

"Yes, ma'am. When you're ready, so is your coffee." And sure enough, it was. A fresh pot hung over the hot coals.

"You were mighty quiet makin that coffee."

"The way Stately built this fireplace made it easy. Open on both sides. I didn't have to come in here to get things going. Oh, and I made biscuits."

"Biscuits?" I cocked my head to one side. "I bet they're like rocks."

"No, ma'am. Tender as a sow's rear, as you would say. Two scoops of flour, one palm of lard, enough soured milk to make a sticky dough. Pat out about . . . oh, so thick. Cut. Bake. I'm a quick study." Del grinned, right proud of himself.

"We'll see if I don't break what teeth I have when I bite into one."

"There's honey too. Robert's wife sent you some fresh honey last night."

"Like I said, we'll see if I have teeth after I bite into one." I shooed him into the next room whilst I relieved myself.

I picked up the dress and apron that hung over the rocker. It hit me I was growin to love this young man like my own. He'd done washed out my dress and hung it to dry so I had clean clothes. Of the things I've missed over the years, kindness seemed to be one I missed the most. Stately never washed a stitch of clothes in all his years, but he was good to bring me a handful of daisies from the field or some sweet-smellin honeysuckle. We'd set on the porch in the evenings, pull the bottom off them honeysuckle blooms, and then catch the single drop of nectar that dripped off. It was better than that hard candy Daddy used to bring me from town.

Things went to runnin through my mind, and I commenced to weigh the good against the bad when it come to Stately. He wouldn't lay with me and give me no child, but he'd sit by the river and lay his head in my lap, his shoulder-length strands of black hair would splay across my lap, and I could comb through them with my fingers. He never lifted a finger to help me in the garden once it was in the ground, but he rarely failed to bring me flowers. He rarely told me he loved me, but he'd say, "You're a fine woman."

It seemed the scale almost balanced. He wasn't the perfect husband. In fact, there were times I didn't think he was much of a husband at all, but I never feared. I never doubted I was taken care of. Stately taught me how to survive on this mountain, and when he died, my heart broke. When I found out about Melba, it broke again.

I supposed Del was right. We'd never know the truth. It had died with Melba and Stately, but I had a decision before me. I could believe that my husband, being the kind man that he was, opted to keep his promise to marry a woman he didn't love, or I could believe that he didn't love Melba at all, and the kiss we never spoke of was just a kind goodbye. I could believe the angry truth that he sinned against the Lord and against me as his wife by fathering a baby and then runnin away like a coward. One minute I wanted to hate him. The next, I just wished he was back in my arms.

Maybe this was the decision the good Lord was waiting for me to make. Maybe, just maybe, He was waitin on me to let go of the bitterness I'd held deep in my heart for years and never admitted. *You might still be waitin, Lord, cause my heart is in a pickle.* Or maybe He was waitin on me to confess my own sin.

I watched through the window as Del made his way toward the garden. Then I got up and dressed. I picked up the ledger and opened it. I turned past the letter to Melba, the one about the two dollars. I wondered why Stately never took it to town to mail it. There were lists of chores to be done. Some had a line drew through them, like diggin a cistern and addin a pump, while others never got done.

I stopped on a page filled with the purtiest handwritin ever. Stately could pen right pretty letters on a page. I put my spectacles on and pushed them tight against my nose. Then I went to readin as best I could.

My life is a shambles. My chest aches like someone has jabbed a knife through my heart. Shame. Disgust. These are the things that overwhelm me. The thought that I not only ruined my own life, but Melba's, our son's . . . and Nerva's. It's more than I can bear.

I set there, tears drippin down my cheeks. If I'd only known. I could have comforted him if he had only told me. If Stately would have said one word, I would have tried to understand. I loved him and I mighta forgave him. I'd have not spent all of them years wonderin if I was a good wife or if Stately really cared. I'd have not spent the years after he died angry at his death.

213

I was seein things about Stately that I could never understand. Things that tormented him, drove him to make bad decisions. He was a man with a troubled soul. But just when I might have found an ounce of sympathy for him, that woman showed up again—the woman he *loved*.

I laid my hand on the pages of the ledger and toyed with the paper. It come to me, something my momma used to say when I was little when she caught me in a lie. "Oh, what a tangled web we weave, when first we practice to deceive."

Stately chose to live with a burden all his life. All he ever knew was to deceive himself and me. He believed a lie—that somehow his takin care of me would cover the wound. I guess he thought that was his redemption. And yet he still chose to suck the life outta a livin woman only to leave an empty shell of a person.

These was not the words I expected to find in this ledger, but the more I thumbed through, the more I saw a tortured man.

I turned a few more pages and managed to read a little more.

She is a beautiful woman. I do not deserve her. Golden hair, eyes blue as the river, and all I can do is admire her from a distance. I watch as she washes in the river. I peer at her from the fields. She is a gentle soul. She works hard to please me, but my heart cannot be pleased.

I'd seen enough. Read all I cared to read. I'd learned a lifetime about the man I called my husband in those few minutes. There was never a hope of my love pleasing him. Never any hope.

I eased across the room, laid the ledger down, picked up the box, and wiped it clean with a cloth. Its wood glowed with a reddish tint. On each side of the back, it had two small gold hinges. I spit on my apron and shined them, using my nails to scrape away the dirt from the crevices. The front latch held the lid closed with a small hook.

I stared at the box and wondered what it held that had meant so much to Stately. What could be so important that he'd swear me to secrecy for all these years? What really was his secret? Gold? Murder confessions? What?

I pulled the hook off the latch and opened the box. It was filled with hay, and I wondered if I dared dig through it. It took me a spell, but I finally inched my fingers through the straw to uncover the contents. Tears filled my eyes. I'm not sure if it was because Stately had hid the contents for so many years or if I was afraid of what I'd find. What I'd kept behind a promise for years.

I tinkered with the contents, picking up each item and eyeing it. I looked hard at every piece and shook my head—a satin bag, a small piece of coal, and a letter. I unfolded a paper, the edges tore right crooked. Picking up the ledger, I thumbed through until I found the place the page might have been torn from. It fit. Stately had ripped it from his ledger. The ink was smeared in places, like it was wet from tears. I tilted it toward the light, carefully twisting around so I could see each word.

My dearest Melba,

There are days when I figure work is the most healing thing. The more I work, the less I feel, and yet for Nerva, there is little I can give. I care for her, provide for her, and I do, in a way, love her. But there is this darkness, a hurt in my heart, like a knife stabbing clean through it. An emptiness that can't be filled. A sadness that I have bore since leaving Lexington.

I was a coward to leave you and our child. I was a greater coward to marry Nerva—a decision that has eat at me every day of my life. It took my joy, and it gave me fear. A fear that maybe what I'd done would be found out. I hid my love for you. Lied to Nerva. That has built a wall in my heart that nothin can break down. Guilt lives there now. Guilt does so much to a man. If Nerva knew, she'd be destroyed. She's done her best to be a good wife to a man who can't love her. I never wanted to break her, so I've cared for her, provided for her, kept her close in my heart. But that is as far as my heart will let things go.

Guilt tears a man down and eats him from the inside out. Guilt steals the joy from your life. And I am overcome with guilt. Then there's you . . . the woman I love. This secret can never be let out. I've done my best to keep it hid, and I know Nerva must know deep down in her heart, but she can't come to grips. So we let it lay, never broachin the subject. This is my sin. This is my secret.

I could see Stately was right. Guilt does terrible things to a body. When you let it live inside you, never sharin it with a soul, each day that passes takes a little more of your soul.

My heart ached once more. It ached because the man I loved had never cared enough to tell me the truth. To ask me for forgiveness would be wrong? Killin me would have been more merciful than the torture I was goin through now.

I squeezed the note into a ball. Wadding it up didn't seem like enough, so I put the crumpled paper back in the box. I untied the gold roping and opened the satin bag. It held a pocket watch. My bent fingers eased around the top and opened it. A photo of Melba and her baby. Reality shot through me, and that knife Stately claimed was stabbed into his heart was really stabbed in me. Stabbed and then twisted in my gut.

I shuffled through the hay and pulled out the piece of coal. From that worthless coal streak. I dropped it back into the box.

"This! Stately Jenkins! This is what I promised to keep. Your sin! Your shame. Your lie." I felt my anger rise and creep from my toes to my head. There was so much runnin through my mind I couldn't decide if I was angry at the lie or disappointed that there was nothing of value in the box. Nothing of value. I'd fallen hook, line, and sinker into Stately's lie, and I'd made it my own by promising to keep a secret. I slammed the box shut.

What was he thinkin? Was he assumin that when he died, the first thing I'd do was open up that box? Stately knew me well enough, had lived with me long enough, to know in his gut I'd be true to my promise. The man I'd spent half my life with confessed I was nothin but a . . . scapegoat and a keeper of his lie.

"An apology might have shown some mercy," I shouted.

I swiped my tears and rested my hands on the lid. I knew what needed to be done. I just had to figure out how and when.

My momma always told me not to tell your business to every-body comin and goin, for folks would promise you the moon and then stab you in the back. She taught me the value of a promise and the strength in keepin your word.

"If you don't think you can keep a promise, don't make one, for it will burden you," Momma said. "And if you let it slip, guilt steps in, and there are always consequences to pay when guilt becomes your bedfellow. First, you lie to hide the fact that you let it slip. And you know what happens with a lie, don't you?"

"Yes, ma'am. You end up tellin another one to cover the first one," I said.

Momma lifted me to her lap. "So don't make a promise you can't keep. You think on it before you say yes. A promise is your word. The good Lord never broke a one of His promises. You remember that."

I won't never forget that talk with Momma. Her words were buried deep in my heart. When Stately laid dyin in my arms, my mistake was to not think about whether I could keep his secret even though I didn't know what secret was hidden in his box. Gold? A weapon? Seed? The good Lord knew what was in that box. He knew it was every bit of Stately's sin, but I'd made that promise without thinkin it through, and Momma was right. It had haunted me ever since. It took my life, and the sad thing was, I let it.

I pushed the hook onto the latch and set the box back on the hearth. I took the doily, covered the box, and then set Daddy's Bible back on top.

"Mamaw Minerva, you ready to eat breakfast? Eggs are get-ting cold," Del hollered from the other room. "Coffee is tepid.

You can drink it without blowing." He stuck his head around the door. "Need help?"

"Yes, I'm ready." I swallowed hard, determined not to let him see my hurt.

Del took my arm and walked me to the table. He glanced at my legs and feet. "Woo-ee, those legs are pretty swollen today."

"Yep, and my feet feel like I'm walkin on glass shards."

He set a plate with a biscuit and honey in front of me. I eyed it. Despite how my stomach turned at the thought of food, I took a bite.

"Hmm." I opened my mouth and showed him my teeth. "Did I lose any teeth?"

Del let out a laugh and pulled up his chair. He took one of the biscuits and bit into it. "Not so bad, huh?"

"No. Not so bad for a beginner. You got enough lard to make them soft. Good job, son."

I eyed him for a minute and made the first clear decision I'd made in months. A smile stretched across my face, so big it made my skin itch. I decided to call him son.

THIRTY

I DID THE BEST I COULD to eat a whole biscuit. These days my stomach just couldn't manage holdin anything. If I eat much, it tended to make me lean over the porch rail and vomit. I know what it is. It's my body tellin me the time is drawin close.

I hobbled out to the porch, my feet bulgin the sides of my shoes. It was like walkin on mashed taters. Every step, I could feel the squish of the water under my skin. And over the last day or two, that swellin had crept up my legs. Even my hands and arms were roundin out. I eased into the rocker. Satchel curled his tail around my feet and rested his chin on my knees. He looked at me with them big ole brown eyes, and I could have swore he had tears drippin from the corners.

"You know, don't you, boy? You know my days is numbered." I scratched his ears. "Don't you fret. Del will see you are taken care of. Don't you cry for me."

The hound whined. His tongue eased from his lips and licked at my fingers.

I did my best to get in a good breath, but it was growin harder by the day. My chest rattled like the rattler on a snake.

"Del! You close by?" I shouted.

He come to the door. "Well, look at you. Toddling out to the porch without help." He knelt and picked up my feet, eyein the

219

size. "Might be best if you don't walk too much on these feet till the swelling goes down."

"It ain't gonna go down, Del. You know that. And that's why I want to talk to you. It's time."

"Time?" He sat next to me. "We got all kinds of time."

I patted his hand and smiled. "I like your enthusiasm. But there are some things we need to talk about. Startin with Stately's bones."

Del squirmed in his seat. "I'm so sorry Colton had the gall to do such a hideous thing. Robert and I shoveled his remains onto a blanket and wrapped them till I could rebury them."

"That's what I want to talk to you about. Or one of the things. Is it bad to change a place where a body was laid to rest?"

Del cocked his head to one side. "You mean, move his remains? It's not a common practice, but since we have the situation we have, I don't see a problem moving Mr. Jenkins."

"I ain't never been known for doin what most folks do, so I'd like you to hitch the wagon and take me down to the river. There's that big wisteria that blooms right beautiful. You know the one. That's where I want to put Stately." I took Del's hand. "That's where I want you to lay me."

Del hung his head. His fingers gently rubbed my knuckles. It took him a minute to find the words. "Mamaw, I can bury Mr. Jenkins wherever you like."

"But I want you to bury me there too. Not right on the bank. Lordy, I'd never want to wash outta the ground durin a flood. But up a bit. Just at the edge of that wisteria. Do you understand?" I squeezed his fingers.

"Yes, ma'am."

"Now, if you will, hitch that wagon. I want to go down to the river and find the spot so you'll know. Will you do that?"

Del didn't utter a word. Instead, he headed straight to the barn to hitch up the mare. I waited till he was a good distance, then I made my way into the house and slipped that box into a cloth bag. I opened the ledger, dug out the pencil that was pressed into the crease, and jotted a few lines.

I, Minerva Jane Jenkins, leave my house and land, all that belongs to me, to Delano Rankin, my grandson. I know my mind is good, for the pastor agreed. Everything I have is to be given to Delano to do with as he sees fit. I leave him Satchel too, who is to be buried at my feet when his life gives out. Ruby is her own caretaker, but if he could watch after her, that would be nice. May the Lord bless and keep you.

Minerva Jane Jenkins
This 23rd day of July
1902

I pushed the pencil back into the bend of the ledger and closed it, then slid it into the bag. I heard Del pull the wagon alongside the steps, so I made my way back to the porch.

"My, my," he said. "Your head is harder than a rock. Didn't I just ask you not to walk much on those swollen feet?"

I nodded and inched down the steps, bag danglin from my elbow.

Del took my arm and helped me into the wagon. "Are you sure you want to make this bumpy trip down the hill?"

"Sure as the sun shines."

The next thing I knew, Del heaved Satchel into the seat next to us. The hound circled three times before he pushed his rear against my side to make room.

"You comfortable?" I asked. He let out a groan and plopped his chin on Del's leg. Satchel rolled them brown eyes back and stared as if to ask, "Did you expect less?"

When I glanced into the back of the wagon, I saw a shovel and the wool blanket from the barn. I elbowed Del. "That Stately?"

He smiled.

"That was a perfectly good blanket, you know."

Del busted out laughin. "Isn't this supposed to be a reverent time?"

"Pffftttt!" I sputtered. I guess that was all it took to get Del chucklin all the way to the river.

The wagon bumped and bounced down the windin trail to the grassy meadow by the river. There were no purple wisteria blooms this time of year, but that vine stretched all over the side of the hill and up into a big white pine. The grass blew to one side with the gentle summer breeze, and if you turned just the right way, you could catch a spray of water from the rapids. I leaned back in the seat and lifted my head toward the sun.

There's something about the mornin sun that seems to pull all the bad stuff from your body. It's like it wraps around every bone and gently rubs. A body can feel every chill bump raise on their skin from the warmth.

I sighed. "Ain't it beautiful? Ain't it comfortin?"

"Indeed. It's a beautiful field and a beautiful morning. I'm blessed to have it with you."

"You know, Delano Rankin, if I was a young thang, I might just pursue you."

"Well, that's good to know." He went to laughin again. "You decided where you want to—"

"Plant Stately Jenkins," I interrupted.

"I would have been a bit more reserved about my choice of words, but yes, do you know where you want to *plant* Mr. Jenkins?"

I couldn't help myself. Giggles climbed up my throat, and there was no stopping them. I giggled and laughed like a little girl. "What good is life without laughter, Del? It ain't no good. This is all a little bittersweet. I'm comin to grips with the bitter and trying to take in the sweet." I lifted my hand and pointed to the base of the wisteria. "Over there. They's a view of the river that will take your breath."

In that moment, I decided there was no reason to be sour at Stately. He'd been a man plagued by fear and lies, and that took his happiness. That guilt was on Stately. I'd made myself a content but lonely life. My humor was used on the hound. When he showed his teeth, I took that as he was laughin at me. Still, I felt sorry for Stately—and I felt a little sorry for me.

I was standin with one foot in the grave. Bein mad at the world wasn't gonna make a difference. My regret was that I didn't make my way off this mountain into the arms of friends after Stately's death. That guilt was on me.

Del commenced to dig a waist-deep hole, and I was right proud I picked a place close to the river so the soil was soft. When he was done, he crawled out and took Stately's bones to the grave, then dropped back into the hole. He gently placed the wool blanket neatly in the hole. It took him a spell to cover it, and when the dirt was heaped on top, he swiped his forehead with his sleeve.

"Do you want to say any words?" he asked.

I stared for a minute. "Nope. They were said years ago. Get me out of this wagon." I hesitated. "I changed my mind."

"Figures. You still want out of the wagon?"

I shook my head and set right firm. I looked over the heaped-up mound of dirt that once again covered my Stately and sighed. "Stately Jenkins, I've been run through the briars and back these last couple of months. I've tried to hate you. Despise you. But I'm seein things is what they is. I'm offerin you forgiveness. You heard me, you old cuss. I forgive you, and that forgiveness is as much for me as it is for you. There you lay with nothin. But here I stand with a boy who loves me. I reckon that cancels out the hate. I forgive you."

Del stood with his head bowed and his hands clasped behind his back. "That was very fitting."

I reached toward him, and he lifted me out of the wagon. I held his arm tight and commenced to move off ten steps, then I laid flat on the ground. "Take that shovel and dig around me."

"What?"

"Dig around me. I want you to take the grass off the top of the soil so you know exactly where I want to be laid out when I go."

Del stood eyein me before he lifted the shovel to mark my spot. "Now I think you're crazy."

I went to gigglin again. "Just want things made easy for you."

Del rolled his eyes and cut into the soil around me. He helped me up and commenced to cut the sod off my spot.

"Just stack it right there. Ain't no need to toss it. You can just plant it right back on top of me."

"All right. This isn't funny anymore," Del squawked.

"I didn't mean it to be funny, though my wit comes into play every once in a while. I'm just makin sure things is prepared."

"Mamaw Minerva . . ."

"Del, you hush. The truth is, I ain't gonna see the end of July. I probably won't see the end of the week. I know that, and so do you. You can hear my breathin. And I remember sittin by the bedside of my own mamaw when she was dyin. That death rattle was the same. You just humor me as I make my way to the golden gates and know I ain't scared to die. I'm ready. I know the good Lord has prepared a place for me. My hope is they ain't no steep hills."

Del didn't utter another word. Instead, he did what I asked, and when we were done, the settin sun glistened off the water. Crickets commenced to sing, and the dew wet our skin. It was a beautiful sunset, the way the evening light bobbled over the mountains behind us. And I was grateful. Fulfilled. Happy to have these last few minutes with my friend and my grandson.

I laid my head on Del's shoulder and rested, and when I opened my eyes, I was covered sweetly by Momma's quilt on my bed.

THIRTY-ONE

DEL SAT, HEAD DROOPED, in the rocker by my bed. Even in his sleep, he couldn't sit still. That one leg kept a slow push on that rocker with every breath he took. He'd take a breath, hiss out a soft snore, and that foot would push the rocker once more. Every push brought a squeak from the rungs. I was surprised even I could sleep through that, but despite the noise, the true sound of his breath was comfortin.

Satchel went to howlin. That shrill and long *aaarroooo* scared the tarnation outta me. I nearly come outta my skin. I rubbed my hand over his neck, and I could feel his hair standin up. That howl brought Del outta his sleep too. He came to his feet and rushed to the window.

"It's Robert." He sighed. Once he was over the start, he stretched and headed to the door.

Though my hearin had never been a problem—I could generally hear a June bug bite into a leaf—today things were a little muffled. I watched through the window as Del walked down the steps, pullin his suspenders up over his shoulders. Them two carried on a conversation, and Del pointed toward the river. My best guess was he was tellin Robert my plans. It wasn't long till they both came onto the porch and into the cabin.

"Mornin there, Miss Minerva. How are you feelin this morning?" Robert walked to my bed and squeezed my knee. "My goodness, them legs is mighty swelled. I might just send Doc Ross up here to take a look-see."

"Pastor, you're lucky I ain't the kind of woman to take your remark the wrong way—or your squeezing my knee."

Robert pulled that rocker close to me and seated himself on the edge. "I wanted to let you know that Colton got loose early this mornin. The sheriff and his deputy was loadin him in the wagon to take him to Lexington, and he horse-kicked the deputy, butted heads with the sheriff, and then took off."

My heart sank. All the what-ifs went to swirlin around in my head. I wasn't much left for this world, but there was Del to worry over. "You suppose he'll show up here?" I asked.

"To tell the truth, I don't know. Greed does odd things to a man, and we all know what drives that man is greed. I'd think his common sense would tell him this would not be a smart place to come. That is, if he wants to live."

"If he wants to live?"

"Now, Mamaw Minerva, it's nothing you need to fret over," Del said. "Robert and the sheriff have gathered some men around your place. It's just a precaution. I'm like Robert. I think Colton is smart enough to know not to come here. And, well, if he does, then we'll worry about that when the time comes."

I sat straight in my bed. "I don't want no killin. Is that clear? The man ain't to be killed. He might be a rat's backside, but that don't make him worthy of bein killed. You understand me? In all my years, the only person who has ever died up here was Stately Jenkins, and I ain't about to have anybody other than me be next." My chest went to heavin hard, and the coughin started. I couldn't catch a good breath. It was like my lungs was done full, but not with air.

Del went to rubbin my back and gently pattin me. "Take it easy, Mamaw. No one is going to kill anyone."

"It was just an expression, Miss Minerva. I didn't mean nothin by it." Robert took my hand. "Calm down so you can breathe. Slow, easy breaths."

My heart slowed, and the coughin eased. Robert poured me a glass of water, and I took a sip.

"You all right now?" Del bent down and looked square in my eyes.

I put my hand on his chest and shoved him back. "Your gettin right in my face ain't gonna make things better! I'm tellin you both, there ain't a soul to lay a hand on that man." I couldn't believe I was hearin myself say those words, but they were pourin outta my mouth like honey from a hive. I reckon that forgiveness I give Stately had followed me home. "The worse that can happen is I give him the envelope."

Robert and Del went dead quiet. What had I done? Had I let the cat outta the bag and there was no catchin it? Had I just give up my word to Stately?

Del took a step back. "Minerva, are you sayin there really is a box?"

I went to shakin my head. "I ain't feelin up to snuff. I'm done talkin. Y'all leave me be for a spell." I turned my back to them and pulled the covers up to my chin.

"Miss Minerva, you ain't no child, and now ain't the time to act like one. If there is truly a box with a treasure in it, then we need to know so we can protect you." Robert gently pulled on my shoulder and rolled me toward them. "Miss Minerva? What ain't you tellin us?"

All these years, I'd been faithful to keep my mouth shut. I never questioned Stately. I wasn't sure how I was gonna sidestep this one, but somehow something would have to come to light. And then it did. The answer hit me right betwixt the eyes. It might just work.

"Listen, you two. I ain't gonna say this but once. First off, I said envelope, not box. There ain't no box of gold. It's an envelope. I'm gonna show you, and I don't want to never hear about it again. I

said I could give Colton the paper. Stately just had an envelope."
I pointed to a small wooden basket on my cupboard. "Del, reach
up there and grab that little basket. It's been right there all along.
Even when my house was ransacked, it set right there. Right out
in the open. I told you there wasn't no gold."

Del brought the basket and handed it to me. His hand shook.

"Why you shakin? You think this little basket is filled with
gold?" I asked.

He shrugged.

I fingered through the trinkets in the basket until I uncovered
the envelope with Stately Jenkins's name printed right pretty on
the front. "Lordy mercy, y'all can take a breath. I can promise
you ain't gonna be surprised. Well, on second thought, you just
might be." I pulled out the slip of paper and unfolded it. "Here,
Del. Read this."

Del slowly took the paper and read it.

US Land Grant
Issued by the State of Kentucky
May 15, 1867

*This land is hereby transferred from one Melba Bishop to one
Stately Jenkins and is approved and noted by the State of Kentucky. This grants access to the land and water rights to Stately
Jenkins. This grant allows the owner to provide a small dam to
divert water from the Shoal River Spring west two miles, provid-
ing fresh water to homesteads above Barbourville, Kentucky. This
grant allows the owner full rights and access to divert the spring
flow 3.5 miles through the valley on the west of Shoal Mountain,
opposite the river on the east side of the mountain. This grants
access to the land where the spring will flow, along with a small
vein of coal noted to be twenty feet by four feet, falling under the
limit for state supervision of coal.*

This land grant has been duly appraised and noted within the

State of Kentucky guidelines. This is agreed upon by the US Land Commission. Noted and entered into the records this 15th day of May 1867.

*Deeded and signed this 15th day of May 1867
The Honorable Judge Mason Harvard
Lexington, Kentucky*

Del's mouth dropped open. "A land grant to access a spring—river water? This is what you've been hiding? This is nothing, Mamaw. Why wouldn't you tell us?"

"Because Stately asked me in his dyin breath to keep this secret." I bowed my head, ashamed at what I'd just done. But I'd promised Stately. I'd promised. "Besides, there was that vein of coal, and what if it turned up more coal than Stately anticipated? Coal is valuable. I never searched it out. It never meant nothin to me. Still, it was a small strip of coal that might be worth a handful. Nothin more."

Robert took his hat and balanced it on his knee. He covered his face with his hands and swiped his fingers up into his hair. "Miss Minerva, this is permission to dam up the spring and divert the water. It's not anything to hide. It's the west side of the mountain. Don't come close to the river. And a twenty-foot-long vein of coal ain't enough to wet your whistle. Didn't you know it was worthless?"

"It wasn't worthless to Stately. Folks on the east side didn't want no water diverted, but folks on the west side of Shoal Mountain was dry as a bone. Stately and your daddy, Robert, and about ten others built that stone wall on the lower field that pushed the spring water over toward the other side of the mountain, into the valley, where it runs today. It starts right there at my garden. It wasn't an easy undertakin either. They dug out a byway about as wide as a man is tall from the river to the spring. Built the stone wall. It was enough to sidetrack a little river water along with the spring, but not enough to stop the river's flow. When they were done, folks had fresh water."

All that was true. There wasn't a misleadin word in the story I told them. There were folks on the east side that grew to hate Stately. They thought he'd take their water. What they didn't realize was that small vein of coal runnin down one side of the mountain. I ain't always the brightest coal in the fire, but I was smart enough to know that there could be more to that coal than Stately realized. I didn't fib about that, but I didn't tell Del and Robert about the real box either.

They stood in my cabin, speechless. Dumbfounded, I guessed. It was hard to see if they were mad or disappointed.

"All this pain for a land grant for water?" Del pressed the paper into the basket and set it on my bedstand. "I wish you would have just told me."

"I did just tell you. And just like I figured, it wasn't enough. I tried tellin you all over and over, there wasn't no gold. *'No gold!'* I'd shout. No gold. You wouldn't believe me, so you made up your own story in your head. Seems folks is right good at believing what they want. Don't pay a body any mind when they tell them what really is. I can't help what you believed. That one is on you!

"Stately and Robert uncovered a small vein of coal down below the barn, but it petered out. Wasn't enough there to warrant diggin up the mountain, so they covered it back. Never told a soul on the mountain, to keep people from ravagin the whole side of the mountain. There is your big news. If you don't believe me, make your way down below the barn and dig in behind that stone wall where the creek widens. You'll see."

Del leaned against the fireplace. "Mamaw, it was never about gold to me. I told you that. But your tight-lipped attitude could very well get you killed. It could get us all killed."

"That's why I said give him the envelope if worse comes to worst," I snapped.

Robert stood and headed to the door. "I'll give the sheriff a heads-up. He'll need to know this. Gives him an edge if Colton comes around."

Del nodded and walked Robert to the door. I could hear their talkin, but it wasn't all clear.

"Maybe we can start the word across the mountain that she's given up the box and all it held was a land grant," Robert said. "Sometimes the truth is stranger than the stories. Do you think Colton would believe that if he caught wind?"

"I've known Colton for years, and there is one thing about him. Once he's on a trail, he's like a hungry wolf. He'll stop at nothing. Especially if he thinks it will line his pockets."

"Load them guns Miss Minerva has. I have a feelin if Colton comes, he won't be alone."

I heard their boots on the steps as they headed to the lower field.

I'd done my best to protect the promise Stately made me keep. It might not be right to every man, but I made a promise, and it was important to me. I ain't perfect and I probably ain't right, but my heart tells me that right now my lips is sealed. I'd made my decision. I'd not share this secret as long as there was breath in me. At this point, it made no difference if it was right or wrong. Stately had me keepin a secret that was his alone. It was his own sin, and I had been too naive to know any better. I thought the box held something valuable, when it only held Stately's sin. And to mislead me—have me keep a sin a secret—was about as bad as a man could get.

My chest ached, and my arm felt like a streak of lightnin run up it. I leaned forward in the bed and tried to catch a breath. When the pain stopped, there was no movin my arm. It was limp. I opened my mouth to holler at Del, and not a sound come out. Not a peep. I laid back and waited for another stab of pain, but it never come.

THIRTY-TWO

I SAT SLUMPED IN MY BED. One whole side of my body was like a wet rag, and my cheek felt like it hung to my chest. I reached my good arm over to the nightstand and grabbed the little hand mirror Momma gave me as a child. It was somethin to me that the women from town seemed to know where all my belongins should sit. They'd pretty much put every possession I had right back where it should be. I suppose us women don't vary right much. We all seem to know the proper place for things. It was nice that they'd put my cabin back in order.

I held the mirror to my face and saw how my left eye and lip seemed to drip down like wax runnin off a candle. My fingers on my left hand bent into my palm, and my arm felt like the icy waters of the river.

A tear trickled down my cheek from the eye that drooped. It was time, and I knew it. I closed my eyes and prayed one last prayer.

Good Father, let me last long enough to write out the truth, and then I'll come on home. At last.

I spent the next little bit scribblin in Stately's ledger. It wasn't pretty. The letters were shaky, and I wrote them big so I was sure Del could read the words through the messy writing. When I was done, I pulled myself to the end of my bed and dropped into the rocker. It wasn't easy. My one side felt like a basket of rocks, but

I reckon when you're determined and know your life is teeterin, a body can muster up a mighty strength. I uncovered Stately's box and made sure the ledger laid open to mark the page. My task was done—my confession was written.

I wasn't sure I could pull myself back to the bed. The ache in my chest grew harder with every breath I took.

It wasn't clear to me why dyin had to hurt. Seemed to me a person could just give in and die. Maybe this pain was my punishment. I didn't care to die. Lord knows I've begged for it for months, but there was a certain sadness about lettin go. I'd only just found a man I could call family, and Del was right. Family ain't always blood . . . it's who's in the heart. The women from town had befriended me, and I was only just getting to know them. Then there was Robert Jr. and Miss Cherry. The man was the spittin image of his daddy, and that brought warm memories to the surface. I guess I was gettin just a hint of what my life could have been . . . had I . . .

I'd been faithful to the good Lord and read my Bible. Behaved. Kept my promise. But in doin so, I'd missed a lifetime of joy, which made me a bit sad. It was water under the bridge now. Too late to change things. Momma was right, regret is an ugly bedfellow, and I did have a few regrets. My body was finally letting go of what was temporal and reachin for what was eternal.

Lord, give me dignity. I leaned forward toward the bed and hoped I'd not end up on the floor with my dress over my head. Wouldn't that be a final hoot—my dress around my head and my bloomers wavin like a flag? In my pain I laughed out loud.

A peck come at my door, and there stood sweet Cherry Blessing. *Thank You, Lord.*

"Have mercy, Miss Minerva." She squealed and ran to me. "What's wrong?"

When I lifted my head, she was bright enough to see what was happenin. Cherry slipped her arm around my waist, and that frail-lookin young woman heaved me onto the bed. She brushed my hair outta my eyes and gently caressed my face with her hands. Then she leaned over me and kissed my forehead.

"Don't you worry none. I'll get the men. But let me check you out. Be sure you ain't got no cuts." She kissed my fingers.

For a minute, I felt such warm love. Love I didn't rightly deserve. But right here in front of me was a woman I'd only just met, who followed that one command the good Lord give. *Thou shalt love thy neighbour as thyself.*

I reckon the Lord granted me just enough ability to utter a few words to Cherry. I pointed to my wardrobe and mumbled, "My dress."

Only by the grace of God, Cherry understood I wanted my Sunday dress. She opened the wardrobe and pulled out the dress. She brushed the dust from it and slipped it over my gown. "Miss Minerva, it's beautiful. Let me wash your face and brush your hair for you."

And she did. In her gentleness and kindness, this sweet woman knew the angel army was on the way. She never argued a word. Instead, she primped me up right pretty.

It took her a few minutes, but Cherry managed to straighten the covers on my bed and scoot me up to sittin. She propped a pillow behind me and tucked the quilt Momma made me around my legs. "Don't you leave me yet! I'm going to get some fresh water. Look at me, Miss Minerva. Don't you leave me yet. Promise me."

I smiled an oblong smile, and she squeezed my fingers.

"I'll be right back." She picked up my washbasin pitcher and headed out to the pump.

It seemed a bit ironic that here I was in the midst of dyin, and somebody else was askin me to make a promise. This time I took Momma's advice and thought it through. I never answered Cherry. Never agreed. Lord knows the promise I made to Stately Jenkins has been a burr in my patootie. I wasn't about to make another promise I might not be able to keep.

I could feel my feet growin cold and my mouth dryin out. My

eyes closed, but my hearin sharpened. The spring on the door squeaked, and I heard the click of boots, then a man clearing his throat.

I kept my eyes shut. I didn't have the energy to fight no more. The boots come close to my bed. I felt the hot breath of someone leanin over my body. I cracked open an eye to find Colton's ear close to my nose, listenin to see if I'd passed.

"Diss-appointed?" I hissed.

Colton's head jerked upward, and he took a step back. I could tell he thought I was gone. The color of his face, whiter than a cloud, proved that. I felt a surge of strength, and though my words were weak, I found the wherewithal to get them out.

"Still searchin?"

"Old woman, you know you can't take it with you. What good is that gold gonna do you in the grave?"

I nodded, then curled my finger for him to come close. I slowly reached to the nightstand, picked up the envelope Del had laid there, and handed it to him. "No gold . . . water . . . it's . . . precious, you know. And there was a little vein of . . ." I gasped for a breath.

"Of what? A vein of what? Gold?" Colton set down on my bed and grabbed my shoulders.

The pain was unbearable. Just his squeezin on my shoulders felt like knives stabbed in deep. I coughed and gasped again. It seemed the good Lord was going to play a little cat and mouse with Colton. Make him teeter just a little. And I had done decided I wasn't about to give up my spirit until I saw that rascal get a little of his own.

"Coal. Wasn't much . . . biiiggger than the porch. Stately said it wasn't enough to light a fire through the winter." My chest ached, and it grew harder to suck in any air. "Del can ex . . . ppplain. I told himmm . . . earlllier tooddaayy." My voice rasped. I'd done used up what voice was left in a dyin body. Hardly a whisper could ease out.

Colton stared at the envelope a minute before he tore into it. The good Lord granted me one last look at the face of a disappointed man, and I thought, *Vengeance is mine, saith the Lord.*

"A land grant? A land grant for . . . water?" Colton's voice raised, and he hauled off and kicked the chair. It hurt everthing in and on my body, but a laugh belted outta me.

I nodded a weak yes. "A lllaand gr . . ." I couldn't finish the word.

Colton's anger raged. He stomped across the room, took that bearlike hand, and commenced to squeeze my throat.

I didn't fight him. Didn't argue. I was ready. I closed my eyes and waited for the gates of heaven to open. I knew I'd see Momma and Daddy. Though Stately Jenkins I wasn't so sure of. But now was not the time for me to play judge and jury. I couldn't lay no guess on Stately's makin it through the gates with all his deceivin and lyin.

Right as I saw the clouds separate and heaven take shape, I heard a scream. There was rustling and a thud.

My eyes closed as my heart took one more punch of pain. I felt my back arch and my fingers separate and stiffen. My hands quivered from my wrists to my nails. *Oh, for Pete's sake, just take me, Lord. Just take me.*

I managed to push open my eyes and catch a glimpse of Miss Cherry knockin the whiz outta Colton with my cast-iron skillet. Satchel bolted through the door and leaped into the fight. Of all the growlin and yelpin, screamin and cussin, I'd never heard the likes between man and beast.

Colton swiped his face. A line of blood streaked down his cheek. He climbed to his knees and lunged toward Cherry, grabbin her around the legs with one arm and snatchin my fireplace hook with the other. He rammed it at Satchel. My dog yelped but held his own. Miss Cherry let out a scream that echoed across the gap, and with one more swing, she come up under Colton's chin with that skillet. She sent him flyin backward into the hearth. His chin rested against his chest, and his arms and legs were sprawled out like a pelt to be dried.

Cherry crawled to the side of my bed and laid her head against my arm. I struggled to pull my hand up and cup my fingers around her soft cheek. Her face pressed deep into my hand.

It was growin dark in the middle of the day, and just before my eyes closed, I noticed Stately's box and ledger layin upside down next to Colton. Right by his side. Right out in the open. Even in the irony of the mess, that box remained closed—latched. A sign to me that the promise I'd made to Stately was safe.

Before my eyes darkened and my mind slipped, it came to me that the good Lord had a sense of humor layin that box next to Colton. It looked innocent—like a casualty of the battle that tore my cabin apart again. This time, though, it was just fine.

I sighed and smiled.

THIRTY-THREE

"MAMAW? MAMAW? Open your eyes. Can you open your eyes?" Del gently patted my cheek.

Things was comin back to me. I heard Del's voice gnawin at me, draggin me back from naught.

"Please, Mamaw. Minerva Jane! Don't you die! I've only just found you. Please don't die."

I slowly moved my fingers, then a little strength come to me to lift my hand. I gave Del's cheek a weak slap. I guess the good Lord saw fit to give me enough strength to speak some. I took advantage whilst I could.

"Shoulda left me at death's door." I took in a gulp of air, and still it wasn't enough to fill my chest. I felt like I was breathin in water.

Del rubbed his face, then let out a hearty laugh. He slid his arm under my back and lifted me against his chest. It was a tender, sweet hug. I felt his breath against my shoulder and his tears dampen my neck. I hadn't deserved Miss Cherry's kindness, and I surely didn't deserve his. I inched my hand around his waist and took in every ounce of genuine love I could. It seemed like a lifetime's worth.

It occurred to me, after I got over bein mad that the good Lord didn't go ahead and take me, that in His leavin me here for a bit longer, I might feel what it was like to be loved. Del was, in my eyes, a special grandson, and he also represented true love. Human love. Kind love.

His tears proved he cared nothin about my secret other than the fact I was his mamaw. Not by blood but by somethin stronger. By compassion. By kindness. By heart. That outweighed bein blood relatives. I took in his hug and let it simmer its way into my memory. It meant something special, and I was grateful.

"Del, Miss Minerva needs to rest. Lay her back. I fluffed up her pillow." Cherry gently loosened Del's arms, and Robert eased me back against the pillow.

"Colton?" I could barely whisper.

"Well, Miss Cherry here took care of that little issue. And the sheriff has Colton bound and on the way to Lexington," Robert said.

Del chuckled. I looked in the direction of my skillet on the floor. It was like the Lord give Del the intuition he needed to know my thoughts.

"Your skillet? All the better for the wear. You said it was a good skillet. Enemy better sleep with one eye open with your friend around. I suppose you were right. Cherry proved that point." Del squeezed my hand.

I took in a long, hard breath. It was like something was keepin the air from comin into my chest.

"Miss Minerva, no one was killed. Isn't that what you wanted?" Robert crossed his arms and leaned against the rocker.

I nodded.

Del pulled that envelope from his pocket. "Seems you shared your secret with Colton. By the looks of the finger bruises around your neck, he didn't take well to the news of a land grant."

"Doesn't look like he was especially happy," Robert said.

"I can say for sure," Cherry said. "The Lord played a little cat and mouse with him just for Miss Minerva. That's how I could get in a good swing with that cast-iron skillet. Folks can do amazin things when they're afraid. I was afraid." She dabbed my forehead with a damp cloth.

"Colton won't be escaping this time," Del said. "The sheriff made sure he was under heavy guard. And you'll be happy to know, he was so angry about that land grant that he started ranting about Melba."

It was all I could do to keep my eyes fixed on Del. I tried to turn to my side, but he had to ease me over.

"I guess you'd like to know what he said about Melba?" he asked. He brushed my cheek with his hand. "Seems you and I were right. Stately is my grandfather. Colton had additional papers in his pack that proved that."

I wasn't surprised—not after all I'd put together about Stately. Still, it stung my heart.

"Melba fell in love with Stately and he with her," Robert continued. "He fathered Del's daddy. And when Melba told him she was with child, Stately wanted to take her away."

He'd wanted her over me. I knew that in my heart all these years. I knew. I felt like I'd won the war since Stately married me and not Melba. But I was wrong. Deceived by lies. Used by greed and selfishness.

"Still, he married you and brought you to this mountain," Del said. "He must have felt something."

I knew what he felt—a promise. He felt a promise to keep Melba safe. All I was, was a means to an end. A way he could keep his own promise. It didn't matter anymore. I had more important things waitin for me.

I rolled my head toward the window and gazed at the mountains lifting high above the valley. There is nothin worse than bein rejected. A body can walk away from a situation with a good mind, but to be pushed out, shoved away, especially when you long for the relationship—that's hard.

A breeze rocked the treetops gently, and I longed to soar on the wind. This just made me want death more. A peaceful end to the rejection I'd felt for years.

I snubbed as tears filled the corners of my eyes.

"I promised I'd not tell you any lies," Del said.

I blinked in approval.

And there it was once more. A promise. Was the good Lord tryin to drive home a lesson to me?

I knew it in my heart when I saw Melba kiss Stately. But I imagine the heart hides the truth when it sees there's pain.

I stared at a string on my quilt, wonderin if I pulled it whether it would unwind just like my life had. Would it pull out in one long strand, or would the thread twist and coil into a bunch? My breath came harder, and I realized it was time to just give in.

Del shook his head. He gently brushed his knuckles up my arm—a tender gesture of apology. "Mamaw, I'm sorry. I wish . . ."

I shook my head to let him know it was fine. There was a peace about me. It'd been a long time comin, but betwixt Del and Colton, I guessed I'd come to accept things. Didn't make it any easier. I guess before we leave this earth, the Lord wants us to settle up. I supposed I'd just settled.

"Melba was afraid her husband would find out Stately was the father and kill him. That's why she sent him away. That's why he . . ." Del hushed and eyed Robert. I could tell by his expression he'd said more than he wanted. Besides, he knew I'd already come to grips with this. There was no need to say it again.

The same thoughts run over and over in my head. I knew why Stately married me. It covered his lie. Protected him and Melba.

I wrapped my fingers around Del's wrist. After all these years, I finally knew the truth that had nipped at my heels. Everthing I'd pushed behind me, brushed off as something I'd done wrong, fell away from me like chains fallin off a fence. The ironic thing was that the secret I kept was nothin when held up to the one Colton had let out of the bag.

"And Miss Minerva." Robert leaned close to me. "Colton admitted to tryin to make you look like a crazy woman."

I took in a breath, and my chest rattled. I knew that sound. I knew a death rattle when I heard it. I coughed.

"Yes, ma'am. He spilled it all. You were right. Can you forgive us for wondering?" Del whispered.

I pressed my fingers to his wrist.

"Well, let's look at the silver linin." Cherry dabbed my face again. "The truth is out about Mr. Jenkins and the grant. I believe Miss Minerva would say, 'Whoop-de-doo! I guess we're supposed to be all happy?' But right now all this mess needs to hush up, and we need to be sure this wonderful lady knows how much she is loved."

"Miss Minerva, we aren't supposed to be all happy," Robert said. "You've been wronged. It hurts. We hurt with you. But through all of this, I believe you have found a family. You are our family." He took my fingers and gently rubbed them.

I tried to listen. All this time I'd been beggin the Lord to take me, and now I was clingin to every second so I could take in my newfound family.

A while back, I'd come to the conclusion that I wasn't goin to spend my last days with Del growlin over what was. It is what it is. I gained this young man outta all this mess, and I got Miss Cherry and Robert. They've stood with me over the last weeks. And that fear, the one about rottin where I fell and died—well, I suppose the Lord decided that wouldn't be right, and He fixed that for me. I just prayed that He wouldn't let me die alone.

The Lord didn't give me everything I wanted, but He'd provided what was best. Who could ask for more? I was surrounded by good folks who in the last couple of months of my life have filled me to overflowin.

I dropped my hand to the side of my bed and felt the furry ears that stayed by my side. My fingers tapped gently against the bed. Satchel eased under my hand.

"Satchel. Come here, buddy. I don't believe Miss Minerva will mind if you lay on her bed." Robert slipped his hands under the dog's belly and gently lifted him.

Satchel whimpered as he crawled over my legs and stretched out the length of my body. His head rested on my stomach.

"Satchel took a hard blow from Colton. He'll be happy to lay next to you." Del lifted my hand and laid it on the dog's head.

I mustered all the strength I could to move my fingers and give him a scratch. His tongue lapped out of his mouth and tenderly licked against my arm. I'd said before, faithful to the end. If only we could all be that way.

I felt a great surge of hurt rise up in my heart. It wasn't a pain that any doctor could fix. Nothin a smile would console. I felt grief. Grief for these people I would leave behind. Grief for an animal that loved me when no one else would. I felt my tears pile up like wood by the fire.

Sobs loosened from the deepest part of my soul. Years' worth of heartbreak rumbled to the surface like a mighty thunderstorm shakin the very roots of the mountain trees. My chin shook, and my lip did its best to hold in my slobber. But it couldn't.

I'd planned it all out. How I'd die. How this would end. I'd done let Del know he was to take care of Satchel, give him a good, warm spot to stay until the Lord called him home. He was supposed to live out his life chewin on bones and lettin out howls that would stand your hair on end.

"I know you had things all planned out, Mamaw. It's fine. I'm fine. I'm grateful for you and the joy you've given me in this short time." Del caught one of my tears on his finger.

He leaned into me, our foreheads touched, and for every tear that fell from me, two fell from him. My heart was plumb broke.

"The Lord is my shepherd . . ." Robert did his best to be the preacher he was meant to be. I couldn't fault him for his tryin to comfort me.

"Rii . . . vverrr?" It was all I could do to utter the word.

"River? Yes." Del kissed my head. "I will take you to the river just like you asked. You know, it's the strangest thing. I noticed yesterday new wisteria blooms coming on that vine. They're small. Might not amount to much, but you can't deny they are blooms."

I shook my head.

"Miss Minerva, you want to go to the river, don't you?" Cherry pushed Del up and toward the door. "She wants to go to the river. Bring the wagon. Robert, grab them quilts."

It was just minutes until I heard the wagon pull to the porch. Cherry rushed out, and that sweet woman was barkin out instructions like nobody's brother. It was sweet that she instinctively knew my mind.

Del come inside and slipped his arms under me. He gently lifted me off the bed while Robert picked up Satchel. I realized in that moment, Del had picked me up and carried me more times than I could count. The sign of love is the one who carries you through.

Cherry laid a pillow in her lap, and Del eased me down in the wagon, restin my head on the pillow. Cherry's fingers cupped my chin as she dabbed the slobber my numbed mouth couldn't hold. Robert laid Satchel next to me, and off we went. For a moment, I felt the joy of an adventure. My first family outin.

I gazed at the sky. A hawk dipped his wings and caught a breeze that lifted him up and over the pine trees. Ahhh, and the smell of them pines. If this was what dyin felt like, then I didn't mind.

The wagon bumped over the rocks in the path, and Del did his best to take it slow, but in my mind, I was sayin, *Just go! Hurry. Just go.*

It was a funny thing. All that agony of life, all those hurts and hardships, seemed so distant.

Miss Cherry caressed my cheek, and I heard a muted hum seep from her lips, then the words, "Yes, we'll gather at the river. The beautiful, the beautiful river." Her voice was sweet as honey, and every tender note she sung eased my soul closer to heaven. "Gather with the saints at the river that flows by the throne of God." The words were like the puddles of soft rain I splashed in as a child, and I felt this unexplainable joy rise in my heart.

The things around me darkened. I wasn't sure if it was me dyin or the sun settin. I heard the roar of the river. Above me, I saw the sunset. Streaks of orange and red. Fiery yellows. The clouds blended in as though an angel dipped his fingers in them and gingerly stirred, making whips of purple and deep alabaster.

The sound of the river was something to behold. Its wash melded with the soft hum of Cherry's voice, and I was cuddled, lulled, embraced by nothing short of pure love.

Del spread a quilt on the ground, and they eased me out and onto it. Robert lifted me enough so Del could pull me against his chest. They laid Satchel next to me, and the dog took one long breath and sighed. He nuzzled tight against me. My old hound holdin faithful vigil for an old woman.

THIRTY-FOUR

I NEEDED THIS TIME BY THE RIVER. It was kind of Del, Robert, and Miss Cherry to see to that. Memories flooded me, and I cried. When I finally reached up to Del, he just rocked me in his arms.

Oddly enough, I could have sworn I remembered bein a baby and havin Momma rock me in her arms. I remembered her rockin me at night when I was a wee little girl, and I remembered how she held me in her arms the night before Stately Jenkins moved me from Lexington. I guess a momma's rockin never stops with her youngins. They're always a momma's child.

They say when a body is about to die, their life passes before them. I could never imagine how that was possible, but maybe it was just like this. Sweet memories of happy moments with Satchel. Rememberin Momma rockin me. Feelin them times when love was most important.

I reached toward Robert and Miss Cherry and motioned them to sit. They come as close to me as they could. A giggle seeped outta me.

The grass rustled as two deer eased from behind the trees. It was like they'd come to meet me. Take me where I needed to go. They were a beautiful sight. Long legs, slender but strong. I was happy to see them. They were always a peaceful sight. It seemed fittin that they would see me off.

Miss Cherry pulled a blanket over me and tucked it under my legs. I saw her eyein Del, as if to say it was time to take me back.

Del begin to slip from behind me. "Mamaw, you're cold, and we really need to get you back to the cabin."

I shook my head.

"You want to watch the sunset?" he asked.

I managed a smile. The three of them eased me to where I was lookin over the river. We huddled close and held hands. Miss Cherry hummed some more of that sweet hymn. I gazed out over the river to one side and up the hill toward the house on the other. The sun hugged the summit. It glistened off the water like stars fallin to the earth. Lightnin bugs flickered across the field, and the song of the frogs was never prettier. My senses opened up, and my sight sharpened. I could see clearly the line of mountain peaks and the brilliant orange blaze in the clouds. A flock of geese sailed in their V shape, their calls echoin over the ridge. Would I see them from glory?

The water danced over the rocks, and the eddies spun in circles, calling down unsuspecting insects for the trout that leaped outta the wash. And the smell of the wisteria . . . The last sweet scents of their blooms tickled my nose.

I suddenly realized just how lucky I was. I didn't need Stately. He'd given me a good life—not a loved life, but good. I had all I needed, though certainly not all I wanted. Stately died holdin a secret that I thought was in that box. It was really what *he knew* that I knew. He carried that secret to his grave. God rest his soul.

Over the past few weeks, I'd learned that I didn't rightly owe Stately a thing. I was a good wife, never unfaithful—at least not in body. I suppose I could be unfaithful in wishin for love, but I couldn't say that was wrong. Folks wish for things every day.

My breath grew slow. I pulled my hand to my throat and gasped, then coughed. The air I longed for just wouldn't come.

The Lord spoke to my soul. *Just let go. I have ahold of you, Minerva.*

It suddenly come to me, there was no need to fear death. Leastways not when you were surrounded by the folks you love. And I was. It was obvious the good Lord was waitin for one last thing. Was He waitin on my surrender? And I thought I was the stubborn one. Seemed He was a bit more stubborn than me.

I'd loved this Man, this Father, my whole life, and when no one else was around, He'd hovered close.

Minerva?

I heard that still, soft voice nudge me, and it was like the day I stepped from behind the pew and went to the preacher, askin to be pushed under the water. *I hear.*

I took in a long, hard breath—a gulp—and I grasped hold of Del's shirt. The pain in my chest was almost more than I could take. I grunted.

What's to come, Lord? I thought.

What's not to come?

Will I see the stars?

She takes her place in the night sky, queen of the stars.

A smile tipped my lips. *Will I see the sun over the mountains?*

When morning takes her first breath.

What about Your promise? I asked.

It's never broken.

So, Lord, You will answer me one last question before I go. How long does a body keep a promise?

How long?

My eyes closed, and I raised my hand to take hold of the outstretched hand of the Lord.

To the grave, Minerva Jane. To the grave.

I ain't never felt such peace as this, as I let my hand drop gently into my lap.

THIRTY-FIVE

GOLD ON THE MOUNTAIN

By Delano Rankin, *Lexington Weekly Standard* Reporter
Lexington, Kentucky
March 1903

The best way to begin is with the end. As you read this final editorial about Shoal Mountain and the treasure hunt for the stolen gold, you must know that this is the end. It's the end of the search for the gold, the end for the dearly departed Minerva Jane Jenkins, and the end of my time at the *Lexington Weekly Standard*.

It was a long few months that led this reporter into unexpected territory. Mrs. Jenkins, Pastor Robert Blessing Jr., and I have solved a decades-long mystery about the stolen gold from the wealthy Bishop family. You have followed the stories I've written about the woman I've come to call Mamaw. You've learned about the dishonesty that came from an employee of this newspaper. I hoped that you grew to love the individuals and the story on Shoal Mountain. There's no need to visit there. There's nothing there but a few small farms. There's no gold on the mountain, nothing to seek unless you long for a quiet stay along the river to fish.

As I conclude these articles, the chapter on the Bishop gold is officially closed. All findings are reported to state authorities, the dishonest employee is incarcerated, and the box of gold, nonexistent.

Colton Morris's trial came

and went. The entire ordeal took three months. I will admit it was a blur since there were so many charges against Mr. Morris. Libel. Stealing and falsifying public records. Harassment of a citizen of Barbourville. Arson and attempted murder. It would be more to guess what Mr. Morris had *not* done. None of it made much sense.

It seemed wrong to be a witness at the trial and the reporter covering the same story, but my publisher insisted I could remain professional and cover just the facts. I referred to myself as "the primary witness" to keep that objectivity. The city of Lexington wouldn't care about the "who," only about the "what happened." It seems Minerva Jenkins was right about so much. Few care about the person, just the secrets against them.

Because I knew Mr. Morris personally, the judge's sentence struck hard at a once strong friendship. I felt a great sense of sadness as the judge slammed the gavel onto the desk and said, "Forty years." That would be a lifetime—if he would even survive that long in the bowels of a filthy prison. Despite my attempt to remain professional, it was—is—

still personal. Though I felt a rush of relief, in some respect there was a deep sense of deception and loss from one who was once a trusted friend.

This ends the official story of the Bishop-Jenkins family. The mystery of the gold is solved, and we are left with nothing more than a broken and twisted love story.

However, before I close this last article, I feel it is essential that readers grasp the facts that this story—any story—is undergirded with the lives of real people. In some cases their stories are joyous, and at other times, as in this story, they end somewhat tragically. This is why it is crucial I close this article with my personal view. It is important to this reporter that what you have gleaned from these stories is that truth always wins out.

Therefore, it's only fitting that I share the last of my adventures on Shoal Mountain, although it is somewhat sad. Robert Blessing continues to serve as the pastor of the Barbourville Independent Freewill Baptist Church, and he and Cherry run the local general store. As a favor to me, they stand watch over the Jenkins homestead until I can return.

As for me, there is no question

about what lies ahead. I've given up my home in Lexington. This no longer feels like home to me—my soul longs for the mountain air and a slower-paced life. More so, my heart wants to know more about the friends and memories of my family.

I loaded the wagon with my few possessions and took time to walk the streets of Lexington. This city is growing. Industry, a new word to this part of the country, is cropping up. I feel sure that neither this city nor this newspaper, nor even you, will recall Delano Rankin in a matter of years. With that, I made one last visit to the cemetery to say goodbye to my parents and thank them for the life they provided me. I couldn't help but make my way to the river—to the road by way of Mrs. Jenkins's

family homeplace—to honor her and her parents.

I wish to thank my readers for their faithfulness to this newspaper and my writing. I can safely offer you a few final words I hold to from Minerva Jane Jenkins. "Ain't that the most beautiful sunset. Look how them colors mix together, twirlin and twistin, formin steps into the gates of heaven. That's what I love about these here mountains. A body can't get no closer to heaven than this. We can only hope the good Lord pulls open a hole in the clouds and yanks us through."

May your days be the colors of sunsets and may the door to heaven open wide for you, until another day.

—Del "Jenkins" Rankin

Even as I gazed across the city from the river's edge, I missed the mountain. Could this city boy become self-sufficient on a quiet and secluded summit of the mountain? I supposed only time would tell.

I stood under a big oak and stared across the water, wondering if this was where Minerva first felt the sting of betrayal. She had entirely made my life worthwhile. Had I done the same for her? I had been the bearer of bad news, the one who brought trouble through her door, unbeknownst to me . . . the source of her hurt. Yet, at the same time, it was a redemptive moment. A moment when she was set free.

I took the land grant and the Last Will and Testament of Minerva Jane Jenkins to the city assessor's office and hoped that this hand-penned, chicken-scratched note would serve as truth enough to gain access to the official records of Stately and Minerva Jenkins. Turns out, thanks to Robert Blessing Jr., the assessor took both my word and Robert's telegram, granting me access to the records. Not only that, but he deeded the land, all of it in Stately's name, to me. A sole survivor. In a matter of months, my life had changed more than in the previous thirty-plus years combined.

Stately Jenkins wasn't at all the man Minerva had believed him to be, but in truth, are any of us? Records proved there was a nice vein of coal on the land that would have provided well for Minerva until her death. Still, Stately sat on a land grant worth more than he'd see in a lifetime just to protect his lie. So the question was, why did he not do the right thing and give an explanation to Minerva to provide for her? We will never know. Stately took that explanation to the grave. My best guess is humans, in their frailty, do the unexpected in the raw moments of life. Perhaps that was Stately's excuse.

I remembered the words Minerva's daddy shared. *Learn to look beyond what is temporal to what is eternal.* It must have meant a lot to him that she looked to the eternal. I'd never thought about it much myself, not until Minerva Jane Jenkins.

I sat down days ago and began to thumb through her Bible. It became clear what Minerva saw in her daddy's words. I would spend more time not just thumbing through the aged pages and reading the softly penciled notes in the margins, but I planned to read the pages. Each one. There must be more here, and as I found it I would allow it to change my soul. After all, Minerva taught me to pray, and she never once veered from the words she read and believed in those pages. I think that was why her life was so long and, though she may not have seen it, so rich.

I handed over the final story to the Lexington paper about the people of Shoal Mountain and prayed it would come across as a boring place to live. The people there were strong and faithful, and even though they may not have been blood, they were, in a sense, family. If there was a need, it was met because that was what they did. They cared for their neighbors. Minerva recognized she'd secluded herself from that love after Stately died. I wouldn't make that mistake, thanks to her.

There was a genuine naivety that could easily be lost because of strangers who might disturb the life there. My hope was that people stayed away from the innocence that dwelt on the mountain. It behooved no one to interrupt it.

It took me a significant amount of time to open the box that Mamaw Minerva had left under her daddy's Bible, then to read the last pages she wrote in Stately's ledger. As I read them, she left me with a smile.

How long do you keep a secret—a promise? Only in the true spirit of Minerva Jane Jenkins would she be able to make me laugh out loud in the moment of her loss. Only in her stubbornness, her determination to keep a silly promise she should have never made, would she be able to accomplish this.

At the cabin, I sat in my chair at the window, the box perched on my knees. It was a beautiful box, though not ornate at all. Its wood had aged, and the color had deepened to a beautiful mahogany. I couldn't help but run my fingers over it, pondering what this box held that was such a secret. Pushing the latch to one side, I let it slip open. I hesitated. Were some things best left alone?

I lifted the lid. Inside was a satin bag that held a pocket watch. When I opened the watch's cover, I found a photo of Melba and her infant son—my daddy. One final slap in Minerva's face. And finally, a lump of coal.

A lump of coal! Probably a hint from Stately to Minerva of his hidden wealth. He had been too proud and selfish to share with her. But what good is a hint without an answer? It remains unknown why Stately seemed to save this gift to provide for her after his death. Yet his sin would be exposed if he shared the real value and that it came from Melba. Minerva never knew what value that land grant held, only that Stately had told her the coal wasn't enough to warm her through the winter. Yet another lie. He appeared, by all rights, to be a man who wanted to do right by Minerva but couldn't bring himself to let go long enough to show he could be a good man.

The last few pages of the ledger held Minerva's final words, written the day before her death. She left me her farm, the land grant, the cat, and Satchel. Satchel was her most valued possession of all the things on the mountain. In her eyes, Minerva left me all she ever knew she had. Despite that, it was her words that brought a smile to my face. Her words that meant more than a land grant and a stint of coal she had no idea held a fortune or would provide for me the rest of my life. It was her words that made Minerva Jane Jenkins worth more than gold.

My dearest Del. It ain't your fault, child. It ain't your fault about the family you come from. You remember that. What matters is the family you make, and you have made me family.

When Stately Jenkins died, he made me promise I'd keep this box a secret. I never asked but once what was in it, and he said gold. I believed him. Never had no reason to doubt.

I never wanted that box or his secret. But I got it. Never knew what was in the blessed thing until Colton come round. That box only held truth. The truth you searched for was knowin your family. For me, truth was accepting I was a tool used to cover a sin. I suppose Stately didn't lie, there was gold in there—a gold pocket watch. Sure wasn't no hidden treasure like Colton thought. I'm still befuddled by the lump of coal, but I figured Stately was a little outta his mind anyway. I was smart enough to know it was worth a little, but not bright enough to see past my grief and take hold.

The truth is, the box everyone searched for had no meaning. No worth. Only to Stately. It was his burden, sin, wrongs—however you see fit to label it. But you remember this. My life was made richer than any box of gold when you stepped onto my porch. My heart grew to love you not as a grandson but as my son. This is worth untold riches to me. It's sure far more valuable and well worth the wait.

I do hope you'll forgive me that I didn't share this box with you whilst I was around to see you open it. Partly because I couldn't bear to see the look on your face when you saw the same truth I saw. But mostly because I made a promise, and no matter what a body tells you otherwise, a promise is your word.

I gotta chuckle as I write this because my promise was never broke while I was alive. The words as to what or where this box was never passed over my lips. But now that I'm gone, you can read this and know I was a woman of my word. Nary a word about the box left my mouth, but I figure a note don't count. Seems old Stately needs to know it was me that had the last laugh.

How long do you keep a secret, my son? How long? How long do you hold on to a promise, even when it's killin you inside?

You're best to remember this, for in the short time we had together, I found a lifetime of love. I loved you. I truly loved you.

~Mamaw

I learned that gold comes in many forms. Sometimes it's in the precious metal, and other times it's in the wisdom and love of our elders. Gold is found in the relationships we build, the time we spend with those we love, and our efforts to bring others into our lives. Gold is found in laughter and tears. It's inside every smile, every good deed, and every ounce of hope that we cling to. Gold is found in those worn spots on the floor by the bed, where we go to our knees and speak candidly to the Lord. Gold is found in the legacy we leave behind. Within these things, there is more gold than the world can hold. Mamaw Minerva Jane was a box filled to overflowing. I was richer for having known her.

I allowed myself one last look at the scribbled words on the ledger page before I closed the book to put it on the shelf. Running my fingers over the penciled words, I wondered how I'd ever keep them from fading from the page.

It wasn't hard to answer Minerva's question. She'd asked it repeatedly during my time with her on the mountain. My sadness had left me as I penned my final article, but what would never leave me was the warmth and joy of Minerva Jane Jenkins, her crackly laugh, and her fiery spirit.

Mamaw had a way of looking at life—the present and the eternal. She gave me things to think over. Things that would change my past life, adjust my present life, and alter my eternal life. Funny thing was, she didn't thump her Bible to teach me. She taught me through love and example. She proved the value in forgiveness, the strength in your word, and the gold of family. Her life was not always internally peaceful, but she never veered from the life that would come.

How long do you keep a promise, Minerva? To the grave. All the way to the grave.

EPILOGUE

"Josiah Jenkins Rankin! Supper!" Mae grabbed the rope on the bell and yanked. "Bring your sister too."

The children's heads popped up over the dip by the big oak. The swing Minerva had loved hung from the limb overlooking the river. I'd replaced the ropes and seat since the years of weather and rot made it less than safe for the children. When we repaired it, Mae took the first swing. She crawled onto the seat and giggled like a little girl. I pulled her back and then pushed hard. She squealed as she leaned back to pump the next sway of the swing. I could see through Mae why Minerva had loved this swing.

I'd come to this mountain a reporter, left a changed man. Somewhere along the way, I'd met this woman who lived around the bend of the river. Like Minerva, her heart was innocent and pure—a trait that seemed untouched in the people on the summit. I married her, and we'll raise our children in that same spirit—the spirit that soars on the breeze right into the Lord's hands.

I looked over the ridge at the river. Robert and I had worked hard clearing the brush and trees. I wanted Mae to see the blue of the river when she walked out on the porch hugging a warm cup

257

of coffee. But I guess, if the truth were known, I wanted to keep a clear view of that wisteria and the treasure that lay at its roots.

"You'll always miss her, you know." Mae slipped her arm through mine and smiled.

"I know. Can't help but. It gives me peace to know she would be happy seeing us here. If you could have only known her."

"I do know her. Every time I see you. Every time I tuck Jane into bed or pull Josiah out of that stand of vines in the back. I know Minerva Jane, and I'm so glad I do." She motioned me into the house. "Supper's ready."

She kissed my cheek and herded the children to the water pump to wash them up for supper. I'd added running water to the house, a real luxury on the mountain. It wasn't hard with the spring and pump so close. But Mae continued to pump water and carry it inside. I wasn't sure if she did it out of habit or out of love for a woman she'd never met.

The grass had long covered the mound of dirt that blanketed Minerva. Daisies and black-eyed Susans had taken root around her grave. I'd done everything she asked. Or almost everything. When Robert and I dug Minerva's grave, we inched over to Stately's resting place. Colton had done the work of digging up Stately and throwing the bones at Minerva's feet. A sick gesture to make an angry point. I'd wrapped all I could and buried his bones where Minerva asked, yet neither Robert nor I had a hard time making the decision to pull Stately out. We just pulled the blanket from the hole and laid it to the side. After the people on the mountain went home from Minerva's funeral, Robert and I moved Stately back to his original spot—hidden in the vines behind the house. It seemed appropriate that a man who caused such loneliness sleep with his own.

Old Satchel died a couple of months after Minerva, the cat not long after that. Robert sent me a wire to let me know that Satchel had passed while snuggled in Cherry's arms. Seemed he never recovered from Colton's stab to his ribs, but I believe the dog probably grieved himself to death. After all, Minerva was all he had. He'd been a faithful animal. Robert and Cherry buried Satchel close beside Minerva. Not only what she wanted but more than fitting. The two were reunited.

The sun began to slowly set over the ridge, and I believe Mamaw Minerva would be pleased that this is how it ended. Her home was filled with love. We'd made changes to the cabin to make room for a growing family. It held a family—one that loved her. I felt sure Minerva would have approved on both counts.

I took in a breath of fresh air and turned to go inside the house. Grabbing the handle, I pulled open the screen door. It rocked on the hinge. I remembered Minerva spouting off that if I was going to own this house, I might consider repairing the door.

I laughed out loud as I held the handle of the wobbly door. I looked over my shoulder at the beauty of the mountains. "How long do you let a door go without fixing it? Answer is—to the grave!"

AUTHOR NOTE

Some years ago, my grandmother died. Oddly enough, it was a joyous transition. My mother and her brothers, sisters, and grandchildren all gathered around the room to walk Grandma into eternity. There was laughter, stories, and tears, but we held tight to the gold that we'd been given in our grandmother. Her time. Her escapades. Her humor. She was a stinker, and some might say she was meaner than a snake (in a good sort of way), but my grandmother left us with wisdom, laughter, and love. Not one of the remaining grandchildren would say otherwise. She has been fodder for tales and inspiration for a life of determination. My grandma was a stubborn woman, but you never lacked for love in her arms.

This story has rolled around in my mind for years, and it's entirely fiction. It is *not* based on the life of my grandmother. However, it is about the gold found in the elderly and my attempt to make you see that treasure. Take time to enjoy the elderly. They are your history. If you let that history slip past without acknowledgment, then something valuable is lost, for a life, a family, a country without history has no future. Talk with the elderly. Walk with them. Get their stories and store them in your heart. You will never find any greater riches than that of lives well lived.

If you stand in conflict with your elderly parents, consider putting that behind you. Replace it with forgiveness and love, for as my grandma used to say, "Regret is an ugly bedfellow. Once the curtain closes on life, things can't be changed, and it's far better to say 'I'm glad I did . . .' than to live with 'I wish I would have . . .'"

There is great value in our elderly. Take time to reap the wealth.

ACKNOWLEDGMENTS

This story has weighed on my heart for several years. I worked for nearly twenty years for a company that provided in-home, non-medical care for the elderly, and my life was enriched. To M. D. and Elvera McCue, who introduced me, trusted me, and taught me to manage an office that cared for the elderly. I am grateful for the opportunity. To Linda Bambino, who later took over that company, securing additional care and services and making the families and seniors needing care a 100 percent priority. To Wendy Smith, who began the rank of caregiver, managing her own growing family and the clients she served with great integrity and dignity, then stepping into my shoes to manage the office upon my retirement. They are in good hands. These individuals changed my life, and I will say without hesitation that you have made the lives of those you care for richer, better, and healthier. Thank you.

To my agent, Bob Hostetler at the Steve Laube Agency, who did not hesitate to bring me on board and serves as my agent and a dear and trusted friend and prayer warrior. I am blessed that God has placed my career in the good hands of a godly and trustworthy gentleman. To Rachel McRae at Revell, a mountain girl who hails from my area in the mountains and who believed in me enough to allow the Appalachian stories to continue. Like me, she knows firsthand about the lives and dedication of the Appalachian mountain people. My love and gratitude will forever be hers. Also, to Jessica English for her hard work to polish and shine this work. Thank you.

To my *prince*—my husband, Tim—my sons, and their wives, who support me and continue to push me to be all I can be. Look where we have come from and where we continue to head together. Thank you. And to my grandsons—I hope you always find joy, fun, and wisdom in Nana and Papaw. To Jeff and Jason (you know who you are) for your sweet support. It means a lot to know that millennials "get" my work.

To my dear friend Robin Mullins, who is not afraid to tell me when a storyline doesn't work and holds me accountable to complete the work I've begun. Her texts asking "Where's Minerva?" kept me pushing ahead. To Stan Leonard and his kindness to help get me over the finish line when it looked out of reach. Thank you both. Without you, this would have been so hard. To Lori Marett, who uses her gifts to help keep my writing on track. She is my dear friend, confidante, and writing buddy. Her eyes see what mine fail to see. I am grateful and honored to share Write Right Author Mentoring Service with you.

Finally, I cannot take credit for a story placed on my heart by the Father above. Oh, Lord, You have heard my prayers to be a writer, and You have answered. May the success and glory be Yours.

Turn the page for a preview of
CINDY K. SPROLES'S
moving novel
WHAT MOMMA
LEFT BEHIND

Available Now

ONE

"They was nothin I could do for her. Her eyes was fixed on the sky and she never moved again. Despite me shakin her, she was gone."

Ely slipped his worn hat from his head and pressed it hard against his chest. "Miss Worie, thangs is what they is. Ain't nothin you coulda done."

The spring breeze whipped my hair around my face, brushin the clay trail of tears from my cheek.

Just the day before Momma was hangin clothes on the line and singin. She didn't seem to have a care in the world. Today she was dead. This didn't make a bit of sense. "Like you said, Ely, it is what it is." I swallowed hard, tryin to be strong.

Ely shoved a flat rock into the soft clay. "This'll mark her till we can make her a cross like your daddy's."

"I never knew what a chore it was to bury a person." I dropped to my knees and gingerly swept the clots of dirt to one side, smoothin the mound that covered Momma. I wasn't sure if I was to be angry or hurt. Either way, my heart was achin.

Ely grunted. "Uh-huh. 'Tis a chore. But you was smart to drop

267

that quilt over her. Kept the buzzards away whilst we dug that hole." He placed his hat back in its spot, pushin his dark, tight curls from beneath.

I stared at Ely, his skin blacker than the rock coal Daddy would bring home from time to time. He was a good friend. Stood by Momma and Daddy through thick and thin.

The sun peeked through the newly formed leaves of the old oak tree, castin a shine on ever one of those curls that boasted around Ely's ears. "You're startin to look a little shabby there, Ely." I smacked at a curl.

He busted into a guffaw that shook ever bone in his body. "You always make a man laugh, Miss Worie. Even now, in the shadow of your own troubles."

"Lordy, lordy. Like you said, it is what it is. Ain't my fault. Leastways I hope not. But I don't understand, Ely. I did everthing Momma ever told me. Never give her no reason to pull such a stunt. I thought my bein good would make up for the boys."

"You stop right there, girl. Ever man makes his own choices. Calvin chose his swindlin and connivin. Justice made his bed with a bottle of hooch. Them ain't your doins. And I feel right sure Miss Louise was proud of you. Ain't many young girls would choose stayin home to help their momma over bein a wife and mother."

I laid across the mound of dirt and commenced to sob. Long, hard wails. Ely stood solid by me, bendin down ever once in a while to pat my shoulder.

It wasn't long before the buzzards went to squallin overhead. "Get way!" I hollered. "Go on. Can't you see we buried Momma?"

Ely took my arm and lifted me to my feet. "She's safe. We buried her deep and covered her with stones and more dirt on top of that. Ain't nothin can get to her." He tugged me toward the house.

"But I've seen them beasts peck at the ground until they dig up what's buried. Buzzards don't care what the meal is, just so it's fresh."

"Like I done said, she's safe. She'll sleep unbothered."

I clapped my hands together and knocked the red clay loose.

"You need to get yourself cleaned up." Ely yanked a dress off the clothesline as we passed. "You stoke that fire in the fireplace and hang the pot. I'll pump some fresh water for you to boil, then I'll send Bess along after a while to bring you some supper."

My legs grew weaker with ever step to the house till my ankles finally twisted and I sat on the ground with a thud. They was no quiet in my stomach either. My gut twisted and churned until I couldn't hold it no more. Ely held my head while I vomited.

"Miss Worie, you been through a lot today. Help me get you inside, now. Come on. Let's go. Get your feet under you. Come on." He slipped his arms under mine and lifted.

I tried to stand but I couldn't. Ely hung the clean dress over his shoulder, then scooped me in his arms and carried me. He turned his head to one side, tryin to get a good breath. They wasn't nothin to say. I knew I smelled like sweat and blood. And I knew the only reason them buzzards was circlin Momma's grave was because they caught the vile scent from my clothes.

Ely stood me by the screen door. His face said everthing his mouth wouldn't. Like what happened here to rip the screen outta the door frame, but in his kindness, he didn't ask. He pulled open the broken screen door and pushed his shoulder against the heavy inside wooden door. It sounded like a wildcat screamin as it swung open on its rope hinges.

"I'm gonna set you in this here chair while I stoke the fire. You ain't in no shape to mess with a fire."

"The pot is already filled. Momma was ready for me to wash clothes."

Ely nodded and headed into the back room. I heard him movin and stackin wood in the fireplace, then they was the puff of the billows. The smell of hot embers filled the house as the fire caught and went to burnin.

Ely laid the dress he'd yanked from the line on the table, then he squatted at my side. "Miss Worie, I'm goin on home. Get yourself cleaned up. You reek of blood. Your purty skin is tainted red." He brushed my hair from my eyes, then kissed me on the head. "Me and Bess will be back later on. You hear me?"

I heard him, but words wouldn't work their way out.

"Worie. You hear?"

I nearly jumped outta my skin. "Yeah, I hear." The words quivered as they come out. He squeezed my shoulder and left.

It didn't seem real. None of it. Worse, it made no sense. I'd gived up everthing—a husband and a new life—to stay and help Momma. She couldn't count on the boys after Daddy died. Half the time Justice was laid out drunk, and Calvin spent his time bein what he called a slick businessman. Daddy called him a liar and swindler. Momma, she called him lost. I couldn't bear her tendin the farm alone. With Daddy dead, it was just me and her.

I ain't sure when I laid down on Momma's bed, but I did. I suppose it was somewhere betwixt exhaustion and agony. I dozed a spell. When I woke up, nothin had changed other than the wet blood all over me had dried. The hope that this was a horrid dream vanished and reality set in hard.

I scrounged up one of my own skirts and an old shirt of Daddy's, then headed to the creek. Despite Ely's best intentions, Momma was smaller than me and her dress wouldn't cover one of my legs. She was a small woman. Tiny in height compared to most folks, but despite her size, she could move mountains when she was riled.

A while back Momma had the boys dam up the creek so we had a clear pool of water. It would fill to the brim of the stacked rocks and spill over. The water Ely set to warmin over the fire woulda been nice, but dried blood washes better in cold water. My clothes was stuck to me, and when I went to pull them off it was like I was tearin ever bit of the hide off my legs. I stepped into the icy waters of Tender's Creek and my skin went numb. It was just one more callus, cause my heart had numbed earlier in the day. Slipping under the water, I opened my eyes to see the streaks of sun and deep blue sky through the clear glassy ceilin.

It would be easy to just take in a breath of cold water, close my eyes, and never see the light of day again. Was it that easy for Momma? What was she thinkin? How could she pull the trigger?

My lungs went to burnin, longin for the spring air, and despite my thoughts to breathe in the creek, I found I didn't have the courage. My head popped above the water and I took in a gulp of mountain air. I wasn't good enough for Momma to make her want to live, and I was too much of a coward to take my own life. "What use am I?"

I scrubbed the blood from my face and arms. My teeth went to chatterin like a squirrel gripin at its mate. Easin out of the pond, I pulled Daddy's shirt over my head, then slipped on my skirt. My skin now harbored a grayish blue. I run my fingers through my wet, curled strands of hair, then quickly braided them. The damp from the braid soaked the back of my shirt.

How does a person do such a thing? How do they get in such a dark hole that they can't see the light of day, the sun bouncing off the summit, or even hear the soft song of the mockinbird? How can they possibly want to let go of the tender smell of honeysuckle or not want to savor its sweet nectar?

Ely's words echoed in my head. *"This here ain't your fault."* And he was right. If I was one thing, I was strong. Momma raised me to be just that. She always said, "Take a day to mourn your lot, then shovel it over your shoulder and move ahead."

I'd missed my chance to be a wife and a mother so I could help her. That was water under the bridge, as Momma would say. But I was no quitter. Never had been. At seventeen, I'd manage just fine.

The longer I pondered the choice of givin up so much, the madder it made me. Momma was always a givin woman. She always took others over herself, until today. Today she turned selfish and greedy. Today she took ever dream I ever had. All my hope. All my desire. And she bled it out on the ground with one pull of the trigger.

I wiped the tears from my eyes, straightened my shoulders, and walked to Momma's grave. In one swift motion, I drew back my foot and kicked the stone Ely had stood at the head of her grave. It toppled over. As I walked away, I spit.

Cindy K. Sproles is proud of her mountain heritage. Born and raised in the Appalachian Mountains, she has a desire for the "old ways" of the mountain people and life to never be forgotten. Cindy is the cofounder of Christian Devotions Ministries and serves as a project manager for Lighthouse Publishing of the Carolinas (LPC Books). She is the director of the Asheville Christian Writers Conference and executive editor for ChristianDevotions.us and InspireAFire.com, as well as a mentor and editor with Write Right, a private editing service.

Cindy is a storyteller, speaker, and conference teacher. She is also a bestselling and award-winning author. Her first novel, *Mercy's Rain*, was named IndieFab Book of the Year, and *Liar's Winter* was named the Golden Scrolls Book of the Year and was a Carol Award finalist. Her devotions have been published across the Eastern Seaboard, and she writes monthly eldercare articles for *The Voice* magazine.

A mother of four and nana of two, Cindy lives in the mountains of East Tennessee with her husband.

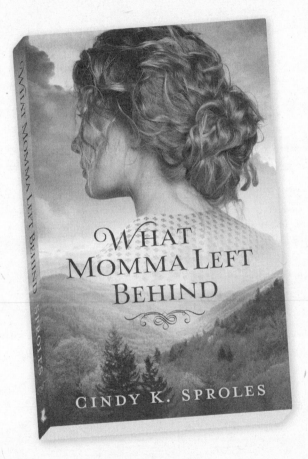

CINDY K. SPROLES

Speaking and Writing from the Heart

GET TO KNOW CINDY AT

CindySproles.com

- Sign up for her newsletter
- Read her blog
- Learn about upcoming events

f cksproles

𝕏 CindyDevoted